Juda

Nothing Else Mattered!

"Why don't you both go—together?"

"Together?" Romina ejaculated, and she saw the look on Merlin Forde's face was one of sheer astonishment.

"Yes," the General answered. "Why don't you go out as tourists? Cairo is very pleasant at this time of the year, and you could be—let me see—brother and sister, having a holiday together. Why not?"

"Why not?" Romina exclaimed furiously. "Because—"

The protest she was about to make died away on her lips. It struck her suddenly that, distasteful as the suggestion might be, it was eminently a sensible one.

If she was to discover how and why Chris had been killed, nothing else mattered.

Also by Barbara Cartland

THE FIRE OF LOVE

BARBARA CARTLAND

DANGER BY THE NILE

 AVON PUBLISHERS OF BARD, CAMELOT, DISCUS AND EQUINOX BOOKS

AVON BOOKS
A division of
The Hearst Corporation
959 Eighth Avenue
New York, New York 10019

First Avon Printing, September, 1967
Third Printing, October, 1971

AVON TRADEMARK REG. U.S. PAT. OFF. AND
FOREIGN COUNTRIES, REGISTERED TRADEMARK—
MARCA REGISTRADA, HECHO EN CHICAGO, U.S.A.

Printed in the U.S.A.

CHAPTER ONE

"No! No! Alex . . . no!"

The protest was not vehement, and the man whose lips were very close to Romina's smiled a little smile of triumph before he answered:

"Why fight? You love me—I know you do. Stop fighting, Romina, and let us be happy. I will teach you what love really is—glorious, wonderful, overwhelming."

The deep voice with its faint accent was hypnotic. So was the soft, experienced touch of his hands, and Romina felt herself drifting into a No-Man's-Land of warmth and feeling.

She was too tired to fight any further. It was so much easier to let things take their course, to allow Alex's voice to soothe her fears and her scruples.

A warm tide was sweeping her along. It seemed to her that his hands were like water rippling over the soft surface of her skin.

His mouth no longer burned hers as it had done earlier. Now his lips seemed to linger possessively, sapping her strength and the last remnants of her will-power.

Quite suddenly, there was a clatter—sharp and decisive.

"What was that?"

Alex sat up abruptly, as if his body instinctively reacted to a signal of danger.

Romina raised her head. She was lying on a deep-cushioned, red-velvet sofa by the fire, and looking across the sitting-room she saw that the door which led into the small hall was ajar.

"It must have been the letter-box," she said faintly.

As she spoke she somehow thought that she heard soft footsteps. They were running down the long corridor on to which the door of the flat opened. Or was she imagining it?

"The letter-box?" Alex repeated.

Romina looked up at him and realized how tense he was.

"Let me see what it is," she suggested. He obeyed her without argument, moving off the sofa, and she swung her feet to the ground.

5

The soft diaphanous dress she had worn to represent a wood nymph was crumpled and disarranged. She dragged the pleated chiffon around her impatiently, feeling a sudden disgust with herself and her acquiescence to Alex's love-making.

'How could I have been such a fool?' she asked silently.

Her head felt heavy and she was a little dizzy. It must have been the wine she had drunk at the Ball. She usually drank very little but there had been a continual flow of champagne into her glass. She could remember telling Alex she did not want any more.

'Why did I let him give me so much?' Romina demanded of herself as she walked into the hall which was large enough to contain only a chair, a gold console table and a wire letter-box attached to the door.

She turned her head and looked back.

Alex was standing in front of the fire, pulling into place the elaborate velvet and embroidered uniform he had worn for the Ball. A Russian nobleman of the seventeenth century was how he had described himself—and it was impossible to argue that he did not look outstandingly handsome and distinguished in the flamboyant, fur-trimmed coat and high red-leather boots.

"I was right," Romina called, "it was a letter."

"At this hour of the night?" Alex questioned.

Romina glanced at the clock hanging on the wall. It was nearly half-past two.

"How extraordinary!" she exclaimed. "I never thought of that."

She opened the wire cage and took out the letter. It bore her name in a bold, distinguished writing which she recognized only too easily. There was no stamp on it.

"It is from—" she began to say, and then checked the words, for underneath the letter was something else—a telegram. In its yellow envelope, it had not been so noticeable.

The telegram must have been there when she came back to the flat, she thought. She had been too intent on listening to Alex and feeling his arm propel her eagerly towards the sofa in the sitting-room to notice it.

"You are lovely—lovely," he had said. "I thought I should go mad with those people all around us. I was unable to touch you—to kiss you."

She had been amused and intrigued by the passion in his voice and by the desire in his dark eyes.

Now she felt a sudden shiver pass through her body. How could she have overlooked the telegram—and what had it to

6

say? She did not know why, but she had a definite foreboding that it contained bad news.

Slowly she opened the envelope.

"What is it? Who is your letter from?" Alex asked.

Romina did not answer him. She was staring down at the telegram in her hands, her face suddenly drained of color.

"Romina, come back!" he commanded.

She must have heard him, because she raised her head and looked across the intervening space.

He was standing in the semi-darkness of the sitting-room, the glow from the fire and the light of one small lamp illuminating his clear-cut features, the dark hair swept back from his forehead, the full sensuous lips.

She looked at him for a moment, and then as Alex asked impatiently: "What is it? What is keeping you?" she went back into the sitting-room.

"Get out!" she said. "Go—and go quickly!"

"Romina—what are you talking about?"

He was obviously shocked and puzzled at the sudden change in her behavior.

"You heard what I said," Romina replied. "I do not want to talk . . . I do not want to explain. I just want you to . . . go . . . now!"

He looked down at her hands and saw she was holding a telegram and a letter.

"You have had bad news?" he asked. "And who could have put the letter in the box?"

"Never mind," Romina answered. "Please do as I ask, and at once."

Her voice had a sharp edge to it which told the man listening to her that there was no point in arguing. He picked up his coat from the floor where he had flung it as they entered the room.

"I will telephone you tomorrow," he said.

"No—don't do that. Please leave me alone," Romina replied.

She did not look at him as she spoke, but turned her head away so that all he could see was the soft curve of her cheek and the disheveled curls of her fair hair.

He moved towards her, hesitated a moment as to whether he would touch her, and then, resisting the impulse, walked from the room and into the hall. It was only when his hand was turning the handle of the Yale lock that he looked back.

"You have made me very happy tonight," he said softly.

He heard the sitting-room door slam as he let himself out into the corridor, and there was a frown between his eyes and

7

his lips were set in a hard line as he walked down the thick carpet towards the lift.

Behind him in the room he had just left Romina walked very slowly toward the fireplace and sat down in a low chair. She gazed across the hearth-rug at the sofa with its crumpled cushions and then suddenly she bent her head and covered her face with her hands.

At ten-thirty the next morning the telephone rang in the office of General Fortescue. He lifted the receiver.

"I am engaged," he said sharply.

"Yes, I know, sir," said one of his secretaries, "but I thought you would like to know that Miss Huntley is here and wishes to see you urgently."

The General hesitated a moment.

"Ask her to come in," he said at length, and put down the receiver. He looked across the room at a man leaning against the mantelpiece. "She must have heard."

"I presume they would have wired his next of kin," the man replied.

"Yes, I suppose so," the General agreed.

The man at the mantelpiece straightened himself.

"Well, I had better leave you for the moment," he said. "But there are still some things I wanted to discuss."

"No, don't go," the General answered. "Romina may have something to tell us—one never knows."

"I should think it is unlikely," was the reply. He moved away from the desk just before the door opened and Romina was ushered into the office.

The General's first thought was that he had forgotten how lovely she was. Then he realized that the black dress and coat she wore threw into relief the perfect clearness of her skin and the pale gold of her hair. He expected her to look unhappy, but he was rather surprised at the darkness of the lines under her blue eyes.

"I am sorry to interrupt you, Guardie," Romina said as the General rose and kissed her cheek.

She and Christopher had called him that ever since they were children, and the General felt his heart twist at the pain in her voice and the unshed tears in her eyes.

"I was expecting you," he said quietly.

"You know, then?" Romina asked.

"Yes, I know," he replied.

"Who told you?" she inquired, and added quickly, "Oh, of course, you know everything. I only got the telegram last

8

night. It may have come earlier, but I was not at home."

"Who sent it?" the General asked.

"The British Embassy in Cairo," she replied.

"Yes, of course," he said. "They would have to notify them."

"They?" she questioned and raised her eyebrows.

"I do not need to tell you," the General said, his hand on her shoulder, "how sorry I am about this. I know, Romina, what it means to you. You and Chris were so close and fond of each other you might have been twins."

"Don't let us talk about it for the moment," Romina said with a little catch in her voice. "I came to see you for another reason. I came to tell you that I am leaving for Cairo almost immediately. You see, I know there is something wrong. Chris did not die of dengue fever as they say here. I am sure of it."

"What do you mean?" the General asked.

"I think he was murdered," Romina said, "and that is why I am going to find out the truth for myself."

"No!"

The ejaculation seemed to echo round the walls, and for the first time since she entered the room Romina turned her head and saw that she and the General were not alone.

A man was standing in an alcove beside the door so that he had been behind her as she entered and she had no idea he was there.

She took a quick glance at him and decided she disliked him. He was thin and wiry, with dark hair, and the look on his face was decidedly cynical, if not sardonic.

"Who is this?" she inquired.

"I'm sorry, Romina, but I have not had a chance to introduce you. This is Merlin Forde, a very old friend of mine and also a friend of Christopher's."

"I have never heard my brother speak of you," Romina said almost accusingly.

"Nevertheless," Merlin Forde answered, walking towards her, "we were good friends. We were at Oxford together and have met fairly frequently since."

"It is odd that he has never talked about you," Romina said. "I knew all his friends."

"Perhaps he had his reasons," Merlin answered. "But I assure you that I am extremely upset at the news of your brother's death. Christopher was a splendid fellow."

"Thank you," Romina said with a faint inclination of her head.

9

Then she turned her back—somewhat pointedly, Merlin thought—and said to the General,

"You see, Guardie, I have reasons for believing that Chris may have been murdered."

"What makes you think such a thing?" the General asked.

"I had a letter from him," Romina answered.

"A letter?"

It was Merlin Forde who spoke, not the General, and there was a sudden note of excitement in his voice.

"When did it arrive?"

Romina looked at him with dislike.

"Forgive me," she said, "but I would really like to speak to my guardian alone."

She saw Merlin Forde's eyes turn towards the General and a look passed between the two men that she did not understand.

"I want to know what is in that letter," Merlin Forde said almost beneath his breath.

Romina threw him a look of disgust. At the moment she hated all men with a bitterness which seemed almost physical.

"Sit down a moment, Romina," the General said gently. "I want to talk to you."

"Alone?" Romina inquired.

"If you insist, after what I have to say," he answered.

He glanced again at Merlin Forde and then held out a chair for Romina next his own, sat down himself and took her hand in his.

"Merlin was indeed a friend of Christopher," he said, "and just before you arrived I had told him of your brother's death. Like you, he jumped to the conclusion that it was unnatural. He had already asked me if he could go out to Cairo to investigate the matter. So you see, my dear, that he is vitally interested in anything you may have to tell us—anything which may give us some idea as to what happened to Chris."

Romina glanced at Merlin Forde suspiciously.

"Is he one of your men?" she asked. "Do you really trust him?"

She spoke as if she would be surprised if the reply was in the affirmative.

"I have known Merlin as long as I have known you," General Fortescue replied, "and I would trust him with anything—my life, if necessary."

Romina gave a little shrug of her shoulders.

"Very well, then," she said. "I suppose he can listen."

She bent her head and opened her handbag. Merlin Forde

withdrew discreetly towards the fireplace. The General sat back impassively in his chair.

Romina took out the letter she had received the night before.

"This came last night," she said.

"By post?" the General inquired.

"No," Romina answered. "It was put into my letter-box at two-thirty—almost exactly."

"How do you know? Were you up at that time?"

Merlin's voice from the fireplace made her turn her head sharply.

"Yes, I was," she answered. "If you want to know, I had been to a fancy-dress dance."

"Were you alone?"

The question made her stiffen as if she resented the impertinence of it.

"I cannot see that that is any of your business," she replied.

"I was only wondering who else was there when the letter arrived at such an unlikely time," was Merlin's answer.

She hated him for being so perceptive as to realize that there was something strange about the delivery of the letter, but she had no intention of satisfying his curiosity.

Besides, the very thought of Alex made her feel sick inside.

She drew the closely-written pages out of the envelope, then, to her surprise, the General asked gently:

"Was anyone with you, Romina?"

"Yes, there was," she said almost defiantly. "Someone who brought me back from the dance. He . . . I . . . asked him in for a drink."

She felt the color rise in her cheeks as she spoke and hoped that the man standing at the fireplace had not noticed, while she loathed him for having caused her embarrassment.

"Do I know him?" the General asked. "What is his name?"

"I expect you have heard of Alexander Salvekov," Romina answered lightly. "He is to be found at every party."

She was aware that once again the General looked towards Merlin Forde. But he merely said in a non-committal voice:

"I have heard of Count Salvekov. He is frequently in the newspapers."

There was silence for a moment before the General said:

"The letter from Chris—that is what is important, isn't it?"

Romina took a deep breath. She had to steady herself to fight back tears which pricked her eyes at the sight of her brother's writing. She had to force herself to focus on the

11

words he had written so lightheartedly only a few days ago.

She read aloud:

"Rom, darling,

I am keeping my bargain and writing to you as I promised. There has been rather a gap between this letter and the last, but I have been madly busy and in hiding. I have stumbled on something wildly exciting, and I think—although I can hardly believe it is true—that I have got the story of the century in the bag. Anyway, expect fireworks and the falling of many august heads, for this is something really BIG."

"He has written 'big' in capitals," Romina broke off to explain. "He has underlined it three times."

Neither of the men spoke, and she continued:

"I am sending this to you by a friend whom I can trust—and there are not many. At the moment I don't even trust the Post Office. Be kind to him if you happen to meet him. He is as black as coal—but his heart is pure gold.

Expect me when you see me—and I don't want the red carpet and a brass band to meet me at the airport!

Bless you, darling, and take care of yourself.

Yours,
Chris"

Romina's voice broke a little on the last words, and then her little chin went up as if she defied herself to break down.

The General put out his hand.

"May I see the letter?" he asked.

Romina passed it across the desk to him.

"There is an address at the top," he said.

"We know it!" Merlin said.

"It is pleasant all the same to know that our informants did not make a mistake," the General replied.

"Is that all you have to say?" Romina inquired, a passionate note of protest in her voice. "Can't you see that whatever Chris had discovered was dangerous?"

The two men didn't answer and she went on:

"I have warned him often enough that he would go too far in his search for a story. Or was it that? Was he working for you, as well?"

She asked the question sharply, and the General's eyes met hers frankly.

"Not directly," he replied. "Chris would not work for me directly and I didn't want him to. As you know, he liked being a writer and a journalist. He wanted to be a freelance so that he could roam over the world—finding a story here and a story there. And I never interfered."

"But he brought you back information?" Romina inquired.

"Yes, and very useful information it often was," the General said. "But primarily he wanted to write—he wanted to discover news. The job he did about the arms to Cuba had nothing to do with me."

"But he often reported to you, all the same," Romina insisted.

"I can say he told me many things I wanted to know," the General replied.

"Well, then, what had he discovered this time?"

The General spread out his hands in a gesture of helplessness.

"I only wish I knew," he said.

"But you must have some idea," Romina told him. "He saw you before he went to Cairo."

"Yes, he saw me, but he did not tell me what he expected to find—or, indeed, what he was looking for," the General answered. "He only said he had a hunch there was a story in the East—perhaps a number of stories, and he was going there just to have a 'look-see.' "

"He told me the same thing," Romina said.

"What was his bargain with you?" Merlin Forde asked.

"It was a private pact we had," Romina answered. "He promised that he would write and tell me what he was doing."

"In exchange for what?" Merlin inquired.

It looked for a moment as if she would not answer him, and then she said in a cold voice:

"If you must know, he had spent a great deal of money on his last trip to Cuba. Our trustees, of whom Guardie is one, are not particularly pleased when we overspend. So I lent him what I could spare until next quarter's allowances come in."

"If he had told me," the General said quickly, "he could have had all he wanted."

"That is exactly why he did not bother you," Romina answered. "And it did not matter one way or another—I had quite a lot of money in the bank, as it happened."

She looked down, and continued:

"It gave me an opportunity to extract from him a promise to write to me. You know how much I disliked his disappearing over the horizon and not having the least idea where he was."

The General spread the pages of thin paper out in front of him.

"No code, I suppose?" he said. "You did not have any way of communicating secretly with each other?"

"I wish we had," Romina answered. "Chris never talked about anything until, as he put it, he had it 'in the bag.' That is why I know that he must have been absolutely sure of what he had discovered to write this—"

She broke off to point to a page of the letter spread out in front of the General and read aloud:

"Expect fireworks and the falling of many august heads. What does that mean? What can he have found out?"

"What do you think, Merlin?" the General inquired.

"It could be so many things," Merlin Forde replied; "—illegal arms—slave-traffic—dope! The East is full of stories, and Chris might have got on the trail of one or a number of them."

He walked across to the desk and stood looking over the General's shoulder.

"I suppose Salvekov did not read this letter?" he asked casually.

"Of course not!" Romina answered. "I would not have shown it to him—he only knew a letter had arrived. And I did not open it until after he had left."

"And the telegram?"

"He did not see what was in that either. I . . . I just asked him to go."

Romina knew that Merlin Forde's eyes were watching her as she spoke, and she could not prevent a faint patch of color from creeping into her cheeks.

'Damn him!' she thought. 'What business is it of his? How dare he look at me like that?'

Because she was uncomfortable, her voice was almost aggressive as she said:

"Well, I am leaving for Cairo tonight or tomorrow morning, as soon as I can get on an airplane."

"You will do nothing of the sort!"

Merlin Forde's ejaculation was so positive that she looked up at him in astonishment.

"You will only make things more difficult," he stated. "I'm going to find out more of Chris's death, and I'll let you know as soon as I can exactly what happened."

The manner in which he spoke, as if she was a misbehaving schoolgirl, took Romina's breath away.

To give herself time, she bent forward and took up the

14

pages of her brother's letter and put them back in the envelope.

Then she said quietly, in a firm voice:

"I'm afraid, Mr. Forde, I am not in the least interested in your movements. I am merely informing my guardian that I am leaving for Cairo."

"But I have told you—that is something you must not do," Merlin said.

Romina looked at the General.

"I shall stay at Shepheard's," she said. "If you want to get in touch with me, that is where I shall be for the next week or so, at any rate."

"Now listen to me," Merlin Forde interposed. "The one thing we do not want at this moment is to let anyone think that we suspect that Chris did not die naturally. The General, as he will tell you, has already been in touch with the British Embassy. They were informed of Chris's death by an Egyptian doctor who attended him; and we have learned that he was buried yesterday."

"Then when did he die?" Romina asked.

"According to the doctor, four days ago," Merlin replied. "It was not reported immediately because they did not know his nationality."

"That is ridiculous!" Romina retorted. "No one would be likely to mistake Chris for anything but an Englishman."

"I wonder . . ." Merlin said enigmatically.

"You mean he might have been disguised?" Romina asked. "Yes, of course! I had forgotten. It is just the sort of mad thing Chris would do—pretend to be an Arab. He was very amused that no one recognized him in Bombay when he was disguised as an Indian. But that was a long time ago."

"I think Chris has used quite a lot of disguises one way and another," Merlin Forde said. "But the danger about a disguise is that once anyone penetrates it, they are quite certain that you are out to make trouble."

"What makes you think that Chris might have been disguised when he was in Cairo?" Romina asked.

"Only that he changed his address recently and moved into a much poorer quarter of the city," Merlin Forde replied.

"Who told you that?" Romina asked. "Surely not the British Embassy?"

"No, it was somebody I spoke to on the telephone this morning," Merlin replied. "He had seen Chris about a week ago, just before he came home."

"Did he tell you anything else?"

"No, because he did not speak to Chris. He only happened

15

to recognize him in a café in a rather disreputable part of Cairo, and followed him back to where he gathered Chris was staying."

"But why didn't he speak to him? Chris might have told him something."

"He was just interested because he recognized Chris," Merlin told her. "It is one of the rules that our men do not interfere unless they are asked to do so."

Romina clenched her fingers together.

"If only Chris had not been so independent," she cried. "Sometimes I used to ask him if it was wise to take unnecessary risks—he went right up to the front line in Korea. But he would not listen to me. I think it was danger that attracted him more than anything else."

"Of course it was," the General agreed. "Your brother was a very brave young man—and in some ways a rather stupid one. He would not listen to me either—I talked to him often enough."

"Well, I am going to find out what happened," Romina said. "I am not going to sit down and let him be murdered in cold blood. And I want to finish the job he started."

"But you *can't*," Merlin Forde said, and he thumped the table with his fist. "You are a woman. What do you think you are likely to discover?"

"Women have managed to do a number of good jobs before now," Romina retorted angrily. "Why, some of the best spies in the War and the bravest people in the Resistance Movement were women, weren't they, Guardie?"

"They were, indeed," the General agreed. "I think you owe the opposite sex an apology, Merlin."

"All right, I apologize," Merlin Forde said impatiently. "But for God's sake stop Miss Huntley making a fool of herself and rushing off to Cairo with a flaming sword in her hand and giving everyone a chance to cover up their tracks and disappear."

His words made sense, and if Romina had not been so angry she might have listened to him. As it was, he had annoyed her and aroused her temper so that now nothing he could say would alter her decision.

She rose to her feet.

"I am afraid we must agree to disagree," she said. "Guardie, darling, I will keep in touch with you. If I want your help, I shall not hesitate to ask for it."

She pulled her coat around her, and started to put on her gloves. As she did so, she heard with a sense of satisfaction Merlin Forde saying in an urgent whisper to the General:

16

"Stop her! You have got to stop her!"

The General looked up at him and then at Romina. A faint smile curved the corner of his lips.

"One minute, Romina," he said. "When you arrived just now, Merlin was talking to me about going to Cairo and wondering what would be the best method from his point of view."

He hesitated before he continued:

"You see, Merlin has no particular standing as far as the ordinary authorities are concerned. While you, as Chris's sister, have every right to ask questions as to where and how your brother died."

"Naturally," Romina agreed. "That is how I see it myself. Therefore there is no need for Mr. Forde to put himself out. I will go to Cairo, and I will let you—and, if you insist, Mr. Forde—know exactly what I discover."

There was a note of triumph in her voice, and she felt she had scored once and for all over the detestable young man who had made her feel so uncomfortable.

"At the same time," the General went on as if she had not spoken, "I cannot help feeling that you will be fobbed off with a lot of plausible answers and will find out very little on your own."

"It is not going to be easy—I know that," Romina told him, suddenly serious. "But I will do my best to act intelligently."

"I do not think you will get very far," the General said gently. "Therefore I am suggesting that we come to a compromise. Why don't you both go—together?"

"Together?" Romina ejaculated, and she saw the look on Merlin Forde's face was one of sheer astonishment.

"Yes," the General answered. "Why don't you go out as tourists? Cairo is very pleasant at this time of the year, and you could be—let me see—brother and sister, having a holiday together. Why not?"

"Why not?" Romina exclaimed furiously. "Because—"

The protest she was about to make died away on her lips. It struck her suddenly that, distasteful as the suggestion might be, it was eminently a sensible one.

If she was to discover how and why Chris had been killed nothing else mattered—not even the unpleasant Mr. Forde.

17

ROMINA propped her suitcase open on the arms of a chair and looked in the wardrobe to see what she should take with her.

She avoided looking directly at Chris's suits, which she had pushed to one side when she came to stay in the flat. This was his room, but she preferred it to the small, narrow bedroom which he kept for his friends.

Her eyes were tense and there was in her heart an ache which was physical in its intensity as she realized that Chris would not come back. Never again would she see him laugh, or hear the clink of the ice as he shook her a special cocktail of brandy, orange juice and cointreau.

"This is rot gut!" he would grumble. "Why don't you have a whisky and soda?"

"I hate whisky!" she would retort. "I'm not the whisky-drinking type—hard riding and hard swearing."

It had been a joke between them that although she looked so fragile and feminine, she was really almost as tough as he was—and quite as quick when it came to intelligence.

She could out-ride, out-ski and out-walk every other woman he knew; and, more important, she could keep up with him. That had been one of the things which had made it possible for them to work together.

Romina had given up her flat as she found it cheaper and more convenient to move into the one Chris used when she stayed in London.

She was determined to keep the house in Hertfordshire which, to both of them, was home. It was where they had been brought up, and Romina and Chris had refused to sell it, even when advised to do so by their Trustees.

"It may be too big and expensive, but we love it," Chris said positively, and finished the argument.

Most of Romina's clothes were in the country, and she decided that she would just have to make do with what she had at the flat and buy a few things when she reached Cairo.

She pulled open a drawer and started to take out her nylon nightgowns and lace-trimmed slips.

18

She packed automatically, her mind on Chris, remembering the things they had done together and how they had always laughed at danger. What could have happened? Would she ever know, even with Merlin Forde to help her? Was there any likelihood that they would find out the truth?

She grimaced as she thought of the journey that lay ahead. What could be more disagreeable than to be saddled with a man whom she already disliked—a man with whom she felt she had nothing in common?

But even going with Merlin Forde was better than not going at all; and above all things she wanted to get away from London at the moment. Her thoughts slid away from the reason for this and it was almost a relief when the doorbell rang.

She glanced at her watch, and wondered who it could be. It was half-past twelve. Mrs. Robins, who looked after the flat for Chris, had already gone and there was no one else to answer the door.

The bell rang again impatiently, and Romina crossed the small hall and opened the door.

A youth stood outside, holding in his arms an enormous basket covered with white paper, which she recognized as coming from a very expensive Mayfair florist.

"Miss Ro . . . Romeena 'untley?" he asked, mispronouncing her Christian name.

"Yes."

"Sign 'ere."

He thrust the book towards her and she scrawled her signature. Then he put the heavy basket into her arms.

" 'Bye, 'bye," he said cheerily, and went down the corridor whistling.

Romina carried the flowers into the sitting-room and set them down on the low coffee-table which stood in front of the fireplace. For a moment she just stared at the wrappings, and then almost roughly she ripped them off.

They had covered a basket of purple and white orchids—a magnificent, incredibly expensive gift.

Attached to the handle of the basket was an envelope. Romina detached it and opened the small, tightly-closed envelope with fingers which seemed suddenly stiff.

The name on the card inside leaped up at her, and above it was a message:

*"In sweet memory of a very wonderful evening, to
the most attractive girl in London."*

19

Romina stood very still. She felt as if the message seared its way into her mind and made her feel more humiliated than she had done before. It was not his fault—it was hers. She should have known better; she should have had more self-respect.

"I hate him!" she said aloud; but she knew it was herself she despised.

She took the card, tore it into a dozen small pieces and threw them into the fire which Mrs. Robins had lit.

She looked down at the orchids. There was something lush and exotic about them; something which reminded her of Alex's experienced, sophisticated kisses—of his hands caressing her, of the deep insistent note of passion in his voice.

With a little sob, she picked up the basket and threw it across the room—threw it with all her strength so that it bounced against the wall near the window and tipped over, the orchids spilling out on the carpet and lying there in a distorted way as if their curved and parted tongues protested against such treatment.

Without looking at them again, Romina turned and ran from the room back into the bedroom.

'I must get away,' she thought. Alex would be ringing her, she was certain of that. He had talked of their dining alone together that night, and she knew he would expect her to be eager to accept his invitation.

'I must get away . . . I must get away. . . .' The refrain repeated itself like the sound from the wheels of a train.

She started to pack without worrying whether her things would be creased or what she should take.

And then the doorbell rang again. She stood still, her heart thumping.

Could he have come to call on her? She looked at the time—it was only twenty minutes to one. It was very unlikely that he would call without telephoning; then again, he might have rung when she was out. But nothing had been said about lunch.

She could not risk it; she could not open the door and find him standing there with that smile on his lips, that look in his eyes. It would make her feel cheaper than she felt already.

The bell rang again.

It must be Alex, she thought. And yet he would be very unlikely to stand outside a door that had not been opened almost immediately in welcome.

Perhaps it was another message from him?

With an effort, she pulled herself together and walked into the hall again. She had an absurd desire to shout and ask

20

who it was. Equally absurdly, because she knew she was being theatrical and foolish, she opened the door just a crack.

'If it is Alex, I shall close it quickly and refuse to talk to him,' she thought.

But it was not Alex who stood there; it was Merlin Forde.

"I began to think I had come to the wrong place," he said.

"What do you want?" Romina asked. "I thought you were going to telephone to tell me the time we were leaving."

"May I come in?" he asked mildly.

She realized how rude she was being and felt apologetic.

"I . . . I am sorry," she answered. "I am not thinking very straight this morning."

"No, of course not," he said in a voice which was unexpectedly sympathetic, and she knew he thought she was referring to her unhappiness over Chris.

Because she was embarrassed at her behavior, she was brusque.

"Come in, if you want to," she said, "but I have only just got time to get my things packed."

He shut the door behind him and put his hat down in the hall. He was not wearing a coat, she noticed, although the wind was cold.

He moved into the sitting-room before she remembered the mess she had made with the orchids. She saw him glance at them, then look away.

"Will you have a drink?" she inquired. "Whisky, or a cocktail?"

"Whisky, please."

He moved towards the fire, holding out his hands to the blaze.

"This is Chris's flat," he said, making it a statement rather than a question. "Why are you staying here?"

"I live in the country," Romina answered. "I gave up my place nearly a year ago. Chris is so seldom in London that it was ridiculous for us to be paying for two when one would do quite well."

She handed him a whisky and soda.

"Thank you," he said. "I came to tell you that our plans are changed."

"Changed?" Romina asked sharply. "I must warn you that nothing you will say will prevent my going to Cairo, whatever you decide to do."

"No one is trying to prevent you," Merlin answered. "But I have had a talk with the General. I think I have put forward a far better scheme than he suggested."

21

"Does he think so?" Romina asked sarcastically, thinking this young man was bumptious and over-sure of himself.

"He does, as a matter of fact," Merlin replied.

Without being asked, he sat himself in an arm-chair by the fire, and Romina was glad that he had his back to the orchids.

"Well?" she prompted.

"I have thought things over," Merlin began, "and I don't think we are going to get very far as ordinary tourists. To begin with nobody—neither friend nor foe—is likely to get in touch with us. Secondly, one of our people in Cairo is already ferreting out all that can be discovered from the quarter where Chris was living."

"I wish he would leave it alone," Romina said angrily. "I want to see for myself. I do not want strangers covering trails and making it difficult before we arrive."

As she spoke she realized that what she was saying was rather silly and ineffectual. Of course someone experienced was likely to find out far more than she could ever do.

And because she did not want to appear too foolish, she said quickly:

"All right—forget what I said, and go on."

She saw a glint in his eyes, and he continued:

"I have therefore suggested something to the General which I believe may get results if we are lucky. But it means an added amount of danger as far as you are concerned."

"I am not interested in danger," Romina snapped. "I want to find out what happened to Chris."

"You certainly have his tenacity—whether it is a good thing or bad I would not know."

"Tell me your new plan," Romina suggested, feeling that she could not bear to be either praised or censured by the self-assured young man sitting opposite her.

Merlin sipped his whisky.

"In the late editions of the evening papers," he said, "it will be announced that a Greek-born millionaire—Nickoylos—has arrived in London from America to make an offer to one of the big gambling combines in the West End. The Press will hint that the offer is in the region of half a million pounds."

"Who is he?" Romina asked. "And where does he come into the story?"

"You see him sitting in front of you," Merlin replied with a grin.

"You?" Romina cried. "But why? What is the point?"

"I thought you would ask that. Mr. Nickoylos is going to

22

have quite a sensational past—in fact, to put it bluntly, he is going to sound somewhat of a cad and an adventurer."

"But is anyone going to believe this?"

"They certainly are," Merlin answered. "Nickoylos has booked a suite at the Savoy; and Lucien, who as you know owns most of the gambling halls in London, has already received an offer."

"Suppose he decides to accept?" Romina asked.

"Negotiations take a long time," Merlin answered. "Besides, unfortunately Mr. Nickoylos has to leave London tomorrow morning for Cairo."

"I see . . ." Romina said slowly. "You are building up a new character, someone who will be of interest to the people in Cairo who may be responsible for Chris's death?"

"Exactly," Merlin replied. "The more disreputable he seems, the more likely that 'birds of a feather will flock together.' Remember your Nannie teaching you that?"

"Where do I come in?" Romina asked quickly.

"Where do you think?" Merlin said. "You are Nickoylos's girl-friend."

He allowed the information to sink in for a second before he went on:

"Now it is up to you whether you can act the part. We cannot afford to slip up—you know that better than anyone—and I presume you know the type of woman who would interest a man like Nickoylos?"

"Flashy, common—and, I imagine, very young," Romina said slowly.

"You are more clever than I thought," Merlin approved.

She flashed him a glance of dislike before she said:

"I suppose I could do it. I shall want the right sort of clothes—"

"I have thought of that," Merlin broke in. "You will arrive at five o'clock this afternoon from New York. You have a slight American accent, but undoubtedly you started life in Manchester."

"I think it is rather risky," Romina said, feeling that somehow she must find fault. "It would be quite easy to check that I had not arrived at London Airport."

"But you will," Merlin answered.

The smile on his lips made her think that he was delighted to be able to contradict her.

"You will catch the two-thirty plane to Glasgow. It arrives—I think I am correct in this—at about a quarter to four. You will then pick up a Pan American plane as it comes in and arrive at London Airport on schedule."

"You think of everything," Romina said.

"There is always the possibility that people on the plane might remember you," he said, "but it is unlikely. Film stars off-duty look pretty scruffy and unimpressive anyway. Wear dark glasses and a handkerchief round your head. And a good mink coat—you have got one, of course?"

"As a matter of fact, I have."

"And when you get to the Savoy we can give you the full treatment—false eyelashes, a touch of peroxide on your hair, and all the usual accessories required by a baby doll of the type you will personify."

"Thank you very much," Romina said. "But do you think all this is really necessary?"

In answer, Merlin dropped the slightly annoying tone he had used until then and said in a very serious voice:

"You knew Chris better than I did. Do you think he would have said he was on to something big unless he was sure of it?"

"No, that's true," Romina said. "Chris always laughed at his successes, and pretended there had been no trouble at all."

"That is why I am taking no chances. If Chris said it was big—it was big. It is no use expecting this to be a Sunday School treat or a little skirmish with some half-witted bank robbers. He must have got on to the big boys, and we have got to appear big enough to interest them otherwise we are going to get exactly nowhere!"

"I think you may be right," Romina agreed.

"Then why not change your mind?" he asked. "Leave it to me. It is quite unnecessary for me to take a woman to Cairo, there are certain to be others only too eager to befriend a millionaire."

"I have every intention of coming with you," Romina replied coldly. "And if you are afraid I shall let you down, you need not be. Chris taught me years ago to think myself into the part I was playing."

She hesitated before she continued:

"I did do one or two things with him which we did not want Guardie to know about, so I did not mention it this morning. But actually I was with him when he discovered what was happening on the Turkish borders—and he said afterwards that if I had not been there he might never have got the story or got back alive."

"I am not doubting your ability," Merlin said icily. "I am only suggesting that if you are keen on knowing exactly how your brother died, I am very much more likely to find out without the hindrance of having anyone else with me—man or woman."

Romina got to her feet.

"You have made it very clear, Mr. Forde, since the first moment we met, that you do not want me tagging along. I could say the same thing. I intended to go to Cairo alone. However, I am well aware that two people on the same mission scrapping amongst themselves would be quite ridiculous. We will go as you suggest."

"Very well, then," Merlin said.

He put his hand in his pocket and brought out some papers.

"Here is your passport," he said. "Luckily the General had a photograph of you. It is made out in the name of Romina Faye."

"Why the same Christian name?" Romina inquired.

"Something I always insist on," Merlin answered. "After all, millions of people have the same name—there is nothing in that to draw suspicion to the person concerned. But I have found that unless one is very experienced, it is awfully hard in an emergency to remember a false name. One instinctively starts to sign the name one has had since birth."

He smiled, and then continued:

"By the time you finish the final 'a' of Romina you won't forget that you have to sign 'Faye' and not 'Huntley.' Also if you are working together and you happen to know someone by their real Christian name, instinctively one says it at some time or another. Then the position can be dangerous."

"Yes, I see," Romina said. "So you will remain Merlin?"

"I thought they went rather well together—'Merlin Nickoylos,' " he said with a grin.

"Well, I must say 'Romina Faye' sounds exactly like a film-star," Romina replied.

"Your last film, in which you were a mere extra, only you won't admit it!—was *Ben Hur* and before that you were in *The Ten Commandments*. I thought that religious touch was rather charming."

"You do not make me sound very glamorous," Romina said.

"But you will look it, don't forget. I am a dark, swarthy middle-aged Greek. Not pure-bred, of course—there will be quite a number of nationalities if you go into my ancestry. And what attracts me are fair-haired, blue-eyed women who are just about as dumb as they are made."

"Thank you again," Romina said sarcastically. "I think I would rather like to invent my own part."

"I doubt if you have time," Merlin said airily. "And now must go. There will be a car downstairs at one o'clock to tak you to the airport. You will have to hurry. And here are th labels to stick on your suitcase—or, better still, I will do tha for you while you take this ticket and put it in your bag."

Romina opened the ticket.

"Why, it is from New York," she exclaimed.

"Of course," he answered. "You will have arrived fron New York on another Pan American and stopped off i Glasgow to see an old friend."

"I must say it seems to be all tied up," Romina said coldly

He glanced at the clock over the mantelpiece.

"You had better hurry," he said. "You have got to be a the airport by two, and you do not want to draw attention b having your name called on the Tannoy or anything lik that."

"No, of course not," Romina agreed.

She turned and hurried into her bedroom, realizing as sh picked up her coat that he was just behind her.

He started to stick the tickets on her luggage and tie label on to the handle.

"Dark glasses?" he said as she put on her mink coat "Have you got any?"

"I expect so," she replied. "If not, I am sure you hav them with you."

"As a matter of fact, I have," he said, "but you might pre fer your own. They would be more comfortable."

"How nice of you to worry about me," she replied cyni cally, and opening the drawer of the dressing-table found a the back several pairs of glasses, her own and Chris's.

She took a pair out of a red-leather case, put them on an slipped the case into her bag.

"What color scarf do you suggest I wear around m head?" she inquired.

"Wear something dark for the airplane," he said, "but i you have something flamboyant, put it on before you get t the Savoy."

She opened another drawer and found what she wanted, dark blue, faintly patterned silk handkerchief which mad her look like dozens of other women who might be travelin at this time of the year. Another scarf, brilliant with flower which she had bought at Hermes in Paris, went into her bag.

"I am ready," she said.

"And on time!" he replied. "Wonders will never cease. always expect to have to wait for my women."

"Then perhaps you are in for a surprise where I am concerned," Romina retorted.

"I think that might be," he answered. "You are rather different from most of the girls I have known. Did Alex Salvekov send you the orchids which do not seem to have met with your approval?"

Romina had not expected the question. For a moment she could not find words with which to answer him.

"He has got rather a reputation with the fair sex," Merlin said conversationally. "I should think it is the first time one of his expensive little gifts suffered such a fate."

"I do not think there is any point in discussing it," Romina said.

"I hope there isn't," Merlin answered. "At the same time, isn't he going to wonder why you have disappeared so suddenly?"

"Alex Salvekov is nothing to me," Romina answered. "I'm not really interested in his feelings one way or another."

"But he will be," Merlin said. "I think it would be a good idea if you wrote to thank him for the flowers and told him you have left London for a few days. You could say you have gone to see your aunt in Bournemouth or Scotland—no matter where as long as he does not try to follow you."

"He is not likely to do that," Romina said sharply.

"I should not be too sure," Merlin answered. "You are a pretty girl and Salvekov must have spent at least twenty-five quid on your floral offering."

Romina pressed her lips together.

She wanted to tell Merlin to mind his own business and not to interfere with her in any way. And yet even though the knowledge infuriated her, she knew that he was right—Alex would think it strange that she had vanished.

"All right, I will send him a note," she said grudgingly. "But as a matter of fact I do not know him very well. I met him at Lady Davidston's a week or so ago. Of course, I had seen him about before that—he was always in the best places."

"He is very keen on Society," Merlin said with a note of derision in his voice.

"Of course—he is gay, amusing and very rich," Romina replied.

She did not want to defend Alex, but at the same time there was something so insufferably superior in Merlin's voice that she felt she had to slap him down.

"A combination that no woman could resist," Merlin said.

Romina felt herself flush not so much with anger but with

27

humiliation because she had been one of the women who had found Alex irresistible.

Without another word she went into the sitting-room and scribbled a few lines. She addressed an envelope, and without putting the letter in it took it back and handed it to Merlin.

"Here you are," she said. "I expect you want to see what I have written."

She spoke rudely, but he took the letter from her and read it carefully as if he considered it of importance. Then he placed the letter in the envelope and put it into his pocket.

"I will see that it is sent round by hand," he said. "You do not want him calling here or making inquiries with the porter downstairs."

Romina opened her mouth to say something, but changed her mind.

Merlin looked round the room.

"Well, I think we have seen to everything," he said. "What about your daily woman?"

"I told her this morning that I was going away," Romina answered. "She is used to our comings and goings and . . ."

She hesitated a moment.

". . . and I did not tell her about Chris. She is devoted to him. She has looked after him for nearly ten years and I could not face breaking the news to her."

She felt rather cowardly as if she had shirked an obvious duty.

Merlin nodded his head approvingly.

"The General has decided there is to be no announcement and nothing is to be said until we get back from Cairo—that is, if we do get back."

Romina glanced at him in a startled manner.

"Do you really mean that, or are you joking?"

"I never felt less jocular," he answered. "I have tried to impress on you that this trip is dangerous—very dangerous. If you would like to change your mind there is still time."

"Now you are merely being insulting," Romina answered, "but I would like to know what I am up against."

"I would like to know, too," Merlin said. "As it is we are just going out into the blue."

"If only Chris were here—he would be thrilled and excited at the thought," Romina said solemnly.

"Everything was an adventure to him," Merlin agreed. "There are few happy people in the world. Why couldn't they have left him alone?"

For the first time since their acquaintance Romina felt herself warm slightly towards him.

"Yes, he was happy," she said. "I have seldom known him unhappy. At least he enjoyed his life—short though it was."

She felt her voice tremble a little. Then almost defiantly she picked up her suitcase.

"I am going now," she said. "Are you coming down with me or do you follow later?"

"I do neither," he replied. "I am going out the way I came in—down the service lift and out through the back door. Incidentally it is quite an easy way of entering the flat and I should imagine it is the way your friend came last night when he delivered Chris's letter."

"If he did, it would have been Chris who told him about it," Romina answered. "He did not sound as if he was anxious to meet anyone or have any questions asked."

"I wish to God we knew who he was," Merlin said. "I have never met a case which was so full of questions without an answer of any sort."

"We must find the answers," Romina replied.

She took a last glance at herself in the mirror. She looked small and pretty but not particularly noticeable.

"I hope I don't meet anyone I know," she said, "it would be difficult to explain why my luggage is covered with American labels."

"Have a story ready in case you do," Merlin said. "You could always have been traveling with a friend who was too sick to go any further."

"I think you are wasted," Romina told him. "You should be writing detective stories."

"I prefer to live them," he answered. "Now come on or you will be late."

He turned and walked ahead and opened the door for her.

"Just walk downstairs and the car will be waiting outside," he said. "It is a gray Jaguar. Try not to say anything to the porter, it is best if he does not notice you."

"He very seldom does," Romina observed. "He is a surly sort of chap who suffers from arthritis."

"Good-bye," Merlin said. "I shall look forward to meeting Miss Romina Faye. You will find Mr. Nickoylos in the Bridal Suite."

As she stepped into the corridor Romina had a sudden desire to draw back. Was she really setting out on this mad, incredible adventure? Would it not be better to do as Merlin suggested and let him go alone to Cairo?

Then as she heard him close the door behind her, she knew it was indeed too late. She had made her decision and nothing on earth would prevent her from carrying out the

29

task she had set herself—to find Chris's murderer and, if possible, avenge his death.

She walked down the corridor feeling rather as if she were going to the guillotine.

There was only one of the small pageboys on duty on the lift. The regular man was at lunch. The boy was licking a lollipop and there was a comic stuck in the pocket of his jacket which Romina was sure interested him far more than the passengers.

They reached the hall and, looking neither to right nor left, she walked across it and through the swing doors.

She saw a gray Jaguar standing outside, a little to the left of the front-door, and walked across to it.

A uniformed chauffeur jumped out to take her case. He put it in the front of the car and opened the door at the back.

Romina got in and let him put a rug over her knees. Without a word, the chauffeur climbed back into the front seat and the car glided off.

The traffic in the Mayfair streets was not heavy as it was lunch-time, and they were soon moving through Knightsbridge and on to Western Avenue.

Romina lay back and closed her eyes. She felt desperately tired.

The night before she had not slept at all, but stayed in front of the dying fire, reading and re-reading Chris's last letter and remembering all they had meant to each other.

At first the shock of learning of his death and remembering the happiness they had enjoyed together made her forget Alex Salvekov.

And then, as the dawn broke, she had gone to the window to look over the roofs at the thin fingers of light coming up in the dark sky and she had felt ashamed as she had never felt before.

Why had she ever got herself into this position? Why had she ever been so weak as to allow him to make love to her?

She did not know the answer.

It was easy to blame the evening they had spent together; the wine they had drunk; the fact that so many women at the party had envied her because he devoted himself exclusively to her.

It was all those things, but much more. Was it her loneliness? Was it the feeling she had had lately of not knowing what she was going to do with her life, of being rudderless?

Perhaps it was because Chris was away and she had not seen him for some time that she felt any love, even the sort offered by Alex Salvekov, was better than none.

30

She did not know what it was.

She only knew that now she was ashamed and sorry. She wished as she had never wished before that she could go back twenty-four hours and relive them in a very different way.

'How many men and women have wished the same thing?' she thought.

Then with an effort she shook herself mentally.

What did it matter except that Alex had left a scar that she felt would be with her for life? He had lowered her standards; he had forced defenses she thought were impregnable.

If the letter from Chris had not fallen into the box at that precise moment what might not have happened?

'No . . . no! I must not think of it!'

Romina almost said the words out loud.

It had not happened, thanks to Chris. But she knew she would never forgive herself because his message might have come too late.

'I will never see Alex again,' she thought; and knew that whatever happened in Cairo she would not be able to go back to Mayfair and her circle of friends if that was her resolution.

Alex Salvekov was the new lion, the new darling, with the gay young married women in whose houses Romina spent a great deal of her time.

He would be at every luncheon party in the smart Belgrave Square area; at the '400' with people whose names would read like a page from Debrett; at the theater, the opera; visiting Cabinet Ministers in the country at week-ends and turning up at political and diplomatic receptions which were attended by the Prime Minister.

Romina tried to remember a party she had attended in the last three or four months when Alex had not been present.

And yet she had never known him well until she had sat next to him a week ago. He had always been busy with some other woman, too busy to notice her, it seemed, until he had asked her out to dinner before the Davidstons' fancy-dress party.

She had imagined there would be a crowd; but to her surprise when she arrived at his palatial suite at the Dorchester she found they were alone.

"The others are going to join us after dinner," he had said quickly as she had looked round in astonishment. "Hugh and Bingo have been kept at the House."

"What about their poor wives?" Romina asked. "Aren't they going to eat?"

"They preferred to wait for their husbands," Alex answered suavely. "And, quite frankly, I was delighted."

"Delighted?" Romina questioned.

"Because I would have you to myself," Alex answered.

She had to admit that he said it well. It sounded as if he meant it.

He was amazingly handsome and his fancy dress showed off his good looks as a dinner-jacket could never have done.

She had thought that she might feel self-conscious in her fancy dress; but by the time that she had had a cocktail and dinner was served in the adjoining room, she had forgotten everything except how interesting Alex could be, and how amusing it was to be flattered and courted by a man who attracted almost every woman in London.

In fact, the evening had been fun—she would not deny it—until they had gone to her flat.

'I won't think about it . . . I won't!' she told herself.

Romina opened her eyes to find she was nearly at London Airport.

The car turned in at the untidy North Gate and moved down the steep hill bordered with advertisements which led to the tunnel. Then through the tunnel to the exit, where they had their first glimpse of the Airport buildings with their fluttering flags.

The chauffeur drove without question to the departure doors of internal flights. A porter opened the door and took Romina's case.

She hesitated a moment as to whether she should tip the chauffeur, and decided against it.

"Thank you," she said, and he touched his cap.

She followed the porter through the swing doors, produced her ticket and had it checked. Her luggage was weighed and she went on the moving stairway.

As she did so it seemed that she was moving from one stratum to another. Her life was left behind; the friends she had known and loved. Everything and everybody was gone.

Romina Huntley no longer existed and Romina Faye had taken her place.

"Think yourself into the part. Think yourself the person you are pretending to be and believe in her," she could hear Chris's voice from the past instructing her. "It is thought that counts."

If he had said it once, he had said it a dozen times.

"It is thought that counts."

Romina repeated the words to herself as she sat down in the crowded waiting-room until they called her flight.

CHAPTER THREE

FROM the moment Romina arrived at the Savoy and asked with her newly-acquired American accent for Mr. Nickoylos she felt as if she had stepped without a script into a part in a rather over-dramatized television play.

She felt almost sick with apprehension as the page took her up in the lift.

Suppose she met someone she knew? What if this all turned out to be a ridiculous farce, and if Merlin was only out for a good time, spending money at what she supposed was the taxpayers' expense?

Then she remembered that her guardian would not have entrusted her so easily to Merlin's care unless he believed in him.

Anyway, she told herself, her tortured questions would soon be answered. The page opened the door of the suite and she stepped inside.

The door of the sitting-room was half open and Romina could see a number of men seated around with glasses in their hands.

A strident voice was holding forth—a voice with a foreign accent overlaid with American which in some clever way seemed self-assertive and full of conceit.

The page knocked on the door.

"Miss Faye to see you, sir!"

There was a moment's silence as Merlin crossed the room, flung open the door and stepped into the *entresol*.

Romina hardly recognized him.

His hair was cut in a different way and he wore long side-whiskers. His skin was darker, and his clothes excruciatingly over-tight and over-smart.

But it was not so much all this as the change in his expression; the way he thrust forward his chin and his lower lip made him seem quite different from the man she had been talking to such a short time before.

"Romina, baby," he exclaimed in an oily tone. He flung his arms around her and kissed her on both cheeks.

33

She stiffened at his touch, then forced herself to relax and pouted her over-red lips into a kiss somewhere near his ear.

"You have arrived," he went on unnecessarily. "And I've been counting the hours until you could get here. Go and make yourself pretty, honey. I will be with you in a few minutes as soon as I have finished with these gentlemen."

He glanced back at the listeners in the sitting room.

"Is your luggage coming up? Good. I will tell the waiter to bring you some champagne. You'll need it after the long journey. I won't be long."

He blew a kiss from a hand which sported a dazzling diamond ring and went back into the sitting room, pushing the door until it nearly closed behind him.

"Sorry, gentlemen," Romina heard him say. "A friend, a very special friend, has just arrived from Hollywood."

"Who is she, Mr. Nickoylos, a star?"

"Now, boys, no questions like that—no encroaching on my private life," Merlin answered lightly. "And no mention in your columns of the lady's presence, please. It could get me into a lot of trouble at the moment if you were indiscreet."

He gave a little laugh, which was a masterpiece of innuendo.

"Heart trouble, or a matrimonial triangle, Mr. Nickoylos?" another voice inquired.

"Now, boys, I am warning you," Merlin replied, and Romina could almost see him wagging his finger at them. "I'm an open book on any other subject, except this one."

There was a burst of laughter as if Merlin had said something which they found humorous because it was incredible.

Romina went slowly along to her room. It was enormous and she realized there was another one of the same size next door and that Merlin was certainly giving the impression of being a millionaire, if nothing else.

There was a spray of orchids in a Cellophane box waiting on the dressing-table, and almost before she had time to take off her gloves there was a knock at the door and a waiter appeared with a bottle of champagne and two glasses.

He poured her out half a glass and she took it gratefully, feeling she was going to need some sustenance before the evening was out.

When the waiter left, there was a discreet knock on the door.

"Come in," she called, expecting someone with her suitcase, but instead she saw a small man wearing a white coat and carrying a small brown case in his hand.

34

"I am the coiffeur, Madame," he said. "I was informed that you would need me."

Romina hesitated.

"I . . . I expect so," she answered.

He shut the door behind him and came into the room.

"It's all right, Miss Faye," he said, "I have my orders."

He spoke in such a low voice that for a moment she hardly understood what he said.

Then he went to the dressing-table and setting down his case opened it. She saw that it contained every sort of make-up—boxes of false eyelashes, hair tints, eye-liners and a variety of lipsticks.

He looked at her hair as Romina slowly undid the colored handkerchief.

"I think I've got the right thing here," he said.

And as she looked at him with a question in her eyes, he added:

"Don't worry, Miss. I really am a hairdresser—or was, for many years."

Romina smiled.

An hour later he took the rollers from her hair and she saw the tinny glint he had given it.

"It will wash out any time you want to get rid of it," he said reassuringly. "But you must re-tint it every time you have a shampoo—I will leave you a bottle of the stuff."

"It is certainly better than peroxide," Romina said, remembering Merlin's words.

"That indeed would be a crime on hair of your texture," the hairdresser said. "And now the eyelashes, miss."

When he had finished with her Romina felt that even her closest friend would fail to recognize her. She looked pretty, flashy and extremely common. There was, too, a sexy look about her which she had never known she possessed.

Merlin had looked in once through the door while they were working, but he had said nothing and disappeared again.

The hairdresser looked at his watch.

"I'd best be going," he said. "I understand you are expecting some clothes to arrive."

"Am I?" Romina inquired.

"I'm sure you are," he answered gravely. "Good-bye, Miss Faye—and the very best of luck."

He held out his hand and Romina shook it. She knew instinctively he was not someone she should tip.

He was an artist in his own way, and she wondered how

many people's faces he had altered until their own relatives would not recognize them.

She had hardly been alone a second before there was a knock at the door and a *vendeuse* arrived with boxes filled with dresses of every sort.

"Good evening, Modom," she said in the exaggerated over-accented voice of her trade. "Mr. Nickoylos told us how your clothes had been left behind at the airport in Hollywood. What a disaster! You must be furious, but we are only hoping we shall find something to suit you!"

She put down the box she was carrying and motioned for a page who was outside to bring in half a dozen more.

"I hear you are off to the sun, Modom. Aren't you lucky? I wish we could all get away from this horrible weather."

"Yes, indeed," Romina answered, and watched with a sense of amusement models which were being brought out from the cardboard boxes for her inspection.

There was nothing she could ever imagine wearing normally—low-coat evening gowns covered with sequins; day dresses that were so tight that she was afraid to sit down in them; cotton frocks with screaming patterns in a kaleidoscope of brilliant colors made her feel that anyone who looked at her would want to wear dark glasses.

With a few exceptions, they fitted her and she felt that Merlin should be commended on having guessed her size so exactly.

It was nine o'clock before she had finished and the *vendeuse* had packed up the dresses which were not required and was ready to leave.

Romina offered her a glass of champagne which she accepted with alacrity.

Then the bill was produced. Somewhat apprehensively Romina took it into the sitting-room.

Merlin was lying on the floor with his feet up, reading a newspaper. He glanced up as she entered, but made no effort to rise to his feet, which Romina realized was part of his new role.

"Well, honey, found anything that fits you?" he asked.

"Some lovely things," Romina answered, "but I am wondering if you are going to be so pleased when you see the bill."

"Nothing's too good for my little girl," Merlin answered.

Romina crossed the room and handed him the bill. She saw his lips twitch for a moment in an amused smile.

Still playing his part, Romina thought, even though, it was unlikely that the *vendeuse* could overhear them.

"Give me a pen."

She went to the desk and brought him back a gold pen which he must have left lying there.

He drew a check-book from his pocket and she saw with a sudden widening of her eyes that it was for a Greek bank in Athens.

'Every detail,' she thought, 'nothing left to chance.'

Merlin scrawled a signature.

"Tell her the shop can cash this at the Westminster Bank in Lombard Street," he said. "And tell them I have taken off five per cent for cash."

It was clever, very clever, Romina thought as she took the check and repeated what she had been told.

"That will be quite all right, Modom," the *vendeuse* said, obviously delighted at having made such a large sale.

Romina saw her through the outer door and then went back into the sitting-room.

"What do we do with all these horrors afterwards?" she asked. "Give them to a theatrical charity?"

Merlin looked up at her from the sofa and his voice was curt.

"Questions of that sort are unnecessary and dangerous," he said. "Romina Faye would not say that."

Romina's eyes widened.

"Do . . . do you mean to suggest that we keep up this . . . this farce when we are alone?"

"Always," he said. "It is the only way. Besides, how do you know there is no one listening?"

Romina looked round the room with amusement.

"Are you suggesting there is someone under the mat?" she inquired.

"Might be," he replied.

She gave a little gasp.

"You mean . . . there might be a microphone, or something like that?"

"Not here," he answered, "at least it is very unlikely. But certainly where we are going."

His voice was lowered and Romina seemed to see clearly, as if for the first time, that they were not playing a farce but it was something deadly serious. They must never, not even for a moment, relax or in any way under-estimate the enemy—whoever he was.

She felt suddenly embarrassed, like a schoolgirl who had giggled out of turn or a child who had made a gaffe.

"I'm sorry," she said briefly. "It will not occur again."

"Go and put your glad rags on, honey," Merlin said with

his assumed accent. "I'm going to order dinner up here. I'm so mighty glad to see you that I'm not going to share you with anyone else—not tonight, at any rate."

"Now you're talking turkey," Romina said. "If there is one thing I really want at the moment it is something to eat."

She smiled and two dimples appeared in her cheeks as she whisked round the door and disappeared.

Merlin looked after her with a little frown between his eyes before he rang the bell.

Later they went from night-club to night-club. At each one Merlin introduced himself to the proprietor or manager and told the same story of how he wished to play his part in London's night-life.

Romina was amazed at all he knew about catering and the sort of entertainment which would attract the richer type of customer.

They were received everywhere with attention and what appeared to be respect; but Romina could not help noticing an occasional look which told her that the men Merlin was impressing were none too pleased at the thought of new competition.

She tried to appear relaxed and gay, but she had been thankful when at last at nearly three o'clock in the morning they had driven back in silence to the Savoy.

Merlin made a scene at the desk because he said he was certain that a cable he was expecting from Athens must have been mis-directed to another room.

Eventually they got to their suite and Romina was almost too tired to say good night. She fell into bed and was fast asleep almost as soon as her newly-colored head touched the pillow.

They had left early for London Airport, but first new suitcases had been bought for Romina's clothes; cables had been sent to mysterious acquaintances in New York; and a telephone call had been made to Lucien to find out if he had yet made up his mind about selling his gambling clubs.

Finally, with last-minute instructions all round and a new spray of orchids for Romina, they started off in an enormous hired limousine which was to take them to the airport.

Romina had a sudden pang of homesickness and fear as the airplane took off.

'What am I letting myself in for?' she asked herself.

Then she put her head back against the seat and tried to sleep so that she would be sufficiently quick-brained to keep up with Merlin's act.

The stewardess brought champagne and while Romina said

"Thank you" for her glass, Merlin sipped his and demanded that it should be re-iced.

'I suppose millionaires do behave like this?' she asked herself and longed to ask Merlin the same question.

She glanced round at the other occupants of the airplane.

They looked ordinary enough—and yet, who knows? One of them might be taking note of Merlin and herself, making inquiries about them, finding out if they were really who they pretended to be.

There was no doubt that Merlin wished to be noticed. He made every possible excuse to ask for things in a loud voice, to complain and say that his seat was uncomfortable. No one on the airplane could fail to hear him.

Their first stop was Rome. They refueled and half an hour later as the airplane rose sharply into the blue sky Romina could see the Colosseum, round, empty and somber in the sunshine.

She had a glimpse of the dazzling whiteness of the memorial to Victor Emmanuel and then as the silver ribbon of the Tiber vanished from her sight they were up in the clouds and heading south.

She had a sudden thrill of excitement. This was indeed adventure. This was something she had never visualized in her wildest moment.

Then she remembered Chris, and a yearning for him made her fight back the tears which came all too easily to her eyes.

In the seat next to her Merlin undid his safety-belt and holding his hand up clicked his fingers aggressively at the Stewardess.

"Champagne," he said. "And quickly. I need a drink."

There was something so arrogant and offensive in his voice that Romina could not help but smile.

She only hoped she could put on as good an act, and although she disliked Merlin she had to admit that in his own way he was magnificent.

The hours slipped by.

Romina glanced round at Merlin and found that he was asleep. Even in repose his face retained the characteristics he impressed on it; the thrust-forward lower lip which gave him a rather sinister, sardonic expression.

'It is extraordinary,' she thought, 'how a man can alter himself so completely without owing anything to make-up save perhaps a slight darkening of the skin.'

With a woman, so many other things were required to play the part—false eyelashes, tinted hair, different colored rouge, an over-red mouth.

She glanced at herself in her hand mirror and wanted to laugh.

The coral of her new tight suit made her hair seem even more tinny than it had been the night before; and a pair of glittering gold earrings which the *vendeuse* had produced to match the buttons and a multitude of dangling bracelets only accentuated the impression she gave of being a showgirl.

Romina put her mirror away and lay back.

She was still half-asleep when some time later she felt Merlin's hand come down sharply on her knee and his voice say:

"Wake up, honey. We are just arriving and as soon as we get to the hotel I will buy you a nice long gin-fizz. They make them in Cairo better than in any other place in the world."

Romina looked out of the window. They were coming down out of the clouds, and she saw Cairo lying beneath her in the last golden rays of the setting sun.

She had a quick impression of high mosques, of flat-roofed houses and a wide curving river; then they were down and taxi-ing along towards the airport buildings which welcomed them with lighted windows.

An enormous car was waiting for them outside. It had been ordered by cable and a smiling Egyptian introduced himself as their guide.

In a few minutes they were traveling along a road on which there was little traffic towards the town.

"Where are we staying?" Romina asked.

"Well, baby, it was a difficult choice," Merlin answered. "I used to stay at Shepheard's in the old days, but it was burned down and they built a new hotel with the same name on the banks of the Nile. Then the Semiramis became smart. But now there is a new hotel altogether—an American one which should make you feel at home. I do not suppose you have heard of it, but it is the Nile-Vista."

"Of course I have heard of the Nile-Vista," Romina replied a little petulantly.

"Well, you know I always expect the best," Merlin said, "and they tell me this is the best, so that is where we are going."

"You are right, sir," the guide interposed from the front seat. "Everyone very pleased and very happy with the Nile-Vista. We book you a good suite—best in the whole hotel."

"There will be trouble if it isn't," Merlin replied laconically. "As I have just said to the little lady here, only the best is good enough for me."

Even if he wished to find fault, it was difficult for him to do so when they were shown up to what appeared to Romina to be an absolutely palatial suite on the fourth floor.

The rooms were not as large as those at the Savoy, but there were big balconies overlooking the Nile; and as she stepped out on one Romina forgot everything but the beauty of the scene that lay before her.

The sable sky was already strewn with a million stars. The wide waters of the Nile gleamed metallically beneath the lights of the bridges and house-boats moored on the opposite bank, while far away in the distance the Pyramids were floodlit against the evening sky.

She stood staring, feeling the sheer beauty of it seep into her like well-loved music.

Then, behind her, she heard Merlin instructing the porters about the luggage, and she came down to earth with a bump.

Almost nervously she turned to go back into the room. Whatever happened, she must not make mistakes now.

The porters shut the door behind them, obviously well pleased with their tips and Romina opened her lips to speak, meaning merely to say how beautiful it was outside.

Merlin raised his fingers to his lips.

"Well, baby, I guess we are going to be very comfortable here," he said and then began systematically to search the room.

It only took Romina a moment to remember why he was doing so; and when she saw him pull open the ventilator and draw something out of it she knew his precaution had been wise.

He twisted something small a little viciously, then replaced it and moved into the next room.

He found another microphone low down in the skirting-board behind her bed and another fixed to the back of the dressing-table in his own room.

Then he smiled at her and before he spoke he drew her out on to the balcony.

"You want to speak, I can see you are bursting to do so. Keep your voice low—nothing above a whisper."

He put his arm around her shoulder as he spoke and drew her close to him.

To anyone watching it would only have been a gesture of affection.

'But who would be watching up here amongst the stars?' Romina thought, and shuddered as if afraid what the answer might be.

She raised her head.

41

"Who do you think put them here?" she asked, hardly breathing the words. "The management?"

Merlin shook his head.

"Most unlikely," he said. "Maybe somebody suspicious, or perhaps just a precaution. Remember we are in a Police State—never forget that for a moment."

"Do you really think that someone knows that we are here to inquire about Chris?"

"No," he answered. "I do not think that—but one never knows. Now, that's enough. It is the greatest mistake to drop out of character, even for a second."

He spoke gently with none of the sharpness he had used the night before and yet it somehow irritated Romina.

"Oh, stop it, darling," she said in what she imagined Miss Faye's most petulant voice would be. "It's too soon to start making love. What about a drink? It's what you promised me."

She saw a sudden glint in Merlin's eye and realized he appreciated she was getting her own back.

Obediently he followed her into the sitting-room and ordered a bottle of champagne while Romina flounced off to unpack and have her bath.

She lay soaking herself in the warm scented water and wondered if, even here, she was observed. Was there a microphone concealed in the pale blue mosaic which decorated the bathroom and made her feel she was floating in the waters of the Nile?

Or was there a peep-hole?

The idea of that brought her hurriedly out of the bath and she started drying herself with the towels which were American size and therefore very small.

She dressed herself in one of her more flamboyant dresses. It was pretty in a rather vulgar way, with a green tulle skirt and a bodice covered in sequins with only one shoulder strap.

"You look like the Spirit of Spring," Merlin told her when she came into the sitting-room.

"I feel more like autumn without that drink you promised me," Romina replied tartly.

He rose to his feet and handed her a brimming glass.

"Do we always have to eat so late?" she asked. "I'm used to earlier hours."

"You may be able to sleep in the morning if you are lucky," Merlin said.

"Oh, I wouldn't want to miss any of the sightseeing," Romina replied, hoping that she would be able to punish him by making him feel tired too.

There was a twinkle in his eye as he picked up the bottle of champagne, and she heard him walk across to his bathroom and pour it down the lavatory.

He came back into the room and set the empty bottle down on the table.

"Come on, baby," he said, "let's go and hit the high spots. There are a lot of things I want to see here. They tell me the night-life equals anything you can see in Paris."

About two o'clock in the morning Romina began to wish that that were so. They had trailed round to at least half a dozen different places, following a dinner which she had found unappetizing and lacking in any culinary interest.

"The trouble with the Egyptians," Merlin said stentoriously, "is that they have quarreled with the French. A great number of the chefs have gone home. I would be willing to wager that this has been cooked by a German."

After that it was champagne—champagne all the way.

Champagne at the oriental night club where one belly dancer followed another; champagne and rather nasty coffee at another place where a boy danced carrying a loaded tea tray on his head; champagne where a variety of fat, rather unattractive young women tried and failed dismally to kick their legs in unison; and champagne in a rather lower type of night club where there was native singing and again more belly dancing.

"Good God!" Merlin exclaimed when they got back to the car, "what you want in Cairo is the kind of joint that I open in most capital cities of the world."

"We should be very pleased to have it, sir," the guide, who had been waiting for them, answered with a smirk which made it difficult to know whether or not he was being sincere. "But now I take you somewhere very nice. It is a club, but that can be arranged, you understand? They gamble there."

"Well, that's the sort of place I want to see," Merlin said. "You have shown us nothing but rubbish so far. Not worth the price of a bottle of Coca Cola."

"The gentleman must pardon me. I was not certain exactly what you wanted," the guide said.

"Well, take us to this other place," Merlin said snappily. "And it had better be good."

It was, in fact, very impressive. What was once a private house or small palace had been converted into a club, but it was obvious there was not much difficulty about becoming a member.

It was packed with people, and Romina guessed that the guide had wanted it to be full before he took them there.

On one floor there were card rooms, on the next a dance band; on yet another there was gambling in what must have been a reception-room when the house was in private hands.

There was an odd mixture of people—men who looked rich, with women blazing with jewels; and others who looked as if they did not have the price of a chip in their pockets. They gambled very intently and appeared to give it much serious thought before placing their bets.

The music of the band came faintly through the big doors which kept opening and shutting, but otherwise there was little sound except from the voices of the croupiers.

Romina's eyes were aching and sore from the cigar smoke. She longed to sit down, but there was nowhere to sit. She wondered how long Merlin would stand watching.

"Would you like to play, sir?" an attendant asked.

Merlin shook his head.

"Not tonight," he said. "Keep me a place at the big game tomorrow. I might take a hand."

"Thank you, sir. You like to play very big?"

"As big as possible," Merlin answered. "It bores me otherwise."

"We will tell some of our members who will be interested," the attendant said. "May I be permitted to ask your name?"

"Nickoylos," Merlin said with an air, as if he was announcing he was the King of England or the Shah of Persia.

He glanced round.

"You must have heard of me," he said. "Tell the proprietor of this joint it might be worth his while to have a talk with me. I'm staying at the Nile-Vista."

He turned on his heel and walked away leaving the attendant bowing, an expression on his face which Romina had begun to expect after people had been talking with Merlin.

She followed him to the top of the stairs. It was a polished staircase with mosaics above the dado and iron banisters carved with Egyptian characters.

There was only one couple walking ahead of them down the stairway, and Romina said with a little catch in her breath:

"Can we go home now? I'm so tired."

Merlin nodded, and she slipped her hand gratefully through his arm.

"I think it was more fun in London," she pouted.

"You are right, baby," Merlin replied, "but we've got to see everything."

44

They took another step, and as they did so, the couple in front of them who had almost reached the bottom of the stairs stood still and they heard the man, who was an Egyptian, say furiously in English:

"Find it, you little fool, find it!"

The woman started looking in her bag.

"It's gone, I tell you!" she cried almost hysterically. "I had it here, but it's gone!"

"You damn little liar, you've stolen it!"

The man raised his hand and slapped the woman as hard as he could across the cheek.

She gave a little sob, and dropped her evening bag which spilled out over the stairs, some of the things rolling on to the carpet below.

For a moment both Romina and Merlin stood there paralysed.

Then, in what appeared to be a single stride, Merlin moved down the intervening stairs and with one strong punch of his right hand caught the man on the chin and sent him sprawling against the wall.

There was a thump as his head hit it, and he lay still, his legs in long pointed shoes spread out in front of him.

The woman stood staring, her mouth open. She was very pretty, Romina thought, with fashionably dressed dark hair and turquoise eye-shadow behind long-lashed frightened eyes. She was about thirty, but her figure was exquisite.

Very slowly she raised a shaking hand to her face which was livid from where the man had struck her.

"He deserved it," Merlin said, almost beneath his breath, and Romina knew as he spoke that he had acted impetuously and out of character in hitting the man. It was not what Nickoylos would have done—he undoubtedly would have walked by on the other side.

The woman did not speak; instead she bent down and snatched up her things off the floor—lip-stick, compact and a handkerchief. She thrust them hastily into her bag.

She looked back for one moment at the unconscious man before she ran as quickly as her high stiletto heels would carry her through the red curtains which hung over the entrance door.

The vestibule and the reception-desk were outside and no one appeared to have seen what had happened. The man still lay with his back against the wall, his head nodding forward on his chest.

Romina saw something lying on the floor. She bent down and picked it up.

"Wait a minute, you have left something," she cried and started to move across the hall after the woman who had just left.

She had hardly taken a step before Merlin caught hold of her wrist and prevented her going any farther.

"Leave her alone!" he said commandingly.

Then they heard voices behind them and someone started to come down the stairs.

Merlin tightened his grip on Romina's wrist and in the passing of a second had dragged her through a door which stood on the left of the hall.

"This is the wrong way," she gasped, knowing that the front door was through the red curtains.

Merlin took no notice.

The door they pushed open led into a passage, and beyond that they could hear the sound of voices and the clatter of cutlery.

Without a word Merlin stalked on, pulling Romina with him.

They passed the open door of a kitchen and a waiter carrying a heaped tray came out from it and nearly collided with them.

"Where is the back door?" Merlin inquired.

The waiter did not seem surprised at the question.

"Straight on, sir. It's on the left," he answered.

Still moving quickly, Merlin led the way and a moment later they found themselves outside the house in a dark alleyway.

There were dustbins and, because they were moving in the shadows, a dog growled at them.

Romina wondered in what sort of filth they were walking, but there was no time to argue.

Almost before she had time to draw her breath, Merlin had pulled her to the end of the alley-way and they were in a brightly lit main thoroughfare with a number of cars moving past them.

Merlin stood on the pavement for a moment, then stepped into the road to signal a taxi. It came to a standstill a few yards behind them and they got into it.

"The Nile-Vista," Merlin told the driver.

"What about the car?" Romina whispered after they had gone a little distance in silence.

Merlin shook his head and she said no more.

When they reached the almost empty lounge of the hotel with its tinkling fountain, Merlin walked up to the desk.

"Telephone the Pyramid Club," he said, "and tell them to

send Mr. Nickoylos's car away. He will not require it any further this evening."

"Very good, sir," the night porter answered in a disinterested voice.

The tired bell-boy took them up in the lift.

As they stepped out on the fourth floor Romina stopped on the small landing where the lifts faced each other.

There was no one about and she felt this was somewhere they were very unlikely to be overheard.

She opened her hand and held it out towards Merlin.

"This is what I was trying to give her," she said.

He looked over his shoulder then picked up a small ring which lay on the palm of her hand.

It was made of gold, or what appeared to be gold, in the shape of a snake's head, and was very like the type of cheap ornament which could be found in every souvenir shop or market stall which catered for the tourist.

The snake's head was larger than one might have expected and on the long red tongue were three tiny pearls.

"Is it valuable?" Romina asked.

"I don't know. I don't think so," Merlin answered.

There was a frown between his eyes which she did not understand.

He seemed about to say something but they heard the sound of a lift rising towards them and he took her arm and led her down the passage towards their suite.

"What made you hit him?" Romina asked.

She had the satisfaction of seeing Merlin look shamefaced. "I always thought the Queensberry rules put one at a disadvantage," he said wryly.

"I thought it was a bit out of character on the part of a Greek night-club owner," Romina jeered.

He opened the door of their suite and switched on the lights. Then he crossed to the desk and stood near a lamp, turning the ring over and over in his fingers.

"Do you think that was what he was asking her for?" Romina asked.

Merlin drew a wallet out of his pocket and slipped the ring into the deepest pocket from which it was not likely to be dislodged.

"Forget it!" he said sharply, and Romina knew it was a command.

"All right, Sir Galahad," she said, and she had the pleasure of seeing him look extremely irritated.

She went to the door and could not resist a parting shot:

"She did not seem very grateful," she smiled.

Without waiting for Merlin's answer she went into her own room and closed the door.

Romina wondered why Merlin had been so interested in the ring. It was obviously rather a cheap one.

She had just finished undressing and was combing her hair in front of the mirror when she heard a door close.

She was certain it was the outer door, and wondered if they had left it open when they entered the suite. Then she remembered that Merlin had closed it and she had seen him put outside the "DO NOT DISTURB" notice.

She put on her dressing-gown and opened the door of her bedroom. It was very quiet. She looked into the sitting-room and there was no one there.

After a moment's hesitation, she went to the door of Merlin's bedroom and listened.

She knocked gently on the door, but there was no answer and she knocked again.

As he still did not reply she opened the door. The room was empty. It was Merlin who had gone out, leaving her alone!

Why had he gone, and why had he not told her he was going?

She felt suddenly furious with him that he had not confided in her. Then her anger ebbed away, and she was afraid—afraid because she did not understand what was happening.

CHAPTER FOUR

Romina was awakened by the sun seeping through the thin silk curtains of the big square window of her bedroom.

She felt fresh and cool, for the air-conditioning had made it possible for her to sleep comfortably with a single blanket on the bed.

Now, looking at the golden sun as it crept in long fingers over the floor and down the side of the curtains, she could almost feel the heat waiting outside, striving to get in.

Then with a sudden jar the events of the night before came flooding back to her mind—the long procession of night-clubs; then Merlin striking out at the man who had hit the woman with the dark hair.

With her eyes closed, Romina could picture the man all too vividly—the thin pointed nose; eyes that were too close together; the tight line of his mouth which had something cruel and unpleasant about it and made one think of sinister, almost evil, things.

She had not realized last night how much his features had imprinted themselves on her mind.

Now it was as if she saw him on a film, striking out at the girl, turning in astonishment as Merlin strode down the stairs towards him; and then the expression of almost ludicrous surprise as Merlin's experienced blow on the chin seemed to lift him off his feet so that he fell heavily against the wall.

And the girl. Romina could remember her, too—the elegantly coiffured hair, the little heart-shaped face which was pretty and at the same time sophisticated.

There was something about her which told Romina irrefutably that she was what was known as 'a lady,' someone of breeding and culture. But even so, what was she doing at the Pyramid Club in company with such a man?

The things which had fallen out of her bag had been expensive. The compact with its butterflies set with tiny jewels Romina had recognized as having been bought at Boucheron. Her lip-stick was gold, too, and her handkerchief had been lace-edged.

The woman had shoved them back into her bag and then run; but not before Romina, with an unfailing feminine instinct for noticing what another woman possesses, had seen everything.

And yet the ring she had picked up had seemed cheap and ordinary. Perhaps it was a native trinket such as one could buy anywhere in Cairo? But perhaps it was something quite different, something as sinister and evil as the lips of the unpleasant man who had got his desserts?

Mentally Romina gave herself a shake.

What was the point of going over this? It was merely an incident, just something which had happened unexpectedly. It was the sort of thing that might happen any night in a club like that, and it was just by chance they had been present and seen it.

There were so many other things to do. To find out about Chris; to learn what had caused his death. But more important at the moment, more near at hand, the reason why Merlin had gone out the night before without telling her.

Romina sat up in bed feeling purposeful and a little angry.

It was inconsiderate, to say the least. Supposing something had happened to him, she would be in a nice mess now.

She got out of bed and drew back the curtains and was instantly blinded by the glare of the sun which seemed to envelop her.

Outside the Nile sparkled and shimmered. The sky was dazzlingly blue, and the traffic a long way below seemed to move with the soothing drone of a bee buzzing amongst the flowers.

There was a faint wind, enough to blow her nylon nightgown against her body, and to carry a small boat with sails of burnt sienna swiftly up the river. She could see two men in it, and thought what fun it would be to be with them, carefree and gay, with the sails slapping happily above their heads.

As if she dragged herself away from the beauty of it all, she turned back into her bedroom and went towards the dressing-table.

She combed her hair, powdered her nose, and put a touch of lip-stick on her lips.

She looked very young and unspoilt, and with a little sigh she thought of the false eyelashes and heavy make-up she would have to apply later.

Over the chair was lying a diaphanous negligée of nylon and lace threaded with tiny baby ribbon that she had bought with the rest of her clothes at the Savoy. It was provocative

50

and intended to be slightly indecent. Romina pulled it around her and then opened the door.

There was no one in the sitting-room and the servants had not yet been to tidy it. Newspapers were scattered about as Merlin had left them the night before. There were some empty glasses on the table beside an open bottle of champagne.

Romina moved quickly towards the door of Merlin's bedroom. She knocked gently, and when there was no answer, felt a tremor of fear pass over her.

Supposing he had not come back and something had, indeed, happened to him and she was quite alone?

She opened the door, and it was with a feeling of intense relief that she saw him sitting out on the balcony having his breakfast.

He was wearing orange-colored pajamas and a ridiculously flamboyant satin dressing-gown of orange and white stripes with orange cuffs and revers.

His dark hair was a little tousled and he looked incredibly un-English and unlike the man she had first met in her guardian's office.

"Good morning."

There was an edge to her voice as she moved across the room and out on to the balcony.

Merlin made no attempt to rise at her approach and she realized with a sense of irritation that he was playing the part of Nickoylos with meticulous attention to detail.

"Hello, baby. It's good to see you," he said.

He waved her to a seat opposite and added:

"I'll order you some breakfast."

"There is no hurry at the moment," Romina answered. "Is it safe to speak out here?"

"Perfectly safe," Merlin answered. "And safe inside, too, thanks to a little toy which I will show you in a minute."

"I am not interested in that at the moment," Romina said sharply. "I want to know why you went out last night and why you did not tell me where you were going. Can't you realize that anything might have happened?"

"So you heard me?" Merlin asked.

"Of course I heard you," Romina answered, "and I think it is extremely unfair of you to behave in such a manner. If you were going out on anything concerning Chris, you might have taken me with you; but if you weren't, and it was an unnecessary risk—"

"You sound rather like a school-mistress," Merlin said with

51

a grin, and she felt she hated him because he was laughing at what had been for a moment a very real fear.

He saw her expression, knew she was angry and said quietly:

"I'm sorry. I'm afraid I'm so used to being independent that I forgot that we are a partnership. Do you forgive me?"

His response was so unexpected that she could not help but feel her anger evaporate.

"I will forgive you," she said grudgingly, "if you will tell me where you went and what it was all about."

Merlin's eyes flickered and she realized that he was wondering just how much to tell her.

"For heaven's sake, be frank," she begged. "We are neither of us in this for the fun of the thing."

"Well, I went to try and find a friend," Merlin said cautiously.

"Has he got a name? Is this idiotic secrecy really necessary?" Romina inquired.

"As a matter of fact it is," he answered seriously. "I am sorry to tease you, but it is a rule that we never mention names unless it is absolutely necessary. His name is Paul. I had expected him to get in touch with me; but he has not done so, and I tried to find him."

"Is he one of Guardie's men?" Romina said.

She realized it was a mistake to press him too far, and before he could reply, continued:

"Well, what did he say?"

"He was not at his flat," Merlin answered. "I think he must have gone away. Some of his clothes were missing, and I could not see a suitcase anywhere."

"So you just came back?"

"Exactly. I just came back by the rather devious way in which I had gone out."

"Somebody might easily have seen you in the hotel and followed you," Romina said accusingly.

"Not the way I did it," Merlin said confidingly.

He glanced across the river and then to Romina's surprise got up suddenly, and moving round the small table which lay between them, bent down and kissed her deliberately on the mouth.

She moved back from him as if she had been stung.

"What are you doing? Why did you do that?" she started to say.

He caught hold of her hand and pulled her to her feet and throwing a casual arm round her shoulders drew her into the sitting-room.

"If you think—" she began, only to be silenced.

He moved away from her and pushed something into her hand.

"Go to the far end of the room, right back, where you cannot be seen and have a look for yourself."

She looked down at what he had given her and saw it was a pair of binoculars. They were quite small and compact, and without a word she did as he told her and stood at the far end of the room and put the binoculars to her eyes.

They were unexpectedly strong, fantastically so, and she looked across the river, finding the first thing in focus was the big 600 ft. tower that she had learned from the guidebooks had only recently been built on the other side of the Nile.

'It contains a revolving restaurant,' she had read, 'and is a great attraction to tourists.'

The windows at the top of the tower seemed to be glittering in the sunshine, but that was all. Vaguely she thought she could see people behind the glass but she could not be certain.

"What am I expected to see?" she asked, taking the binoculars from her eyes and turning to look at Merlin.

He was standing watching her with a rather strange expression on his face.

"I may have been mistaken," he said, "it may have been just my fancy—the sun on the ordinary glass of the tower—but I had an impression that someone was watching us from it with glasses."

"Why should they be doing that?" Romina asked. She could not help thinking that Merlin was being unnecessarily dramatic.

"Of course, I may be wrong," he said, "but it never does to take chances."

"And so you think it eliminates the risk if you kiss me?" Romina said. "I should have thought that was quite a gratuitous piece of over-acting."

"I assure you I thought it was necessary," Merlin said a little impatiently, as if her scruples bored him. "It would be unnatural for the type of people we are supposed to be to sit about talking seriously."

"All right, have it your own way," Romina said. "But I would rather you did not do it again—I very much dislike being messed about by strange men."

She put all the contempt possible into her voice.

Instead of looking abashed, Merlin threw back his head and laughed.

"I do not see that this is so funny," Romina said.

"It's you," he said, "trying to be dignified and crushing when you look about seventeen and as delectable in that ridiculous garment as the fairy on a Christmas Tree!"

"Don't laugh at me!" Romina said, stamping her foot. "I dislike it, and there are far more important things to talk about, as you well know."

As she spoke, she looked round nervously.

"Is it really safe to talk in here?" she asked hastily.

"As a matter of fact, it is," Merlin said. "This is something else I borrowed from Paul. The toy I wanted to show you, but you said you were not interested."

He held out a tiny box with what looked like a compass on top of it.

"What is it?" Romina asked.

"Something I have been wanting for a long time," Merlin answered, "and I'm afraid I have stolen it shamefully from Paul, but he was not using it and I thought my need was greater than his."

"What does it do?" Romina asked.

"It tells you if a microphone is about. I was told the Russians and Japanese use them, but I have never seen one before."

He flicked a switch and the needle on the face of the box quivered and moved only in the direction in which he opened it.

"If there was a microphone in the room," Merlin said, "it would point magnetically in its direction."

"How ingenious!" Romina remarked, interested despite herself.

Merlin slipped it into the pocket of his dressing-gown and picking up the binoculars put them in the drawer of the dressing-table.

"Now we will ring for your breakfast," he said. "Will you drape yourself sensually on one of the chairs on the balcony?"

"I will do my best—I only hope you will not find it too amusing," Romina said, and was annoyed to see him repress a sudden twitch of his lips.

It was bad enough to be with him, she thought, without being incensed at his manner on numerous quite ordinary occasions. Mentally she made up a scathing report on him which she was determined to give to the General when she returned home.

Then, by lying stretched out in one of the chairs on the balcony with her eyes closed, she managed to avoid speaking to him again until her breakfast arrived.

"What are we going to do today?" she asked, sipping some freshly-pressed orange juice which was naturally sweet and looked like a glass of sunshine.

"First, I think we should go sight-seeing," Merlin answered briskly in a tone which told her he had considered everything beforehand and had it all planned out. "You must appear to be keen on seeing the Tutankhamen jewelry. It is the sort of thing which would obviously attract Miss Faye. Then I think the only course is to drive quite openly to the address from which Chris last wrote."

"What? Wouldn't that be giving the show away?" Romina asked.

"I don't think so," Merlin answered. "I shall tell the guide and the chauffeur that there is a journalist who helped me over the publicity for my night-clubs whom I want to contact again. It would be quite useless to disguise ourselves and try to get there. They may be watching out for people doing just that very thing."

"Yes, I can see that," Romina agreed.

"Besides, I'm hoping Paul will have discovered everything there is to discover by that sort of method," Merlin told her. "No, I think we have got to do it boldly with nothing more subtle than a plausible tale as to why we are interested."

"Very well," Romina said, "I had better go and have my bath. I think somewhere in my wardrobe there is a dress even more fantastic than anything Nefertiti wore!"

"Then put it on," Merlin said. "And don't forget the war-paint—at the moment you look rather like the head of the lacrosse team at Heathfield."

Romina had crossed the room as he spoke, and now with her hand on the door she looked back.

"Remind me during the day to tell you how much I dislike you," she said, and heard him roar with laughter as she went into her bedroom.

In a very short frock of nylon with a pattern of vivid blue and white flowers on it and a sunshade of bright pink, Romina looked flashy enough to attract the eyes of all the men as she moved through the big entrance hall an hour later.

It seemed to her there were eyes everywhere—watching her full skirts as she tried to walk like a Hollywood film-star; watching her beautiful legs in her gossamer-thin nylons; watching her pouting red mouth and painted finger-nails. But she wondered whether they were eyes that were not admiring, but merely curious and speculative?

'Imagination!' she told herself sharply. She tried to forget everything except the part she was playing, smiling up at

Merlin, touching his arm with her finger-tips, contriving to look flirtatious.

"Oh, the flowers! What lovely flowers!" she exclaimed outside the door of a shop which opened into the entrance hall of the hotel.

She thanked Merlin prettily when he bought her a spray of orchids and ordered a huge bunch of carnations to be sent up to their rooms.

"I adore flowers," she told him, and for once there was no insincerity in her remark.

Their car and guide were waiting at the back of the hotel which looked over a huge open square where, to Romina's amusement, there were great crowds of people clustered around public television sets.

"The Museum is only the other side of the square," Merlin said, "but I know you don't like walking."

"I hate it!" Romina exclaimed.

She sank down on the seat of the car as she spoke, and held out her feet in their white sandals as if she wanted him to appreciate that nothing so small and delicate could be meant for anything which might be construed as work.

"There is no need for the lady to walk except inside the Museum," the guide said, and ordered the chauffeur in Arabic to drive across the square.

There were flower-beds filled with brilliantly colored flowers and pools with fish darting in and out of the water-lily leaves outside the Museum.

They did not linger because of the heat rising from the ground and moved quickly up the steps and in through the great doorway where attendants were selling tickets and taking into safe-keeping cameras and sunshades.

"Museums are always so gloomy," Romina remarked in the high, rather petulant voice that she felt personified Romina Faye.

"You wanted to see the jewelry, though, baby," Merlin said.

"Oh yes! I love jewelry," Romina answered, and they moved slowly up to the first floor, the guide starting his usual patter about every statue and object.

"We've seen it all before," Merlin said briskly. "The lady wants to see the jewels. Let's go to them quickly."

It was unnecessary for Romina to simulate interest when they reached the corridor where the treasures from Tutankhamen's tomb were on show.

The gold furniture, the lovely colored figures and the carved sarcophagi were almost breath-taking, and she gazed

56

at them rapturously, only remembering now and then to ex-
claim over the value of the precious stones that had been
used.

"That's just what I would like to hang round my neck,"
she managed to say in inviting tones while trying, without appearing to do so, to look at all the objects which were so exquisitely carved and had been preserved in such a perfect
state for thousands of years.

Even Merlin forgot to be blasé and, calling the guide
across to a show-case, he asked one or two interested questions.

Romina had a chance to look more closely at a little model
boat which had lain in the tomb.

It was then, as she stared at it, that she saw on the other
side of the room the woman with the dark hair whom they
had seen the night before.

She looked older and was beautifully dressed in a suit of
white linen which screamed Dior to any woman who had
ever been to Paris. She wore a little hat of white flowers and
there were diamond ear-rings in her ears. Her bag was not
black as it had been the night before, but pale blue to match
her gloves and her pointed high-heeled shoes.

Just for a moment Romina hesitated, and then was quite
sure it was the same woman.

There was no mistaking the dark eyes which had looked so
terrified or the soft cupid-bow lips which wore rather an unusual shade of lip-stick.

She was talking to a man who was much older than herself. He was heavily built, with iron-gray hair and shrewd
eyes.

Romina saw him turn aside to look at something which
had interested him, and impulsively she hurried across to the
woman.

"I'm so glad to see you again," she said. "I tried to catch
you last night, but I was too late. I found a ring after you
had gone—a ring like a snake."

She got no further. The woman in the white suit had the
same look of horror in her eyes which Romina had seen before.

"I d-do not know what you are talking about," she said
quickly, and Romina realized that her lips were trembling.
"Go away, how dare you speak to me!"

She spoke in a low voice hardly above a whisper as if she
was afraid of being overheard.

"But . . . but last night," Romina said, ". . . . the Pyramid Club . . ."

"I have never been to such a place. I do not know what you are talking about. If you do not leave me alone, I . . . I will call the police."

The woman turned and literally ran away from Romina towards the man who was accompanying her and who was standing with his back towards them both, quite unaware that anything had happened.

Romina saw the woman in the white suit go up to him and slip her arm through his.

She appeared to be asking him to come with her to look at something else and he allowed himself, good-humoredly, to walk quickly—too quickly for it to be quite natural—down the long corridor and out of sight.

Romina stood where the woman had left her, too astonished to do anything but stare.

Then she realized that Merlin was by her side.

"Well, have you seen all you want to see?" he asked in a bored voice.

"If the lady will just step inside the next room," the guide said ingratiatingly, "she will see there necklaces of precious stones more beautiful than anything that has been discovered in other tombs."

"Oh, I think I have seen enough," Romina said in the tone of a spoiled child. "Let's go and look at the jewel shops this afternoon. There might be something pretty you can buy me. That's the trouble with Museums—one can never buy anything."

Even to herself she sounded incredibly foolish; but the guide was smiling delightedly, obviously scenting that there would be a commission in this for him.

Merlin glanced at his watch.

"I would like to try and find that chap I was telling you about," he said. "We've got an hour before lunch."

"You wish to go somewhere?" the guide inquired.

"Yes, to the—I think the street is called the Sharia Bein al Nahasseen," Merlin replied.

The guide looked surprised.

"I think, sir, you must be mistaken."

"No, I don't think so," Merlin answered. "It's the address I was given."

"But it is in a very poor quarter," the guide persisted.

"I expect so," Merlin agreed loftily. "This man I'm trying to find is a journalist. He has been useful to me on one or two occasions. When he is writing about a place he likes to get right into the atmosphere, if you know what I mean. Well, I want him to get into the atmosphere of something very different from what he is doing now. Night-clubs—that's my speciality."

"Yes, sir, we all know you are the King of Night-clubs. Perhaps you open one in Cairo?"

Merlin managed to smile enigmatically.

"That depends on whether you can show me something better than you did last night."

"Well, there are many more places I can take you."

"Never mind that now. Let's go to the Sharia Bein al Nahasseen."

"Very good, sir, if that is your wish," the guide said doubtfully.

They got into the car, Romina still puzzled a little over the extraordinary behavior of the woman in the white suit.

Then she decided that the man whom Merlin had hit must have been some clandestine lover, while the man she was with that morning—the older man—was perhaps her husband.

'That would explain everything,' she thought, and made up her mind to tell Merlin of her idea at the first opportunity.

There was no chance to talk intimately of anything now.

Merlin was droning on about how useful his journalist friend had been to him when he had started up a night-club in Paris.

"He will be able to give me the low-down on a lot of things here," he said ponderously, raising his voice a little so that the guide could hear.

"I hope he won't keep us long," Romina said. "I'm feeling quite hungry. You promised we could have lunch in that house-boat moored on the other side of the Nile."

"I believe it's quite a good restaurant," Merlin said. "We'll certainly have a look at it."

They were now driving down narrow, crowded streets filled with donkeys and carts which had to get out of the way of the big car. Here it was very different from the broad modern streets with their brightly-painted new buildings.

This was part of old Cairo with its crumbling walls, peeling paint and dirt, dust and flies which President Nasser had not yet had the time, or money, to sweep away.

The car twisted and turned, narrowly missing a herd of goats and very nearly upsetting a stall filled with strong-smelling native cakes which were fried on a charcoal fire.

Another turn, and the driver said something to the guide who turned his head towards Merlin.

"This is Sharia Bein al Nahasseen, sir," he said. "Do you know the number?"

Merlin drew a piece of paper from his pocket and pretended to consult it.

"I think it's number ten," he said.

They drove on down to where the street narrowed and finally they were forced to get out and walk the last remaining few yards to the house the guide pointed out.

"I will come with you, sir," he said to Merlin.

"No," Merlin replied. "Go with the car, turn it round and get it back up the street so that it's pointing in the right direction when we are ready to leave."

The guide seemed hesitant; but his objections were overruled by Merlin's firm manner and the fact that he had taken Romina by the arm and was picking his way over the dirty stone road away from the car.

Men and women passing in the road stared at them, but they said nothing.

Romina had already noticed that in modern Cairo the children no longer begged but only looked beseechingly instead, with hands that fluttered in the age-old supplicating gesture of an upturned palm.

They found the door easily. It was closed, and the house looked so dilapidated and dirty that Romina wondered if in fact it was inhabited.

Merlin knocked.

There was no answer; and then a man lounging in an open doorway on the other side of the street said something and pointed down the road in the direction they had just come.

For a moment neither Merlin nor Romina understood.

Then the man said something again in Arabic and they saw coming towards them a woman carrying a large basket.

She was dressed in black, but they were European clothes and as she drew nearer Romina could see that her face, too, was European.

She was elderly and almost weighed down by the huge basket filled with food.

She glanced up with sharp eyes at Merlin and it seemed to Romina there was a faint expression of fear in her lined face.

"You are knocking at my door, Monsieur?"

The woman spoke in French, and Merlin replied in the same language.

"Is this your house?"

"It is. I am Madame Goha."

"*Bonjour*, Madame."

Merlin touched his hat with a perfunctory gesture.

The Frenchwoman drew a key from her pocket and inserted it in the keyhole.

"What do you want?" she asked uncompromisingly.

"Can we come in and speak to you for a moment?"

She looked up at him uncertainly. There was no doubt now that she was frightened.

"If you wish," she said, and led the way into the house.

The room beside the front door was the most poverty-stricken Romina had ever seen.

There was a sandy floor with a few very old rush mats on it; a chair out of which the horse-hair stuffing was bulging, another of bamboo; and a table made of cheap wood.

The one decoration on the peeling walls was postcards of France, most of them very old and faded, which had been stuck up in what seemed to Romina a pathetic attempt on the part of the woman to remember the country of her birth.

Madame Goha put down her basket on the floor, eased her aching arms and raised them to pull the black shawl off her head.

She was not as old as she appeared at first; lined and worn, perhaps, with poverty and toil, but actually little more than middle-aged.

"Now, Monsieur," she said. "What is it I can do for you?"

Merlin smiled at her, and Romina guessed he was doing his best to charm her.

"It is very kind of you to let us in, Madame," he said in careful French with an undoubted British accent. "I am looking for a friend who I believe may be staying here in your house. I employed him at one time and I want him to do another job for me—a well-paid job, as it happens."

The Frenchwoman said nothing. It seemed to Romina that she was very tense.

"When I knew him, his name was Christopher Huntley," Merlin went on, "although he may have changed it for one reason or another. Do you know him?"

"He is not here. He is gone."

The woman's voice was flat.

"Then he has been here?" Merlin asked.

"Yes, but he has gone."

"When did he go?"

"Some time ago—I cannot remember."

"He lived with you for a long time?"

"No—a short time. I can tell you nothing more, Monsieur."

There was an obstinacy and blankness about her which told Romina that if they were not careful they would be up against a brick wall.

Without worrying what Merlin would think, she interposed

herself between him and the Frenchwoman and taking off her dark glasses looked her straight in the eyes and said:

"Please, Madame, will you not help us? Christopher Huntley was a very dear friend of mine. He and I . . . were brought up together—we played together as children. We were worried about him and very anxious to get in touch with him."

"I cannot help you, Mademoiselle. He is not here."

"But could you perhaps tell us where he went to? Was he ill?"

"No, he was not ill. He went. That's all I have to say."

Romina felt the tears come into her eyes.

"Please tell us a little more," she pleaded.

She saw the Frenchwoman shake her head, and then she heard a rustle and looked round to see that Merlin had brought from his pocket a roll of notes.

"I am willing to pay for information, Madame," he said quietly.

The Frenchwoman glanced at the notes, hesitated, and then looked away.

"There is nothing I can tell you."

"Just tell us what happened," Merlin said.

He spread out the notes in his hand as if he was playing cards with them. There were five of them, each worth about two pounds.

It seemed to Romina that the Frenchwoman was breathing a little heavily.

Suddenly she went to the door of the room, opened it quickly and shut it again.

"I can tell you nothing," she said. "They came and took him away."

"How long was he here?" Merlin asked.

"About three weeks. He told me he was writing a book and that he was studying the dialects of the people in this part of Cairo. He explained that sometimes he would go out wearing Arab dress so that the people would talk to him more freely. He asked me to tell no one—and I spoke of it to no one, no one at all."

"And then what happened?" Merlin prompted.

"They came for him," the woman said.

"Who were they—the police?"

"No, no . . . men."

"Egyptians?"

"How should I know? I am only a poor widow. They say to me, 'Keep out of the way,' and I stay in here when they go upstairs."

"And he was not ill?" Romina asked.

"No. He walk downstairs with the men, and that is the last I see of him. Afterwards they come back for his things."

"Ah!"

It was a sound from Merlin.

"You say they came back for his things?"

"Yes, Monsieur. They took everything . . . everything he possessed . . . nothing was left. They searched very thoroughly."

She gave a little sigh.

"I can tell you no more."

Romina looked desperately at Merlin. If that was all, what had they gained by coming here? Nothing—except to be certain that Chris had indeed been murdered!

She expected Merlin to give the woman the money and for them to leave; but instead he looked at the five notes in his hand and digging into his pocket brought out another five and spread them all out.

The Frenchwoman looked at them and very delicately her tongue wetted her lips.

"I think, Madame," Merlin said softly, "—I think you are keeping something back. He did leave something behind, did he not?"

"No . . . I have not said so."

"But I think he did. You have something of his, have you not?"

The woman was silent for a moment then once again she went to the door and opened and shut it.

She went to the window where the dirty panes of glass with their cheap lace curtains obscured most of the daylight and the possibility of anyone seeing in.

She stood in the center of the room panting a little and on her forehead Romina saw to her surprise there were beads of sweat which had not been there before.

"Monsieur, I am afraid," she said in a whisper.

Merlin rustled the notes, ten of them, spread out like a fan.

"Who will know?" he asked. "Money is always useful."

"They have questioned me, Monsieur . . . they have asked me over and over again, and I have told them there was nothing."

Romina saw a sudden light in Merlin's eyes, but he said quietly:

"They will never know what you have told me. I swear to you that I will never betray you. And money is always useful—"

The woman seemed to make up her mind.

"It was when he was leaving, Monsieur . . . He came down the stairs—two of them in front of him, and two behind . . . I was hiding behind the door, but he saw me."

" 'There is Mrs. Goha,' he said. 'Wait a minute, gentlemen. I must pay her what I owe her. As it happens, I am heavily in arrears with my rent.'

"He spoke quite cheerily, but I was surprised—although I did not say anything—because he had paid me only the day before. Then he pulled some notes out of his pocket, pressed them into my hand and said, 'Keep it safe, for it is easily spent!' One of the men laughed, but the others scowled and murmured something about getting on."

The Frenchwoman paused. The beads of sweat were now running down from her forehead and on to her cheeks.

"They went out of the door," she said, "and I never saw them again. But when they had gone I looked at the money he had given me. There was a piece of paper with it."

"Yes, a piece of paper?" Merlin said eagerly. "You have got it?"

"Yes, I have got it," the Frenchwoman answered. "But I only just had time to put it away safely. The men came back and went up to his room, searching everything and taking what was left away with them. Then they came down here and went at me."

"They asked you for the piece of paper?" Merlin suggested.

She nodded.

"They told me a piece of his handwriting was missing. They said they wanted it very urgently, and that I must have it. I looked them straight in the eyes and told them I knew nothing about such a thing. I was quite certain he had not sent them. He would not have told me to keep it safe otherwise. And the money he had given me was ten times more than he had ever paid in rent all the time he had been here."

The Frenchwoman glanced towards the heavy basket she had had in her arms when she arrived.

"I have eaten well since then," she said simply.

"And you never told them about the paper?" Merlin asked.

"I said I had nothing," she said. "I was afraid for what they would do to me. And they came back another time, but I stuck to my story, and I think they believed that I knew nothing—even though they were sure that the paper was somewhere about the place."

The woman glanced over her shoulder towards the window.

"Give it to me," Merlin said. "I promise you it will be safer in our hands than in yours."

He held up the notes as he spoke; and like a flash the Frenchwoman took them from his hand and stuffed them down the front of her dress.

Then she went to her shopping basket and drew out an old worn purse. It was almost yellow with age and the leather was peeling off.

She opened it, and Romina's heart sank. What could there be of importance in anything so small?

The woman pulled aside the lining of the purse where it had come apart from the hinge, and she dug her fingers in and drew out a carefully folded piece of paper.

"Take it, and go quickly," she said.

She put it into Merlin's hand, and without looking at it he slipped it into his pocket.

"Thank you," he said. "You have been very kind, Madame. We are deeply and sincerely grateful."

"Yes, thank you very much," Romina said.

As the woman went to open the door into the street, Romina hesitated.

"Please," she said. "It would not take a second—I would just like to see Chris's room, if possible."

"There is another lodger in it," the woman said. "He came three days ago. He said he was a friend of Mr. Huntley, for that matter."

"A friend?" Merlin said sharply. "What is his name?"

"He, too, is an Englishman," the woman said. "And he has an English name—Smith. That's what he said his name was."

"Is he in now?" Merlin inquired.

The Frenchwoman shook her head.

"I shouldn't think so, but I do not know—I have been at the market since early this morning. It is difficult to find things these days—food is dear and scarce in Cairo."

"Please may we go up and see?" Romina asked.

"Yes, but hurry," the woman said. "You have stayed too long—if they come back, they will ask questions."

"We will not be a moment," Merlin promised her.

He did not stand aside for Romina to go up first, and she understood that he thought it best that he should go ahead.

The stairs were rickety and without a banister, but they were tolerably clean, and although the house smelled old it was not unpleasant.

The ceiling on the first floor was so low that it was hardly the height of a tall man. There was only one door opening off a minute landing, which was little more than a standing place for two people.

The door was slightly ajar, and Merlin pushed it open.

Just for the moment the sight that met Romina's eyes made her think it must be some kind of joke.

Then she realized that everything was thrown untidily in disarray.

A chair was upset, the bed turned over, a desk had all its drawers emptied on to the floor, and pieces of paper had been torn from the walls.

Then in a corner Romina saw something else—a man's foot and leg, the trouser of a tropical suit.

She felt as if everything was unreal—a picture which had no depth behind it.

Almost as if she was in a dream she watched Merlin kick aside a chair, climb over a broken drawer towards the corner, and because her own will had ceased to function, she followed him.

She saw Merlin push aside a long strip of dirty wallpaper which revealed the body of a fair-haired man.

He was lying crumpled on the floor and there was a knife firmly embedded in his chest, the blood surrounding it staining his white shirt and tussore coat.

Then she heard Merlin say in little more than a whisper: "Paul! My God—Paul!"

CHAPTER FIVE

MERLIN dropped down on one knee, and Romina saw him feel the forehead of the man lying on the floor and then grope for his pulse.

She felt it must be an instinctive action. There was no doubt the man was dead.

He must have died fighting, but his eyes were wide open and his face contorted with anger. But his fists were clenched as if he was about to strike his opponent when he was struck down himself by the knife which had pierced his chest.

Merlin got to his feet.

"Come!" he said to Romina, and taking her by the arm, started to lead her from the room.

"But we must——" she began to stammer, her voice sounding weak and distraught even to her own ears.

"Be quiet! Say nothing!"

She was hushed into silence by Merlin's command, spoken imperiously, but hardly above a whisper.

He led her out of the room and on to the small landing, closing the door carefully behind him.

Then, because it was impossible for them both to descend the stairs at the same time, he released her arm after giving it a warning pinch and went downstairs.

Madame Goha was standing at the bottom, waiting for them.

"I don't suppose he is in . . ." she began.

Merlin interrupted her.

"Madame," he said, "take your shopping basket and go back to the market. Tell your neighbors as you pass that you have forgotten something, and stay away from the house as long as you can."

Romina, coming down the stairs, saw the Frenchwoman blanch.

"You mean . . . ?" she said.

"There is trouble," Merlin said. "Do not go upstairs—do not do anything but what I have told you. But you must stay away so that if anyone returns they will not know that you have come back. Do your neighbors talk?"

Madame Goha shrugged her shoulders.

"Not if they can help it," she said. "They are frightened, like everyone else."

"Very well," Merlin said. "Go now. Leave the house with us. And hurry!"

Muttering a little beneath her breath, Madame Goha seized her basket from where she had put it just inside the door and passed behind the stairs to where Romina supposed there was a kitchen; they heard her hurriedly emptying things on to a table or into a cupboard.

Romina put out her hand and touched Merlin's arm.

"I . . . I feel faint," she said.

He looked down at her white face, and then to her surprise, he said almost angrily:

"I thought you had more guts!"

His words, spoken contemptuously, were like cold water being dashed into her face.

She felt her anger rise and the faintness pass, just as Madame Goha came hurrying back towards them.

"You are ready?" Merlin said. "Then do as I say. Go back to the market, or visit a friend."

"I understand, Monsieur."

Madame Goha spoke quietly, and it seemed as if she had lived so long with danger that she was past being surprised or even alarmed at anything that had happened. And yet there was a pallor beneath her sallow skin which had not been there before.

Merlin opened the door and the sunshine came pouring in, seeming somehow ironic in its contrast to the darkness and shadow within the house.

"Thank you very much, Madame," Merlin said loudly, enunciating every word so that his voice would carry. "It was very kind of you to tell us about Mr. Huntley. When he returns I shall still be staying at the Nile-Vista. Tell him to get in touch with us at once. And tell him it would be worth his while. I have got a good job waiting for him."

"*Oui*, Monsieur. I will do exactly as you say," Madame Goha replied.

Merlin turned to link his arm through Romina's in an affectionate gesture.

"Now, honey, it's time for our lunch," he said. "Mind where you are walking, you don't want to have a sprained ankle. It's about time President Nasser got around to clearing up this quarter of the city."

Swaggering as he walked, and talking in a loud voice, he led Romina back to the car. He helped her in, threw a handful of small coins to the children who were clustered around it, and got in himself.

"The Nile-Vista," he said to the guide.

The car had been turned round as Merlin had ordered, and they set off down the narrow streets, hooting incessantly at the pedestrians and the laden donkeys who found it almost impossible to let them pass.

They had gone some way before Romina realized that her teeth were chattering and that she was very cold. She clenched her hands together in an effort at self-control, envying Merlin the ease with which he was lying back in the car and talking affably with the guide.

"You have found the gentleman you were seeking?" the guide inquired.

"Unfortunately, no," Merlin answered. "The woman who keeps the house told me she thinks he has gone away for a few days. He must be hard up to lodge in such a filthy place. It will be bad luck if he doesn't return in time to snap up the job I have to offer him!"

"It will indeed be unfortunate for him," the guide said, his curiosity obviously making him speculate how much the job would be worth.

It was not long before they were out of the crowded streets and into the broad road which ran alongside the Nile and on which the new big hotels had been built.

"Well, here we are," Merlin said unnecessarily as they reached the Nile-Vista. "I suppose you want to go up and titivate before lunch? For Heaven's sake don't be long—I'm so hungry I could eat a horse!"

He helped Romina out of the car, feeling her ice-cold fingers tremble in his, and then arm in arm marched her towards the lift and up to the fourth floor to their suite.

Romina thought she had never been so grateful for the solitude of an empty room. It was with an effort that she reached the bed and managed to throw herself down upon it.

She closed her eyes, unable to speak, unable to think for the moment of anything but the knife thrust in the man's chest, and the bloodstains all round it.

She heard Merlin go into his own bedroom, then return, and there was the clink of a glass.

"Drink this," he said, and put the glass into her hand.

"What is it?" she asked weakly.

"Brandy," he answered and, realizing that her hand was

69

still trembling, he took the glass from her and held it to her lips.

She managed to gulp some of it down and felt it move like a flame through her body.

"That's better," she said after a moment and took the glass from him.

"Finish it," he said, "and do not speak yet."

He disappeared again and she guessed he had gone to fetch the little machine which would tell him if there was a microphone working in the room; the machine he had borrowed from Paul.

She remembered now—Paul would never need it again.

Merlin came back as she had expected and moved around the room with the instrument and slipped it into his pocket.

"It is all right," he said. "Are you feeling better?"

"Who could have done it? Why did they kill him?" she burst out.

"That is what we are going to learn now," Merlin answered.

He drew from his pocket the tightly folded little wad of paper which Madame Goha had given him.

"I had forgotten about that," Romina exclaimed almost breathlessly.

She put the glass down beside the bed, and would have got up if Merlin had not sat down beside her.

"Sit quietly and lie back. It has been a shock."

"Of course it has," Romina said crossly. "I am not in the habit of seeing dead men—let alone those who have been murdered!"

"I know," Merlin replied. "We will talk about that later. But now let us see what they were looking for."

He started to open the paper carefully.

"You mean," Romina said in a voice of horror, "that Paul was killed because they—whoever they may be—were looking for that particular piece of paper?"

"I'll answer that question when we have read it," Merlin said a little grimly.

He smoothed out the paper, and Romina bent forward.

At the sight of Chris's writing on the paper she felt her eyes fill with tears, blinding her.

"Read it to me," she murmured.

"The paper appears to have been crumpled up before Madame Goha folded it as it is now," Merlin said reflectively. "It is my belief that Chris was in the middle of writing this when the men came for him."

"He must have snatched it up and thrust it into his

70

pocket," Romina said. "That was why he was able to mix it up with the money and hand it to her as he did."

"That is what I thought," Merlin agreed. "And now let us see what he was writing."

He read the first line to himself, then said aloud:

"It starts off abruptly. There must have been sheets before this. I imagine that this was his report either to your guardian or perhaps to his newspaper. I'm guessing, of course, but I think this was his rough copy which he would have coded later."

"It must have been very important," Romina said, "for Chris to take the trouble to make a rough copy. He nearly always wrote everything straight on to his typewriter."

"I think it was very important," Merlin agreed. "Now listen to what he says."

He cleared his throat and read aloud:

"... a fantastic, incredible plan which might through its very ruthlessness succeed. Now to the stuff itself. There is no doubt in my mind that it originally started in China. Anyway, it was grown in the paddy fields, but only in small quantities, and those who were distributing it became greedy.

"Now they are producing it here. It is very habit-forming—even quicker than cocaine or heroin.

"Distinguished people in many countries are, however, being enticed or tricked into sampling it. To them it is known as 'Yin'; and the password—the key which unlocks the secret—is in the form of a ring with ..."

Merlin stopped reading and turned over the page, but it was blank. He turned back again to study what he had already read with a frown between his eyes.

"Then it was dope Chris was after?" Romina said.

"A fantastic, incredible plan!" Merlin said almost as if he was speaking to himself. "And a new drug. No wonder Chris said it was a big story!"

"Is that very sensational?" she asked timidly.

"Not only sensational," he said, "but terrifying. Can't you understand what he says?—that the narcotic is being grown here as well as in China; obviously along the Nile."

Merlin paused and looked out of the window towards the sunshine.

"This means ruination and death to thousands, if not millions, of people," he said, "unless it can be stopped."

"Was Chris trying to stop it?" Romina inquired.

"I imagine so. The production is at present in its infancy; in other words, as he says very clearly, they have not yet got

71

sufficient supplies. My God! We must do something about this!"

"Whom do you mean by 'we'?" Romina asked.

"All the decent-thinking, clean-living people in the world," Merlin replied.

"But how?"

"That is the whole point," he said. "If the International Anti-Narcotics Bureau start looking for them, it may send the leaders underground. That was obviously why Chris was proceeding so carefully. He wanted to be able to pin-point the men responsible."

"Surely," Romina asked, "the police or the members of the Bureau you just mentioned would be far more effective in finding these criminals?"

"It sounds much more sensible to put it into their hands, doesn't it?" Merlin said. "But if Chris had thought that, he would have got in touch immediately with one of the heads of the Anti-Narcotics Bureau. But sometimes it is safer and quicker to work alone. These people must be very clever and subtle."

"What makes you so sure of that?" Romina asked.

"Because the police and the International Anti-Narcotics Bureau have done a magnificent job in clearing up Egypt," Merlin said. "For these people to be able to operate under their very noses in this country means . . ."

He paused a moment, pressing his lips together.

"Means what?" Romina prompted.

"It means that 'august heads will fall,' as Chris wrote in your letter. There must be some top people in on it—people of importance, not only in Egypt, but perhaps in every country in the world."

Merlin walked across the room, moving restlessly like a caged tiger.

Romina suddenly gave an exclamation.

"Merlin, I have thought of something! The ring—do you think it was the ring we picked up? I have not had a chance to tell you, but something very strange happened this morning."

Merlin swung round to face her, and she told him what had occurred in the Museum and what the woman in the white suit had said to her.

"Are you sure of what you are saying?" he asked when she had finished.

"Absolutely certain," Romina replied. "And I saw the terror in her face when I mentioned it—just as she looked terrified last night when that man hit her."

Merlin drew out his notecase and feeling deep down in the inner pocket pulled out the ring.

In the daylight the rubies in the snake's eyes seemed to glitter evilly, and the pointed red tongue holding the three tiny pearls held a new significance.

"It could be that," he said.

"It could indeed! If it was not something wrong, why should she have been so insistent that she had not been there? Besides, she was frightened—really frightened," Romina said.

"I wish I had realized this was going on," Merlin said. "Which woman was she?"

"She was wearing a white suit," Romina said, "and a hat with little flowers, and diamond ear-rings. She looked rich and very elegant—you must have noticed her. There was a man with her—it was when he turned away, as I have told you, that I spoke to her—he was short and rather stocky, with grayish hair."

"Was he wearing a yellow carnation in his button-hole?" Merlin asked quickly.

"Yes, I think he was," Romina replied. "Why?"

"Our guide pointed him out to me," Merlin said. "He told me that he was a German financier making a trade visit to this country. He told me his name—but I've forgotten it. Our guide seemed very impressed because he had recently spent a day with President Nasser, or something like that—you know how the man gossips."

"And you think the woman," Romina suggested, "was his wife?"

Merlin looked at her and sat down again on the bed.

" 'August heads'—'august heads in every country.' And how better than to work through a woman?"

"Do you think that she is an addict?" Romina asked.

"Perhaps on the road to becoming one," Merlin replied. "The man she was with at the Pyramid Club might have been a distributor. He looked the type of chap who would be ready to take anyone's money. Or there might have been more to it than that."

Merlin hesitated before he continued.

"He was angry with her for having lost the ring—perhaps because these rings are in short supply. Or, what is more likely, he loaned her the ring so that she could procure the stuff from another distributor or some special rendezvous."

"It is terrifying!" Romina exclaimed.

Merlin got up again.

"I'm only guessing," he said. "And now we are going downstairs to lunch."

73

"But I can't . . . I can't face the restaurant," Romina said.

Her voice was strained and her face so white that Merlin, after a moment's hesitation, gave in.

"It is out of character," he said rather sharply. "Nickoylos is the type of chap who would want to show off—to be seen in public. But still, just this once we will lunch up here."

"Thank you," Romina said meekly. "And while you are ordering it, could I . . . could I please look at Chris's writing again?"

Once more Merlin hesitated; but then he handed the piece of paper to Romina, and went from her bedroom, shutting the door behind him.

A few minutes later she heard him giving his orders for their lunch to the waiter in the sitting-room.

She smoothed out the paper, hardly bothering to read the words. She concentrated on Chris's firm, bold handwriting.

"Chris . . . Chris . . ." she whispered, and now that she was alone the tears poured from her eyes and ran down her cheeks.

She wanted to kiss the piece of paper, to hold it close to her; but instead, because it was so important, she looked at it for a long time and then laid it on her bed and walked towards the dressing-table.

Almost brutally she wiped away the tears from her cheeks and with a powder puff repaired the damage they had done to her make-up. Her eyes looked a little red, but glasses would hide that. She put more red on her lips, feeling as she did so that she was going into battle on Chris's behalf.

"We will find them," she whispered. "We will find the men who killed you and Paul. And they shall suffer for it . . . oh, my darling, they shall suffer for it!"

She heard a sharp knock on the door, and started to her feet as Merlin came in without waiting for her to reply.

"Lunch will be here shortly," he said. "I talked a lot about your having a headache in the sun, and I have sent a message to say that we will not require the car until about half-past three."

"Thank you," Romina said. "That will be a respite but I'm quite all right now."

"I'm glad of it," Merlin said. "I thought you were going to fold up on me!"

"I'm sorry," Romina said humbly. "But I had not expected to see anything so horrible as that man. Was he a close friend of yours?"

"He was," Merlin said briefly.

74

He sounded so disinterested that Romina looked up at him and said scornfully:

"Don't you care? He was your friend . . . you knew him . . . don't you care if he was killed like that?"

"Of course I care!" Merlin answered. "But this is not a moment for sentiment. I cannot afford to jeopardize your life as well as mine by doing anything which might attract attention to us."

"Do you think we might have been followed, then?" Romina asked.

"I've thought that from the moment we left London, although you considered many of my precautions were ridiculous. But now we know these men are completely ruthless— they killed your brother and they killed Paul—and they are aware that somebody has got a piece of paper which incriminates them. They will never rest until they find it."

"What are you going to do with it?" Romina asked.

"I'm going to destroy it," Merlin said.

"Destroy it?" Romina cried.

"Of course," he answered. "It is only in story books that people are stupid enough to carry incriminating evidence about. I know what it contains, and so do you. The piece of paper is no longer important to us. What really matters is whether we can communicate what we know to those who can make the best use of it."

"To Guardie?" Romina suggested.

"Among others," Merlin said. "But, like Chris, I'm not certain that the time is right. Perhaps it would be better to carry on the investigations to find out just a little more so that when the powers-that-be do strike, they strike effectively."

"But that will be dangerous," Romina said.

"Very dangerous," he agreed.

He turned his head as if he heard something, and said in a different voice:

"Now come on, baby. Come and make an effort to eat something. You will feel better and I have ordered you a cocktail which will put you right on your feet."

Romina could see no reason for him to speak in such a manner until, a few moments later, she heard a sound outside the door and realized that the waiter was returning.

'Merlin's hearing must be very acute,' she thought, and felt inadequate to cope with everything that was happening.

But because she knew she must, she walked into the sitting-room and allowed Merlin to ply her with cocktails and afterwards sipped at a glass of iced champagne.

It seemed to Romina that the meal was interminable. Too

many courses; too much to eat; and as she felt nauseated at the very idea of food, it was hard to keep up even the pretense of eating under Merlin's watchful eye.

The waiter brought the coffee and Merlin ordered liqueurs and a big cigar before finally they were alone.

She would have spoken, but as the waiter left the room Merlin put his finger to his lips.

Paul's little microphone-finder was brought out again and only when Merlin was satisfied there was nothing to fear did he speak.

"All right, go ahead."

"I'm sorry—it was not anything important," Romina answered. "I think I was just going to say I was thankful that our lunch is over. I would never have believed a meal could take so long!"

"Well under an hour," Merlin replied.

"It seemed like a chunk of eternity," Romina grumbled.

Merlin got slowly to his feet and smoking his cigar walked towards the window.

"What are you going to do?" Romina asked.

It was a question she had been longing to ask for some time.

"I was just wondering about that," he answered. "I think the first thing to do is to book you an air passage home."

Romina sat upright.

"What do you mean?" she asked.

"Exactly what I say," he answered. "You have played your part—and very well, if I may say so. You have found out what you wanted to know about your brother, and now you must go back."

"So that is what you have been planning, is it?" Romina said, her voice sharpening. "Well, you will have to think again. I have no intention of leaving now."

"There is no point in your staying," he answered, "and please do not be obstinate about it. You came to Egypt to find out about your brother's death—you know all we are ever likely to know. I suggest you go back to London and forget what else you have seen."

"Such as Paul's murder, I suppose?" Romina said sarcastically.

"It is nothing to do with you," Merlin replied.

"Of course it is to do with me," she said impatiently. "He was killed because he was trying to find out what had happened to Chris, that is obvious. He moved into those lodgings because he believed it was certain things had happened there,

76

or perhaps something was hidden there. Can't you see that, just as he was not going to give up, neither am I?"

Merlin gave a sigh and sat down beside Romina.

"Listen," he said. "You have been very brave and done a good job. No one could have done it better. But now there is no necessity or point in your carrying on. What is going to happen is anyone's guess; but whatever it is, it will be tough and extremely dangerous."

"I'm not afraid of danger," Romina said coldly.

"Of course you are!" Merlin said scornfully. "We all are! You saw what happened to Paul—do you want that to happen to you? I shall be frank and say I do not want it to happen to me. I shall do my damnedest to prevent it happening, of course. But there is every possibility of my, and perhaps you, ending up like Paul—sprawled on a dirty floor with an unknown assailant's knife in our hearts."

Romina gave a little shudder, she could not help it.

She could see all too vividly Paul's wide-open eyes and the manner in which his body lay among the debris.

Merlin sensed what she was feeling and pressed home his advantage.

"Paul was a brave man," he said. "He was one of our very best under-cover men. If he could be caught off his guard—as he must have been—there is not much hope for me, and certainly none for you. Go home, Romina, and stop imagining yourself to be the heroine of a detective story."

"I imagine nothing of the sort!" Romina said angrily. "And stop sneering and gibing at me. You are trying to make me agree to something I shall never do, never . . . never . . . never. . . . not if you talk from now until next Christmas! I have come here to find out about Chris; but merely because I have discovered why he was murdered does not satisfy me or make me feel in any way that I have come to the end of the story. I'm staying, whatever you may say or do—do make up your mind to make the best of it!"

She saw she had annoyed Merlin by the almost savage way in which he puffed at his cigar.

Then he said in a voice icy with anger:

"The trouble with you is that you have been spoiled. What you want is a good whipping and to be told to do what is the sensible thing!"

"If I had been sensible I would not have come in the first place," Romina said. "And do you suppose Chris would like to have a sister who always did the right thing and never took a risk? Don't be so ridiculous! And now let us stop wasting time and make some plans. We cannot just sit here and wait to be murdered."

"I've no intention of doing anything of the sort," Merlin answered. "And if you must be so confoundedly obstinate and pig-headed, I suppose I shall have to make the best of it."

"You have no alternative, have you?" Romina said.

Because he looked so discomfited and irritated, she could not help smiling.

"It is rather stupid, if you think about it," she said in a different tone. "I'm hating you because you are trying to save my life. And you are hating me because I will not be saved!"

Merlin had the grace to look rather shamefaced.

"I'm sorry," he said quietly. "I might have known you would be as tenacious as your brother. He would never give up."

"I'm not going to give up either," Romina said, "so do not let us bother to discuss this again. I want to know what you are going to do."

"I suppose I shall have to tell you," Merlin said reluctantly with a faint twinkle in his eye. "First of all, I'm going to send a cable to tell them that Paul is dead—that is essential—and I shall try to include the news that we are on to something big, and that Chris was right."

"How on earth are you going to do that?" Romina asked. "Would it not be possible to telephone?"

"Far too dangerous," Merlin answered.

He got up and walked to the writing desk and picked up a cable form. He sat writing for some minutes with his back to Romina, and then he handed her the form.

She took it from him and read it slowly.

It was addressed to a firm of stockbrokers in London and instructed them to sell certain stocks and shares and buy others. It was signed 'Nickoylos.'

"Is that your code?" she asked.

"It would be a clever man who would break it," Merlin said with a note of satisfaction in his voice. "Only one other person and myself can decode that cable. We will send it when we go downstairs."

Romina looked up at the electric clock on the wall. It was nearly three-thirty.

"Have we got to go out?" she said.

"Just for a visit to the jeweler—you remember you said you wanted to look at some jewelry. Our guide will be very disappointed if he cannot make his commission."

"I will not choose anything expensive," Romina said.

78

"Just keep saying nothing is good enough," Merlin instructed her. "And now you had better change your dress. I feel Miss Faye would not wish to be seen in the same creation twice in the same day."

"You think of everything," Romina said, and made the statement sound anything but a compliment.

She walked towards the door and turned back.

"Merlin," she said in a low voice, "will they tell Paul's parents how he died?"

Merlin stubbed out his half-finished cigar in the ash-tray.

"Listen, Romina," he said. "If you are in this, as you insist on being, you have got to be tough. Paul took risks in his life knowing exactly what they were and what the consequences might be. He was unlucky. He is the last person who would want anyone to mourn over him, to be upset or frightened by his death. Forget him—forget what you have seen. Remember what you are supposed to remember. Madame Goha told you that Chris, whom you have known since you were a child, has gone away for a few days. Can you do that, can you put everything out of your mind? Can you erect a barrier between your brain and your heart? I try—I try very hard."

"Well you must be superhuman," Romina said accusingly. "It is impossible for anyone to have no ordinary feelings about death and murder."

"But if one does have ordinary feelings about death and murder, then it is best to take an airplane back to safety and sanity. There is a Comet going in the morning."

"Damn you!" Romina said, suddenly losing her temper. "Damn you for always having an answer and for being so clever that you appear not to care about anything!"

She went out of the sitting-room and slammed the door behind her, but by the time she reached her bedroom she was ashamed of her outburst.

Merlin was right, of course he was right. They were playing a dangerous game and it was no use letting one's feelings make one so soft and vulnerable as to become an easy prey of those who apparently found killing an essential part of their job.

First Chris and then Paul. Would Merlin be the next?

Romina felt herself shiver, although the sun was pouring in through the open window and made the room hot and rather airless. She realized that she could pull the glass door to and turn on the air-conditioning.

She was still cold from the shock of Paul's death and despite all that Merlin had given her to drink she felt she might easily slip into unconsciousness.

With a tremendous effort she forced herself a choose a dress which was flamboyant. She decided on a peacock blue organza which was embroidered with tiny white flowers and had a large white collar which framed her neck and accentuated the curves of her breasts.

It took Romina a little time to get ready—to rearrange her hair, to change her eye shadow to one which matched the dress, and to find a white sun-shade to match her white bag and gloves.

"I'm ready," she announced when she returned to the sitting-room and found Merlin lying back in a chair, his arms behind his head and his eyes fixed on the ceiling.

It was an attitude she had found him in once or twice before. She guessed it made it easier for him to concentrate. Everyone had a particular pose they assumed when they were thinking, and this was Merlin's.

But in the split second before he realized that she had entered the room she saw by the grim expression on his face that what he was thinking about was none too pleasant.

"Ready?" he questioned, springing to his feet. "That's good. You look an eyeful, if I may say so."

"Thank you," Romina replied. "I feel rather like a Windmill Girl on a holiday. I honestly do not believe my closest friends would recognize me."

"Let us hope they do not," Merlin said. "They might be rather surprised at the company you keep."

He also had changed his clothes, Romina noticed. She was amused to see how rakish and vulgar his red waistcoat looked with his thin gray suit, and how too much jewelry of the expensive gold kind could turn a man who usually looked a gentleman into an obvious bounder.

They went from the hotel into the heat outside and told the guide to take them to a good jeweler.

"Some of the best are in the hotel," Merlin said in a low voice to Romina, "but like all guides he will know someone who will pay him a bigger commission than the more reputable dealer. Let us sit back and see what happens."

They drove to a large and rather pretentious shop not far off the main thoroughfare but near the crowded native streets which catered for the tourist.

They were bowed politely to comfortable seats, and mint tea was brought, as was the custom.

Romina was amused to see the guide hovering anxiously in the background watching everything they handled in case the shopkeeper pulled a fast one on him as well as on them.

They looked at amethysts, pieces of turquoise, rubies

which were of a doubtful quality, and emeralds of a beautiful color but were badly flawed.

There was nothing of value, but the prices were astronomical. Romina managed to pout effectively and say there was nothing as nice as what she had seen in Paris and that she had much preferred the brooch which Merlin had refused to give her in London.

The shopkeeper began to be despondent and finally Merlin bought a ring which had a number of aquamarines hanging from it and which was described as a 'harem' ring.

"It is rather sweet," Romina said, "but I don't really think it's good enough to wear with my other aquamarines."

"It's only a little souvenir," Merlin said soothingly. "I like rings. I have often thought of buying another, but I have never seen anything as good as mine."

He held out his hand to show the flashing diamond on his little finger.

"It is very good stone, sir, very good indeed," the jeweler said.

"By the way," Merlin continued, "while I am here tell me if these stones are real."

He drew his note-case from his pocket, and with a little feeling of tension Romina watched him take the snake ring from it and hold it out towards the dealer.

The man turned it over in his hand and drew the inevitable jeweler's glass from his pocket and put it to his eye.

"Yes, the rubies are real, sir. So are the emeralds, but they are only chippings. There's no intrinsic value. It's amusing, very amusing."

He spoke quite dispassionately and returned the ring to Merlin.

As he did so, Romina happened to glance toward the end of the shop to see if the guide was still watching.

She noticed that a middle-aged Egyptian wearing a tarboosh had just come in. It was obvious that he was a customer. He hesitated as if he was wondering which counter to go to, and then, as he looked, he saw the ring in the jeweler's hand being passed back to Merlin and his eyes widened.

Just for a moment he stared. He seemed to be very interested in the ring, and then he turned away.

Another assistant in the shop hurried to attend to him and Romina heard him inquire if his cigarette-case had been repaired.

"It is ready, Your Excellency. Yes, I am almost certain it is ready."

The man wearing the tarboosh sat down in a chair while the salesman hurried away to an inner room.

Merlin put the snake ring back into his notecase and drew out the notes to pay for the harem ring which had already been packaged up for Romina.

They had to wait a few moments for their change; then they got to their feet while the shopkeeper who had attended them bowed ingratiatingly and said he hoped for their patronage on another occasion.

They turned to leave the shop. As they did so they had to pass the man in the tarboosh who was sitting waiting at another counter. The shop was not large and they passed quite close to him.

To Romina's surprise, she saw him rise and brush into Merlin in a quite unnecessary manner. It was as if he deliberately staged the encounter and the awkwardness with which he knocked Merlin's arm.

Then he apologized.

"No, it is quite all right," Merlin answered.

"I think we have seen each other before," the man in the tarboosh said. "Sahara City, perhaps? Ah, well, forgive me. Sometimes I am very clumsy."

"It is quite all right. Please do not apologize," Merlin said automatically.

They went from the shop and the guide took them back to the car.

"You did not find anything you like?" the guide said almost accusingly. "Now I take you to another shop with much, much better stones—fine, beautiful gems of the Orient. Just what the lady would like."

"No, we have done enough for today," Merlin said in a bored voice. "We will go back to the hotel."

"But . . . but, sir . . ."

"The hotel!" Merlin said relentlessly cutting short the persuasion which was obvious in the guide's eyes and on his already plausible lips.

"Very good, sir," the man said in a disappointed tone.

The car started off.

"Why did the man knock?" Romina began, only to feel the sudden pressure of Merlin's hand on her knee and to know that he did not wish her to speak of it.

They drove some way before he said anything; then he addressed the guide.

"Where is Sahara City?" he asked.

The guide perked up immediately.

"Ah, sir, you must go there. You will enjoy it so much. It

82

is a night-club—the best, the most magnificent in the whole world."

"Indeed?" Merlin said.

"It is out in the desert beyond the Pyramids. It is in a tent. The cabaret—ah! you have never seen such a cabaret, not even in London. Beautiful girls, wonderful belly dancers, dancing dervishes, sword swallowers. Sir, it is a place you and the lady must visit."

"We must indeed," Merlin remarked dryly. "We will go to-night."

"Very well, sir. I will order the car. What time?"

"Do we dine there?" Merlin asked.

"Oh, no, sir. It is best to go later. There is food, but it is only what you call supper."

"All right. We will dine at the hotel," Merlin said, "and tell the chauffeur to be waiting for us about ten o'clock."

"Very good, sir."

"There is no need for you to come," Merlin went on. "The chauffeur can find his way, I suppose?"

"Yes, sir. But I am your guide—it is no trouble."

"No. It is unnecessary," Merlin said firmly. "We will see you tomorrow. I expect we will visit the Pyramids."

"But of course, sir. No one can leave Cairo without seeing the Pyramids and the Sphinx."

"That is understood, then," Merlin said. "The car tonight, and you will take us to the Pyramids tomorrow."

"It shall be arranged," the guide said sulkily.

Romina could hardly contain her impatience until once again they were upstairs in their suite and able to speak.

"Do you think that man in the shop was giving you a message?" she asked. "I saw him look at the ring."

"I saw him, too," Merlin answered.

"But you had your back to him," Romina protested.

"I was watching him in the mirror. The ring certainly meant something to him."

"And so he contrived to tell you to go to Sahara City?" Romina said.

"Rather clumsily, I thought. We may be wrong, of course."

"But . . . supposing he wanted to get us out into the desert away from Cairo?"

"Sahara City is a night-club," Merlin said quietly. "I cannot believe that they intend to stab us as part of the cabaret act, whatever else they may do."

"No, of course not," Romina said.

At the same time she was dubious. Sahara City . . . the very name seemed somehow ominous.

CHAPTER SIX

THEY dined at nine o'clock in the big restaurant of the Nile-Vista which overlooked the river.

It was very modern without the air of Oriental mystery in the ante-room, where there were chandeliers like huge earrings of beaten gold set with enormous jewels; and where in the center of it there was a fountain which tinkled musically into a marble basin and which even on the hottest day gave the impression of coolness.

The bar where a great number of people drank before dinner was dark with windows of stained glass; and the faint scent of incense seemed to turn the inevitable whisky and soda into something more potent.

In the restaurant the discreetly shaded lights on every table did not detract from the light-studded river outside where the bridges reflected themselves in shimmering gold on the slow-moving current.

"It is lovely, isn't it?" Romina exclaimed. "But I feel there is hardly time for us to take it all in—there are so many other things to think about."

Merlin frowned a little as if he thought she was speaking out of character.

He was busy doing his usual flamboyant act—sending for the head waiter before he ordered his food; making inquiries as to whether this or that was fresh; asking for *foie gras* from Strasbourg, and then changing his mind, saying he always tried to eat the specialities of the country he was visiting.

It was all very impressive, Romina thought, and envied him the way he seemed to get under the skin of the man he was supposed to represent.

He had new mannerisms, certain ways of saying words which he repeated again and again—the sort of things which would be remembered by anyone describing Nickoylos.

They were as easily discarded as assumed, Romina reflected but they might encourage someone to say: "One would recognize Nickoylos anywhere. He always drums with his fingers on the table . . . or taps the side of his nose as he speaks . . . or pulls at his ear."

Merlin was clever—almost too clever, Romina thought, suddenly afraid that she might let him down. No wonder he did not want to bring her!

She forced herself to flirt across the table with an archness which made her squirm inside although she did it most effectively.

At last dinner was over. The food had not been particularly exciting after all Merlin's consultations and directions, and Romina had the insane desire to suggest that the next job they did should be in France.

She wanted to giggle at her own idea, and then remembered with a jolt the reason why they had come to Egypt.

All day she had been shying away from the memory of Paul's sprawled figure and open eyes. She thought that the full horror of it would not be likely to overwhelm her until later that day or the next as she was still numb from shock.

The question which hovered in the back of her mind was—had Chris died like that?

She remembered his laughter; the way his eyes used to crinkle at the corners when he was amused; his gay and inconsequential air; his enthusiasm for everything, which made all he undertook an adventure.

'I must not think . . . I must not think,' Romina told herself and forced to her lips one of the rather stupid sallies which she felt was appropriate to the brain of Romina Faye.

"It's about half past ten," Merlin said, looking at his watch. "I believe the cabaret starts at eleven, so we might as well be getting there. I would rather like to arrive fairly early. It gives one the chance to see the other people."

"I suppose there is such a place?" Romina said. They were standing by a fountain in the outer hall and no one could overhear them.

"Do not worry, I have checked," Merlin said quietly, and then aloud: "Come on, let's go to this new place—although if it is not better than what we saw previously I shall complain to the Government! It is sheer cruelty to tourists to make them watch bad belly-dancing. Even when it's good, it's none too hot."

"Well, I think it's a change from strip-tease, anyway," Romina answered almost shrilly, so that several guests coming from the dining-room turned their heads to look at her.

They walked downstairs rather than wait for the lift, Merlin smoking a big cigar and Romina stopping half-way down to color her lips in front of a mirror set into a pillar.

She piled the lip-stick on thickly, outlining her mouth even in the corners to make it seem broader and then looking provocatively from under her eyelashes at every man she saw in the hall.

They went through the big glass doors to where they knew the car would be waiting.

The night was warm like velvet against their faces as the car set off at a brisk pace towards the suburbs and on to the Pyramids.

They believed that the chauffeur could talk only Arabic; nevertheless there was no point in taking risks, so they said very little to each other except occasionally in a low whisper which the man in front could not possibly overhear.

The houses grew fewer and Romina saw the first Pyramid suddenly silhouetted against the sky.

It seemed to her that, while they had been driving, the stars had come out in greater profusion than she had ever seen before. Slowly the moon was moving up in the sky to give a pale silvery light which made the Pyramids seem strange and ethereal, like something from a dream world.

The car moved slowly, and unexpectedly they were out in the desert, the sand stretching away from them on the right to the far horizon; and on the left there were three Pyramids, so fantastic in their symmetry that Romina drew in her breath with a little gasp.

"I never thought they would look like that," she said. "It makes me understand many things."

"What?" Merlin asked, a note of curiosity in his voice.

"The way people have devoted their lives to studying Egyptian architecture and the prophecies the Pyramids hold engraved within them . . . the story that they were designed by the Athenians. It is almost inconceivable that such architectural perfection could have come from Egypt or any of the other Eastern countries."

"I did not know you knew so much about them," Merlin said.

"Why should you?" Romina asked. "You know nothing about me."

"I have not really had the chance to get to know you, have I?" he said.

Her eyes were on the Pyramids and she was not listening to him.

"I can understand," she said dreamily, "why anyone who looks at the Pyramids believes in reincarnation. There is something about them which makes one quite certain that one has seen them before. Perhaps I was a slave who helped to build them. . . ."

"Or the Pharaoh who ordered them," Merlin said.

The Pyramids were almost out of sight by now and she turned and smiled at him.

"I think that would be more your role than mine. Perhaps you were not even a Pharaoh . . . perhaps you were an overseer cracking his whip and making the poor slaves kill themselves in their efforts to get those great stones into place."

"You dislike me, don't you?" he asked surprisingly.

She had not expected the question, and for a moment she had no answer.

"All right," he said. "Don't tell me, I know. I have seen it in your eyes and heard it in your voice. I can understand it, in a way. I crossed you, and you are not used to being crossed, are you?"

"You make me sound spoiled," Romina said.

"Well, aren't you?" he inquired. "I suppose every beautiful woman is, to some extent. Perhaps you are more spoiled than most because you have both beauty and brains."

It was a compliment, but he did not make it sound like one.

Romina turned away from him impatiently.

"You are ruining the night for me. I did not want to talk about myself. I wanted to absorb the atmosphere. This is the first time I have ever seen the Pyramids and they have made a tremendous impression on me."

"They are not quite so impressive in the daytime," Merlin said, "with the guides screaming for backsheesh, while the man who lets you ride a camel charges so many piasters that you could buy the beast. Then there is a tiresome little man who runs to the top and back again in three minutes, and asks you as much as a first-class air fare to Rome to do it—"

"Stop! Stop!" Romina cried, half laughing, half annoyed. "You are spoiling everything for me—let me have a little fun!"

Merlin waved his hand towards the desert on the right-hand side of the car. The road was smooth and well made, but it had obviously been laid down straight across the sandy desert which stretched in rippling mounds away into the darkness.

"It is like eternity," Romina said, almost beneath her breath.

"I agree," Merlin answered. "As frightening—and as dull."

87

"Must eternity be dull?" Romina asked, more for the sake of challenging than any other reason.

"Deadly," he answered. "The whole idea must be nauseating to any thinking person, unless, of course, one believes that there is no individual survival."

"In which case there is no point in worrying about it," Romina answered.

"Exactly," he said.

Merlin was quiet and Romina wondered if they had talked too much. The car was a large limousine so it was doubtful if the chauffeur could hear much of what they had been saying, but nevertheless there was always the risk that he understood English.

Romina turned her head.

There was apparently nothing to relieve the darkness. Supposing, she thought to herself, Sahara City did not exist, and this was nothing but a trap into which she and Merlin had walked all too easily?

But then her common sense started a whole train of questions.

Who would be likely to set a trap for them? Who was interested in them? Even if they—whoever 'they' might be—had heard of their curiosity about Chris's death, there was no reason to believe that she and Merlin knew anything more, or were anything but what they appeared to be.

She had always been skeptical of Merlin's idea that they were being watched, that binoculars had been focused on them from the Tower, or that microphones had been planted in their rooms. But Romina knew enough of the East to realize the insatiable curiosity of the Eastern races about everything and everybody.

It was not just because they considered someone dangerous; they wanted to know more about them. In many cases it was just unadulterated interest. But the difficulty was to know where interest and curiosity ended and the campaign of tracking down began.

"Look!" Merlin said suddenly.

Ahead there were lights.

"Is that Sahara City?" Romina asked, a little doubtful. "It does not look very important."

"It doesn't, does it?" Merlin agreed. "But I am informed that it is in fact the most original night-club in the whole world."

"Who told you that?" Romina asked. "A travel bureau?"

"Who is being unromantic now?" he questioned. "I personally am filled with a pleasurable excitement and quite prepared for something if not stupendous, at least unique."

"Well, I hope you will not be disappointed," Romina said as the car drew nearer and she saw that the lights were only a few lamps illuminating what was apparently a large car park.

It was nothing more nor less than a piece of desert which had been used to park cars. There were a number there already and the chauffeur drew up at the far end where a roughly made gateway led on to a path.

They got out of the car and Romina felt the sand fill her sandals and she had to shake it free as she walked, conscious that gritty particles were already scraping the soles of her feet through her expensive nylons.

She was wearing a full-skirted lace dress trimmed with tiny bows of satin ribbon and she shook her skirts after sitting in the car and pulled her wrap lined with silver lamé a little closer round her shoulders.

"Are you cold?" Merlin asked as they walked down the path side by side.

"No," she answered, for she knew it was not the air, which was warm and sultry, which was making her shiver but anticipation of what lay ahead.

They passed through a rough courtyard, with a few slabs of stone laid down the center and two small wooden box-offices which were, however, empty.

Then they heard music and ahead, out of the darkness, was a glow from the great flap of a tent door which was open.

It was just as exciting and unexpected as Merlin had said.

A huge tent, capable of holding hundreds of people, had been erected in the middle of the desert. There was a dance floor in the center and around it were three rows of low sofas and stools with round, beaten brass tables in front of them.

Merlin was welcomed by a turbaned waiter who led them to what was obviously one of the best seats at the side of the dance floor.

On every table which was occupied was a bottle of whisky.

"The price of entry," Merlin said with a little smile, and Romina saw that all the whisky was of well-known British brands.

The cabaret had not yet started although the band was playing.

Romina looked around her. There were very few Europeans present. Nearly all the occupants of the low sofas were Egyptians—fat, prosperous-looking men with dark-eyed women who attempted to look European with a pale face powder and pink lip-stick.

Merlin poured himself out a neat whisky, ordered the waiter to bring Romina a soda for hers and asked her if she wanted anything to eat.

She shook her head.

"Not yet," she said. "What an extraordinary place this is!"

She looked around her and noticed that a number of people were being shown to the seats around them.

Almost before she had time to take everything in, the cabaret started, and, as she had half anticipated, the first turn was a belly-dancer.

There was no doubt that the dancer was very different both in looks and quality from the ones they had seen the night before. She was in fact rather a lovely girl, beautifully dressed in the traditional gown with its flowing panels, and her hair was well dyed to a golden shade which every Egyptian finds irresistible.

The applause when the dance was finished was long, and the next turn was even more sensational—dervishes who twirled and spun with a relentless insistent rhythm which had almost a hypnotic effect on those who watched.

"It is clever, isn't it?" Romina asked.

"Very," Merlin answered.

Three Arab girls came next who balanced chairs and tables by holding them with their teeth. Then there was another belly-dancer, and Romina felt her attention wandering.

She looked round at the absorbed faces of the audience.

It was hot in the tent and some of the men were sweating rather unpleasantly as they poured themselves glass after glass of what they called 'Scotch.'

Suddenly the curtain which had been pulled over the flap at the end of the tent parted and Romina saw a newcomer arrive.

She gave a little gasp as she saw him and put out her hand to touch Merlin on the knee.

"Look!" she said.

He glanced up and saw, as she had seen, the man he had knocked down the night before in the Pyramid Club, waiting to be led to his table.

There was something about the cut of his coat, the tightness of his trousers and the long, thin, pointed toes of his shoes which told Romina that he was in fact a homosexual.

Then she looked at the three men who accompanied him. There was no mistaking the somewhat effeminate voices, their exaggerated clothes and the way in which they walked as the waiter took them to a sofa on the other side of the tent.

"I think this is where we get out," Romina heard Merlin say close to her ear.

"But why?" she asked.

"That type of man will fight like a cornered rat," Merlin answered, "and I have a suspicion that he will recognize me."

Romina watched the four men sit down at their table.

The man they had seen the night before glanced round and started visibly as his eyes came to rest on Merlin, then he bent forward and began to talk to the men with him.

"He has recognized you," Romina whispered.

"I know," Merlin answered. "And now, play up. I want to have an excuse for leaving so early."

He drained his glass with one gulp and, it appeared, became suddenly very drunk.

He thrust his legs out in front of him and complained noisily that there was little room for them. At the same time he put his arm round Romina and drew her close to him.

"Come on, baby," he said, slurring his words. "Let's drink up this bottle and have another."

He filled her glass half-full with whisky and did the same to his own, signaling unsteadily to the waiter.

"Now, we'll make a night of it," he said, and bending his head, pressed his lips in a noisy kiss against Romina's shoulder.

She fought back her desire to push him away and tried to simper her delight.

He drank again; and now to her horror she found he was kissing her cheek, running his fingers through her hair and trying to persuade her in a drunken voice to kiss him properly.

"Come on," he said. "You're my girl, aren't you? Give us a kiss—what does it matter what people think? All the world loves a lover—do you hear that—all the world."

He released her for a moment and lifted up his glass.

"To lovers!" he said in a loud voice, and catching the eye of the woman at the next table, drank to her while her escort glared furiously.

Romina felt that she should take part in the drama.

"I think we should go home," she said. "Come on, let's go back to the hotel."

"If that's what you want, sweetie, I'm only too willing to oblige—only too willing."

He pulled her to him suddenly and kissed her full on the

lips, his mouth lingering on hers as if he was too drunk or too lazy to move quickly.

Romina fought herself free of him, hoping that her anger did not show in her eyes.

"Come on, it's time we went," she said, and signaled the waiter to bring the bill.

Merlin took a large note from his case and threw it down on the table.

"Keep the change," he said to the waiter, as he staggered unsteadily to his feet and waited for Romina to help him between the tables.

"Jolly good show!" he said to another waiter who hurried up, and repeated it over and over again as they wound their way to the exit.

"Jolly good show!—first class!—I'll tell my friends!"

His voice was thick and he slurred every word.

It seemed to Romina that their passage to the door took them an aeon of time. Finally they made it and they stepped out of the glare of the tent into the cool silver of the moonlight.

There were no attendants outside in the courtyard and Merlin took Romina by the arm and drew her behind one of the empty little box-offices.

"What are we doing?" she asked.

"Waiting," Merlin said tersely.

Where they stood in the shadow they could see the entrance to the tent and hear the music.

"Another cabaret turn must have just begun," Romina whispered.

And then out of the tent came two figures.

She felt Merlin stiffen and knew this was why he had been waiting.

They were two of the men who had been sitting at the table with the man from the Pyramid Club. Their drain-pipe trousers, their tight-waisted jackets, their pointed shoes were all too familiar.

And so, Romina thought, was the sudden flash of steel in their hands—the flick-knives of Teddy Boys all the world over.

They moved swiftly and almost silently down the path, breaking into a run just before they reached the spot where Romina and Merlin were hiding, their knives ready in their hands and an expression of evil on their faces.

As they reached the box-office, Merlin stepped out, tripping the first man and at the same time landing a blow on his chin which sent him sprawling across the courtyard. The knife shot out of his hand and clattered away over the flat paving stones.

The other man turned and Romina gave a little scream as she saw the knife flash upwards in the moonlight.

It seemed that it must strike Merlin's chest, but he knocked the man's hand down and at the same time punched him hard in the stomach, causing him to double up with a groan. Once again Merlin hit him and this time he was down, sprawled on the floor like his friend.

There was no sound from either of them.

Merlin stood looking down at them and then his gaze fell on the second man's knife where it had fallen just a few inches from his sprawled body. He bent down and picked it up.

It was a frightening weapon, the blade thin and sharp as a stiletto, as sharp perhaps as the one which had killed Paul.

Just for a moment Merlin held it in his hand and then with a swift downward thrust he stabbed it through the hand of the man who had held it. The man's body gave a little convulsive shudder, but he was half-conscious and did not realize what had happened to him.

There was a sudden burst of applause from the tent behind them. Merlin looked over his shoulder and, drawing Romina from the shadows in which she was standing, hurried her down the path towards the cars.

"We had better hurry," he said calmly, "but do not run—walk."

He moved swiftly, but to Romina it seemed a funeral pace.

At any moment the hue and cry might start. Someone had only to come out of the tent to see the two men lying there. It would be easy to find out who had left before them, to guess what had happened.

They reached the car and Merlin helped Romina in.

The usual attendant was waiting for the usual tip for having done nothing. Merlin put his hand in his pocket and pulled out some silver coins.

As he did so, the moonlight glittered on the ring he wore on his little finger, the ring with the snake's head with three little pearls in its tongue.

The car attendant looked down at it.

"Sorry, sir," he said in English, "but there is none, not tonight."

"When?" Merlin asked.

"Tomorrow, perhaps—if it arrives."

"Where is it coming from?" Merlin asked.

The man pointed vaguely with his hand towards the south.

There was a noise behind them, not loud, but undoubtedly the sound of voices as Merlin got into the car.

"To Cairo," he said to the chauffeur, and they moved out of the car park and on to the road which led towards the Pyramids.

Romina sat for a moment in silence; then, as if she could control herself no longer, the words seemed to burst from her lips, but still she spoke in little more than a whisper because of the chauffeur.

"Why did you do it? Why did you do that to him?"

There was no need to ask what she meant.

"He deserved it," Merlin answered.

"You're as bad as they are," she said.

"What about it?" Merlin asked.

"You enjoyed it," Romina said accusingly. "You enjoyed torturing him like that."

"He deserved it," Merlin said again in a bored voice. "Shall we talk of something else?"

"No, I would rather be silent," Romina said savagely.

She moved as far as she could away from him into the corner of the car as if she could bear no further physical contact with him.

She could still feel his lips on her cheek and on her mouth. She could still feel his arm around her, his fingers kneading her bare shoulder with their caressing insistency.

She could understand now why he had behaved as he had, lulling the men into a sense of security, into feeling they could dispatch him quickly and easily with their knives.

Romina closed her eyes, fighting to see things in their proper perspective. She felt as if every nerve in her body was on edge.

She had not understood, when Merlin had begun to kiss and caress her, why he was doing it. She had felt disgusted that he must touch her; and yet, somehow, she had known that he would not have done it unless it was absolutely necessary. Now she knew just how necessary it had been.

It was clever of him, she thought, to have realized that men of that sort would take advantage of his drunkenness. Just for one moment she wondered what would have happened if they had done what they had intended to do—if they had left Merlin wounded, perhaps dying—with nothing for her to do but scream.

He had been right—of course he had been right—and clever, as he had always been.

And yet for some unknown reason she wanted to find fault with him, to prick his complacency, to hurt him; because she had been forced to be a party to his subterfuge, to endure his kisses, to play the part he had assigned to her when they first left London.

She could feel his lips all too vividly—that long kiss with his arms enveloping her.

She turned her eyes sharply to see Merlin staring at the Pyramids, silhouetted against the window.

She felt suddenly ashamed of herself, ashamed for having attacked him.

Why shouldn't those brutal men with their ready knives suffer? Paul had died from the stab of a knife—and Merlin might have suffered the same fate but for his dexterity.

"I . . . am . . . sorry," she said, her voice low and hesitant.

"There is nothing to be sorry for," Merlin answered. "You were right; it was an unnecessary action. And in this game one should never do anything unnecessary or uncontrolled."

"Do you think that those men have anything to do with those who killed Chris?" Romina asked.

"I do not know," Merlin answered, his voice hardly above a whisper. "They are in the same racket, of course. That is all we do know."

Romina felt suddenly afraid.

It seemed that the long arm of coincidence was making things worse. And yet, if that encounter on the stairs of the Pyramid Club the night before had not taken place, they would not have come into possession of the snake ring—and that, in itself, was a clue they had not expected.

"Shall we have to go back again to get . . . what had not arrived?" she asked a little anxiously.

"I don't think so," Merlin answered quietly.

They drove on in silence.

The car soon reached the lighted streets and crossed the bridge over the Nile, to wind slowly into the semi-circular drive in front of the Nile-Vista.

They got out, and as they reached the hall, Romina looked at the clock, expecting to find it was the early hours of the morning. Instead, it was a little after twelve. So much had happened since they left, and yet it had happened so swiftly.

They went up in the lift to their suite. As they stepped through the doors, Romina would have spoken, but even as she opened her lips Merlin put his finger to his mouth.

She bit back the words, waiting for him to draw the little instrument from his pocket. She watched the needle with interest.

It swung round in the opposite direction to that in which

Merlin was pointing it. This time, it appeared, a microphone was fixed to one of the dressing-tables.

Romina waited for Merlin to find it and disconnect it.

But he paused. He stood for a moment and then to her surprise said in his Nickoylos voice:

"Well, baby, it was an amusing evening. Did you enjoy yourself?"

"It was lovely, but I'm tired," Romina answered.

She watched Merlin walk across the room and open the drawer of the dressing-table.

"Hell! What's going on here?" he said at the top of his voice. "Somebody's been here—my things have been moved! Where's my dispatch-case?"

He stamped across the floor and pulled the dispatch-case from the drawer in the desk where he had left it.

"It's been opened!" he said. "Someone's searched my papers. God damn it, I'm not going to stand for this!"

"But who could have done such a thing?" Romina asked, very conscious that the microphone was alive.

"That's just what I am going to find out," Merlin answered in a furious voice, and picked up the telephone.

"It's Mr. Nickoylos speaking," he shouted. "I want to see the manager—I don't care if he is in bed—get him out and tell him to come up here quick!"

"But I don't understand," Romina said in her Romina Faye voice.

"I understand it, right enough!" Merlin raged. "A man in my position—a man with my business connections—always has his enemies. There's always a snooper wanting to find out what I am going to pay for this, or going to pay for that. People can make money if they know enough."

"But . . . are you quite certain somebody's been here?" Romina asked.

"Certain of it," Merlin replied. "The lock of my dispatch-case has been tampered with. It was locked when I was out. Somebody's been at it—and the drawers have been opened. I wasn't born yesterday, my girl, I can tell you that!"

He picked up the telephone receiver again.

"Have you got hold of the manager?—Yes, the assistant manager will do. He is on his way up? Good, tell him to hurry."

He slammed the receiver down again, looking across the room at Romina, smiled and winked.

She did not know why, but that wink was the most reassuring thing that had happened to her for a long time.

She found herself smiling back, and then her hand fluttered out towards him. At least the microphone could not register that!

His fingers were hard and warm and comforting.

For a moment they stood quite still, looking at each other.

It seemed to Romina that something passed between them—something wordless and very important—although she was not certain what it was.

And then, even as she wondered, there came a knock at the door and they sprang apart.

CHAPTER SEVEN

THE assistant manager was young, fair and obviously Scandinavian. He spoke English perfectly and his manner was polite almost to a formality.

"I deeply regret, sir, that you should feel obliged to complain—" he began as Merlin shouted out that his private papers had been searched.

"What explanation have you got for such an outrage?" Merlin inquired.

"I cannot believe such a thing is possible," the assistant manager answered. "We are always extremely careful in this hotel with the servants we employ; and everything that is possible is done to ensure that the guests are protected from burglars. Are you quite certain, sir, that someone has in actual fact entered this room?"

"If I was mistaken," Merlin answered, "how do you account for this?"

He pulled aside the dressing-table as he spoke and pointed at the tiny head of the microphone attached to one leg. His finger then followed the wire to where a small box a little larger than a matchbox was hidden underneath the drawer of the table, quite out of sight unless one looked for it.

The assistant manager gave an exclamation, knelt down and examined the microphone closely.

"Let us disconnect it before you say anything," Merlin suggested.

He knelt to do so, then raised himself as he asked:

"Well?"

The assistant manager held out his hands in an expressive gesture.

"I have nothing to say, sir. I cannot think how this has happened. I can only tell you one thing—that type of microphone is not used by our police."

"You are familiar with the type they use?" Merlin inquired.

The assistant manager nodded.

"There are times when the police make inquiries about certain people staying in the hotel," he answered; "and we know they use microphones. But I have never seen this type before—never."

"I can tell you something about it," Merlin said. "It's made in Russia."

The assistant manager was silent.

There was no doubting his sincerity, Romina thought, or that he was genuinely perturbed at what had happened.

"I would like to know more about this," he said suddenly, and going to the bedside, rang the bell for the valet.

The man came, an Egyptian who had been on duty the night before. He was middle-aged, with what seemed to Romina to be a straightforward way of looking at whoever was speaking to him.

"Abdous," the assistant manager said, "this gentleman, who is in your charge, has reported to me that his private papers have been tampered with. What have you got to say to that?"

"It is not possible, sir!" Abdous replied. "No one could have got into the room without my seeing them. I have been on duty the whole evening. I have never left the floor once."

"Tell me who you have seen coming in and out of the room," the assistant manager suggested.

Abdous considered before he spoke.

"The gentleman," he said at length, looking at Merlin, "and the lady went downstairs at about nine o'clock. About an hour and a half later, it may have been nearly eleven, I saw the gentleman come upstairs and go into the room. I was working at the end of the passage. I heard the lift and looked out to see who it was and I saw this gentleman quite distinctly."

"Did you come up?" the assistant manager asked Merlin.

Merlin shook his head.

"No, we went straight from the dining-room downstairs and out to the car."

The assistant manager looked at the valet.

"Go on," he said. "What time did the man you saw enter this room go out?"

"He left the key in the door," the Egyptian said. "I passed down the corridor because the bell rang in No. 490. I saw the key hanging there. And about ten minutes later—it might have been longer—I heard a door shut and saw this gentleman locking the door and crossing the corridor to the lift."

"How far away were you?" Merlin inquired.

"I was right at the end of the corridor, sir, but I am sure it was you."

"I'm equally sure it was not," Merlin retorted, and turning to the assistant manager he said: "Now then, how do you account for this story?"

The assistant manager's eyes were on the Egyptian.

"You are quite sure, Abdous, that this is the truth and there is nothing else? You know that you must leave nothing out when you tell me a tale like this. This man you saw did not speak to you—did not give you any money?"

"No, sir, I swear it! I am honest—I have never taken money to let anyone go into an hotel room. My references are good, there was not a fault in them when I came here."

"That is true," the assistant manager said. "Very well—you may go."

The Egyptian looked uncertainly at Merlin and then again at the assistant manager. As neither of them had anything more to say to him, he walked slowly from the room.

As he shut the door, the assistant manager said:

"There is only one possible explanation, sir. I deeply regret having to make it."

"What is it?" Merlin asked sharply.

"It is something which happened once before when I was working on the Riviera. A jewel thief got into the hotel and stole a very valuable necklace belonging to one of our guests. The way he did it was ingenious—and it could have happened the same way tonight."

"Well, what was it?" Merlin asked sharply.

"You say that you went downstairs after dinner. What time was that?"

"About twenty past ten," Merlin answered.

"You had the key of the door in your pocket, I suspect?"

"That's right," Merlin answered.

"And as you passed through the hall you put it on the porter's desk?"

"Again you are right," Merlin agreed.

"Did you speak to the porter?"

"No, I don't think I did," Merlin replied. "I just put down the key and walked on—the way one does."

"Exactly. Well, the porter will have picked it up and hung it on the peg behind him. It would have been the night porter and he may have been busy as you passed and not taken a good look at you. He might not even have seen your face at all, as you did not speak to him. You left the hotel. The thief—that is, the man Abdous saw come up to this room, would have been watching you leave. After a little while he probably went up to the desk and asked for your key—"

Romina gave a little exclamation. She was beginning to see

100

quite clearly the pattern of what the assistant manager was saying.

"I suspect," the assistant manager went on, "that the man who came upstairs was deliberately chosen because he looked like you. We Europeans are rather inclined to think that all black races look alike—well, I have often suspected that we look alike to them. Anyway, the night porter saw a tall, dark-haired man wearing a gray suit—and naturally assumed it was you. So he handed over the key which was asked for."

"It's clever," Merlin remarked slowly.

"Very clever," the assistant manager agreed. "There was nothing to excite suspicion. He left the key on the outside of the door, as you would have done. He had plenty of time —he guessed that you had gone to a night-club. He would have looked amongst your papers, fixed up the microphone and walked out of the door quite openly. He went down in the lift, put the key on the night porter's desk—doubtless waiting until he was looking the other way—and left the hotel."

"But supposing the night porter had challenged him?" Romina asked.

"That would have been quite easy," the assistant manager said. "He would probably have remarked: 'How stupid! I've asked for the number I had in the last hotel I was staying at. My room is No. 224.'"

"You mean he might have taken a room in this hotel?" Merlin inquired.

"More than likely," the assistant manger said. "My experience of criminals is that the good ones are very thorough and very attentive to detail."

"I see," Merlin said.

He walked across the room looking perturbed, then he said:

"Well, my enemies—or competitors—have certainly put one over on me this time. The only thing I can do is to get back to London as soon as possible. There is information in my dispatch-case which could do me a great deal of harm if it gets into the wrong hands—which presumably it has."

"I very much regret that you must cut short your stay," the assistant manager said suavely.

But Romina had a suspicion that he was not as sorry as he appeared to be. Hoteliers do not like people who invite thefts, espionage or trouble of any sort.

"Miss Faye and I will leave tomorrow morning on the first airplane," Merlin said almost roughly. "Will you tell the hall porter to get us two seats? I don't suppose the agencies are open at this hour."

"No, sir, I'm afraid not; but I will see to the bookings myself," the assistant manager said. "And may I, on behalf of the company, express my most sincere regret that this should have happened."

"It's not really your fault," Merlin said half grudgingly. "When one finances big projects, there are always people who try to sabotage one's plans or get on the band wagon. Anyway, I was lucky to be able to spot what they were up to."

"It was indeed very clever of you," the assistant manager approved. "I do not think I should ever have noticed that microphone—it had been so well concealed."

"Well, they won't learn much from now on," Merlin said. "Good night—and be quite certain you get me on the first possible plane."

"Very good, sir," the assistant manager said. "What time would you like to be called?"

"Perhaps you had better ring me as soon as you have got the seats," Merlin said. "There's a plane, I believe, which leaves about nine o'clock."

"That's right, sir," the assistant manager agreed. "But it will mean leaving here about a quarter to eight."

"That'll be all right," Merlin said. "I can promise you that I shall not be able to sleep much tonight."

"I am sorry, sir, extremely sorry," the assistant manager said.

He bowed himself from the room. Merlin and Romina stood silent and still until the door had closed behind him and they heard his footsteps cross the corridor outside.

Romina turned towards Merlin with a worried expression on her face.

"We are not really going?" she asked.

"Yes, we are," he answered. "I've seen the red light tonight, if you haven't."

"But the men with the knives may have nothing to do with it," Romina exclaimed. "It was a private vendetta because you knocked out that horrible man at the Pyramid Club."

"You'll not deny, will you, that he is in on this dope racket?" Merlin asked. "Why do you think he hit that woman in the first place? It is my idea—and I have been thinking about this all day—that he lent her his ring because for some reason he wanted to get her into his clutches. But the ring was very valuable to our Egyptian Teddy-Boy, and he was furious with her when she said she had lost it."

Merlin paused and then continued:

"He's in on the racket, all right. He may be quite a small peddler—or may be a big one; it doesn't matter. He'll not be pleased when he finds out what has happened to two of his close friends. And I am not sticking my neck out so as to be absolutely certain I get a knife in it!"

"You mean—you are running away?" Romina asked him incredulously.

"Of course," Merlin answered. "The clever thing at this game is to know when to retreat. It is only the fools who go on with a sword in one hand and a Union Jack in the other, making a perfect target for anyone who cares to pot at them."

"And Chris . . . have you forgotten Chris?" Romina asked.

Merlin walked across the room to pick up his dispatch-case.

"Don't be a little fool!" he said. "Of course I haven't forgotten Chris—but we are leaving tomorrow morning. Mr. Nickoylos and Miss Faye are going home."

"I'm not going," Romina said fiercely.

"Oh, yes you are! Mr. Nickoylos wouldn't leave his girl-friend behind, you can be sure of that. You're coming with me. The Teddy-Boy and all his friends can wave us good-bye at the airport."

"I don't believe it . . . I just don't believe that we are going to give up now, when we have learned so much," Romina cried, and there were tears in her voice.

Merlin, who had his back to her, looked over his shoulder.

"Give up?" he asked. "Who talked about giving up?"

"But you . . . you said so," Romina replied in a bewildered voice.

"I said nothing of the sort," he replied. "I said we were leaving Egypt—for the moment, at any rate."

It seemed to Romina as if the dark cloud which had slowly encompassed her lifted and let in the sunlight.

"You mean we are coming back?" she asked.

"Of course," Merlin said wearily, as if he was speaking to a rather tiresome child. "Of course we are coming back—at least, I am. You ought to go home, and you know it."

"Oh, Merlin . . . Merlin, you frightened me so much!"

Without thinking what she was doing, Romina ran across the room and flung her arms around him.

"I thought for one moment you really meant to throw in your hand!" she cried.

He put his arm around her; and then as she felt the pressure of it she instinctively moved away from him.

"You frightened me . . ." she said, and her eyes were

103

shining. "You frightened me more than I have ever been frightened before."

"I have been called many things," Merlin said, "but not a coward. At the same time, one of the first things you learn when you are playing at this game is not to be afraid to be called one."

"I didn't really think you would run away," Romina said.

"Nonsense!" he replied. "You were sure of it! Don't try and soft-soap me now. And do you mind getting on with your packing—you won't feel like doing it first thing in the morning."

"Of course I won't," Romina agreed.

She hesitated for a moment and then added:

"I have just thought—I wonder if they have searched my room, too?"

"I expect so," Merlin answered. "Wait a minute, I will bring the microphone-finder just to make quite certain we are not saying things out of turn."

He walked into her room, and the needle on the instrument which had belonged to Paul pointed only in the direction to which he held it.

"Well, that is all right," he said after a moment. "Now look and see if anything has been disturbed."

Romina opened the drawers of her dressing-table one by one.

"No . . . I do not think anything has been moved," she said. "It is rather difficult to know—I'm not as tidy as you are."

She opened a cupboard.

"I really can't be sure."

She hesitated: "They may have looked through here, or they may not. If the microphone had not been there, would you have been so certain?"

"Perhaps I wouldn't," Merlin admitted with a smile.

Romina opened the wardrobe with its big glass door and took out one of her suitcases. She put it on the bed, opened it and then gave a little cry.

Merlin, who was just leaving the room, came back.

"What is it?" he asked.

"Look!" Romina said. "They certainly have been here."

She pointed to the inside of the suitcase.

The lining of red moiré which matched the interior in color had been slit all round.

"They were looking to see if anything was hidden there, I suppose?" Romina said.

"Exactly," Merlin replied, his voice rather dry.

Romina looked up at him quickly.

"Are you worried?" she asked.

"Frankly, I don't like it," he answered. "I think it is obvious from this that they know about Chris's letter."

"But how can they have known?" Romina asked. "You mean that Madame Goha—"

"I may be guessing," Merlin said a little grimly, "but it is much more likely that they extracted the information from her."

"You mean that they tortured her?" Romina asked hardly above a whisper.

"Don't think about it. We've got to get out of here—and quickly. That is all that matters."

He went outside the room to the door which led into the corridor. It was made of stout wood.

"Are you thinking they might burst in?" Romina asked behind him. She had followed him from her bedroom to see what he was doing.

"No—but they might have had the key copied," Merlin answered. "I may be exaggerating things. With any luck they won't know we are leaving tomorrow morning. As you know, I'm always one to take precautions. You sniggered at me before for doing just that very thing."

"I didn't mean to snigger," Romina said humbly. "I know now that you are right. It is just that, until today, when I saw what had happened to Paul and the knives in those men's hands as they meant to attack you, I . . . I . . . I didn't think that anything of this sort existed outside a film studio."

"Well, you know now," Merlin said rather flatly.

He went into his own room and started to drag the chest of drawers into the *entresol* and set it against the door.

"It's not very strong," he said, "but at least it will make a noise if anyone tries to open the door."

Romina felt a little shiver go down her spine.

"I think you're right," she said. "I shall be glad to get away from here."

She went back into her own room and packed quickly.

The dresses which had looked gay, if rather garish, when she had bought them at the Savoy now looked tawdry.

Then, it had seemed rather fun to be play-acting; even though her quest for news of Chris was serious enough. Now the acting had a grim, macabre background which left her merely afraid.

She packed everything, leaving only the dress and coat in which she intended to travel. Then she undressed, put the clothes she had been wearing that night into the case, slipped into her nightgown and her lacy negligée. Then she went to Merlin's room and knocked on the door.

"Come in!" he called.

She found that he had finished his packing and was lying on the bed in his pajamas and dressing-gown. In his hand was a small automatic revolver.

"What are you going to do with that?" Romina asked quickly.

"Nothing," he replied; "at least, I hope that is the right answer. It is merely a precaution. I'm allergic to visitors after midnight."

Romina glanced up at the clock.

"It is nearly two o'clock," she said.

"I know," he answered. "Go and get your beauty sleep. I promise that you'll be all right. Lock your door, all the same."

"I hate being locked in," Romina said almost petulantly. "Besides, how do you know someone won't come in through the balcony?"

"Fortunately that is impossible," Merlin answered. "It is a sheer drop to the street. The fire escape is at the back, on the other side of the corridor."

"Well, that is one consolation," Romina said, trying to speak lightly. "Have you heard about our bookings for to-morrow?"

Merlin nodded.

"Two on the nine o'clock plane," he said. "The assistant manager seemed very pleased about it. I think he is delighted to get rid of us."

"I thought that, too," Romina said with a little smile. "I think in his heart of hearts he believes we are trouble-makers."

"How right he is," Merlin said, looking down at his gun.

Romina followed the direction of his eyes.

"Put it away," she begged. "There has been enough killing and bloodshed for today."

She drew a deep breath and looked around the room.

"It isn't true . . ." she said; "we must have dreamed it all . . . how could it have happened?"

"Go to bed!" Merlin commanded her. "You'll feel better in the morning."

He slipped the revolver into his pocket and rose slowly from the bed.

He walked across the room to where Romina was standing, and to her surprise bent his head and kissed her lightly on the cheek.

"You've been very brave," he said. "Chris would have been proud of you."

She felt the tears prick her eyes at his words; and because she could find nothing to say she smiled at him tremulously and went back to her own room.

She locked the door as he had told her to do and flung herself down on the bed, staring through the uncurtained window at the star-strewn sky.

She felt as if her brain was turning over and over, struggling to remember all that had happened during the day.

How fantastic it had been! The woman with her frightened eyes in the Museum; Madame Goha parting reluctantly with the piece of paper that Chris had given her; Paul's dead face staring up from the floor; the two men running after them from the tent at Sahara City, their knives glinting in the moonlight!

Then, suddenly, she remembered the pressure of Merlin's lips on hers.

She had hated him, and loathed the part she had to play, letting him maul and caress her—until his mouth had captured hers and she felt herself held prisoner by him.

She could feel again her resentment changing to something else; a sudden quiver within herself; a strange sensation she had never known before. And even as she became aware of it, he had set her free.

He had kissed her again just now—a kiss on the cheek. It was a gesture which might have been made by her brother, or an older man. And yet she could still feel the touch of his lips and know the nearness of him.

Romina closed her eyes.

The pictures of what had happened were all encroaching on her one by one . . . the problems that lay ahead were coming nearer, mingling and becoming entangled one with the other . . . the kiss . . . the knives . . . and again, the touch of Merlin's lips. . . .

She awoke with a sudden start. Someone was knocking on the door.

The knock came again, and in a voice thick with sleep, she asked:

"Who is it?"

"It is seven o'clock! I have ordered breakfast. You had better get up," Merlin said, speaking, Romina thought, rather as if he was ordering a squad of soldiers about.

"All right," she answered.

Her dreams were still heavy upon her, and it was with difficulty she forced herself back to reality.

107

Outside, the stars had gone; and the sunshine, brilliant and not yet as warm and golden as it would be later, was glittering over the Nile.

With an effort Romina did not stop and look as she longed to do, but crossed her bedroom to the bathroom where she ran herself an almost cold bath.

Her head felt heavy and she wondered if it was lack of sleep, or the whisky she had drunk the night before.

'I hope we don't have to drink so much today!' she thought; and could not help smiling even while, at the same time, it all came flooding back to her how serious and dangerous the situation was.

By the time she had dressed, breakfast had been brought into the sitting-room and she saw that Merlin had put the chest of drawers back in his room again.

The rolls were crisp, and although the butter tasted rather nasty, the coffee was hot and reviving.

"Did you sleep well?" Merlin asked.

"Surprisingly, I did," Romina said. "And I expected to stay awake all night."

"One never does," Merlin said. "Probably sheer exhaustion—one's mind cannot take in any more unpleasant situations and so it packs up and does not try to cope any longer."

"It is as good an explanation as any, I suppose," Romina said; "but usually if anything worries me I lie awake hour after hour, not feeling in the least sleepy until it is time to get up."

As she spoke she thought that they were 'making' conversation and realized that when she had come into the room she had felt a moment of embarrassment.

It was stupid, of course, but when she saw Merlin she remembered all too vividly not only the kiss he had given her, but the way she had flung her arms around him.

She looked up from buttering a roll to see Merlin's eyes fixed on her critically.

"You have forgotten your false eyelashes," he said.

Romina put her hands up to her eyes.

"How silly of me," she said. "I suppose I was thinking of something else."

"Listen," he said, dropping his voice, "it is of the greatest importance to impress on them that we have really gone, you understand? They must not suspect for one moment that we are not running away. Somebody will be there to see us off, you can be sure of that! They will make quite sure that we get on the airplane—so look as Miss Faye should."

"And how would you expect her to look?" Romina asked.

108

"Rather disagreeable, I think," Merlin answered quite seriously. "She would want to enjoy the holiday, to stay in Egypt and not be particularly interested in her boy-friend's difficulties—except so far as they affected his pocket."

"Yes, of course, you are right," Romina said, almost humbly.

Merlin looked at his watch.

"Hurry," he said, "and then I will ring for someone to take the baggage down."

Romina went back to her room, stuck on her false eyelashes, mascaraed them and paid more attention to her face than she had done before.

As she looked into the mirror, she realized how flamboyant she looked with her brassy hair, over-made-up eyes and pouty, crimson mouth.

"No one could miss seeing me, at any rate," she said to her own reflection.

She put on the red coat in which she had traveled to Egypt and picked up the shiny patent-leather bag which matched her stiletto-heeled shoes.

She was hardly ready before the baggage man was knocking.

"Come on," Merlin said sharply, his dispatch-case under his arm and a purposeful, aggressive manner about him.

The assistant manager with another man who she learned was the manager was waiting for them downstairs.

There were profuse apologies, but Merlin brushed them aside.

"I've had enough of this country," he said in a loud voice. "I shall be glad to get back to civilization."

He paid his bill, querying a few small items, then with a curt nod towards the two managers, he walked ahead of Romina towards the door.

She shook hands smiling, trying to make things a little better by being pleasant. She realized, as she did so, that neither manager thought her of the least consequence and therefore were not prepared to waste time on her. She could not help being amused at their attitude, although it was quite understandable.

She hurried after Merlin, and got into the car.

The guide was sitting in front and expressed deep concern that they were leaving so soon. He tried to talk pleasantly, but Merlin answered him either with monosyllables or with grunts, and finally they drove in silence to the airport.

There Merlin tipped the guide and the chauffeur, and they

moved into the lounge to wait only a short time before their flight was called.

As they walked across the hot tarmac towards the airplane, Romina looked back at the dozens of faces at the top of the airport building watching them leave.

Any one of them might be a killer, intent on murdering them, but frustrated from doing so only at this moment because if he risked firing a shot he would certainly be caught!

"Welcome aboard, Madame," the stewardess said in a quiet, commonplace voice.

Romina thanked her as she moved to her seat.

They need not after all have worried about bookings on the airplane. The third class was packed, but the first class was only half full.

Romina sat next the window and looked out.

"Say good-bye, and not *au revoir*," Merlin said in a loud voice. "We are never coming back to this damn' place, I can tell you!"

Romina felt that his attitude was rather unnecessary now they had left Cairo behind.

She found herself resenting the way in which he summoned the stewardess and demanded champagne almost before they had taken off.

"I will bring you a drink as soon as you can unfasten your seat belt, sir," the stewardess said sweetly.

"Have we got to wait as long as that?" Merlin growled.

"I'm afraid those are the rules," the stewardess replied.

Merlin muttered something under his breath.

"What is our first stop?" Romina inquired.

"I believe it is Athens," he answered. "And I hope we get something to eat before then."

"Breakfast will be served in a few moments," the stewardess told him.

"I really couldn't eat another breakfast," Romina whispered.

He looked at her and gave her a slight frown and she knew that he had some reason for what he was doing.

She tried to look round the cabin and see who else was aboard. As they had walked across the tarmac she had been too preoccupied with her thoughts to worry who else was there.

She thought now that they looked the usual nondescript, rather boring travelers who seemed to occupy every airplane.

But there was a smart Egyptian woman accompanied by an elderly, distinguished-looking man in front of them.

Romina remembered that they had been taken on first by

the officials at the airport, so she supposed they must be important.

Anyway, nobody looked sinister; and it was very unlikely that they would be attacked in an airplane from which there was no escape.

Breakfast was served, and after it was finished Merlin said:

"There is an empty seat behind. I think I will go and sit there. It will be more comfortable."

"And you can see out of the window, of course," Romina said, feeling selfish as she had taken the best place.

He smiled at her reassuringly and she heard him settle himself behind her.

The soft beat of the engines made her close her eyes and begin to doze.

She was suddenly alert, and heard a woman's voice behind her say:

"I must speak to you for a moment!"

"But of course."

Merlin's reply was polite, but Romina could hear the note of surprise in his voice.

"I saw you last night at Sahara City," the woman said. "You left before I did. Let me have some . . . they said none had arrived when I left."

"It was true—they told me the same thing," Merlin answered.

"I don't believe you!"

The tone was suddenly sharp.

"I will pay you anything you ask. Just a little—I've got to have some."

"I'm sorry," Merlin answered, "it was the truth. The man in the car-park told me it had not yet arrived."

"It's a lie! I'm sure it's a lie!"

The voice was almost hysterical.

"Where does it come from, do you know?" Merlin asked, and Romina knew how much anxiety lay behind the question.

"I don't know—and I don't care," the woman answered. "I just know I've got to have it. Are you sure, absolutely sure, you are not lying to me?"

"Have you got a ring?" Merlin asked.

"So you are not trusting me, is that it?" the woman said in an agitated tone. "Here—I have got it somewhere in my bag."

"Who gave it to you?" Merlin inquired.

There was a sudden silence and Romina could almost sense that the woman had gone tense.

"You know I can't tell you that. You know we have sworn—all of us—that we would never reveal—"

She broke off.

"I did see the ring on your finger, didn't I?"

"Yes, of course you did," Merlin answered. "I've got it here—do you want to see it?"

He obviously opened his wallet and took out the ring and showed it to her.

"Yes—yes, it's the same. You do belong—but help me, please help me!"

"I would if I could," Merlin told her, "but I got the same reply as you—it has not arrived there."

"I'm so afraid of not getting any in Europe," the woman said in a desperate tone.

"Why shouldn't you?" he asked.

"I don't know . . . I . . . I only thought . . ."

"You think it comes from somewhere in Egypt?" Merlin said.

"I don't know. I only assumed—because I am Egyptian, I suppose—that there was more in our country than anywhere else, although I have had it in London."

"Where from? And from whom?" Merlin asked.

"I won't tell you!" The answer was almost a snarl. "If I do, you'll get it instead of me. And I've got to have it—I've got to!"

She paused a moment and then said:

"If I thought you were holding out on me, I'd . . . I'd . . ."

"Yes, what would you do?" Merlin questioned.

"I don't know, but I would make you suffer in some way—just as I am suffering now, damn you!"

There was a hurried movement.

Romina realized that the woman was going to her seat.

She turned her head quickly.

It was the woman with the elderly man who had been taken aboard first—the Egyptian woman who had looked so important.

CHAPTER EIGHT

MERLIN came back to sit down beside Romina.

"You heard that, Romina?"

She nodded.

He looked at his watch.

"We shall be in Athens in about half an hour," he said. "I want you to feel ill so that I have an excuse for breaking our journey."

A quick feeling of relief swept over Romina.

She had been afraid that once they returned to England either Merlin or her guardian would have persuaded her not to come back again.

She had realized for a long time that she was holding on to her position in this wild and dangerous adventure by the skin of her teeth.

Then she saw the expression on Merlin's face, and said:

"You meant to stop there all along, didn't you?"

There was a little smile on the corner of his lips which was an answer in itself.

"Why didn't you tell me?" she asked angrily. "I think you are sadistic where I am concerned."

As if her accusation shook him, he said gently:

"No, you must not think that. It is just that I hate making plans too far ahead. It is unlucky. One never knows what may turn up."

"And now that woman has decided you?" Romina hazarded.

He pressed his fingers hard on hers as a message of warning, and she understood that he was afraid to talk in case those in the seats behind might overhear.

She released her fingers and picking up her bag took out her vanity case and looked at herself in the small glass.

She looked, she thought, in excellent health. It was not only the rouge on her cheeks, the crimson of her lips, but there was a sparkle in her eyes which made her face seem radiant.

She dipped her powder-puff into the vanity case and

started to make her cheeks as white as possible. Then she took some of the lipstick off her lips, and putting on her dark glasses, slumped back in the seat.

"Good!" Merlin said appreciatively.

He had been watching every movement she made, and it had the effect of making Romina feel nervous.

Now she opened one eye.

She saw his face and could not suppress a little giggle. It was all so like a game of charades—the kind of thing in which she had excelled at school and which had resulted in her always getting the leading role in every school play.

Then she remembered that she was not at school; their lives were in danger; and she was suddenly very serious.

Merlin rang the bell above their seats and when the stewardess came, he said:

"Miss Romina Faye is feeling very ill. Have you an aspirin, or something like that?"

"Yes, of course," the stewardess answered. "I will bring you some at once."

She came back with two tablets and a glass of water.

"Come on, baby, take these;" Merlin commanded.

But Romina waved her hand languidly and gave a muttered groan.

"Leave them for a moment," Merlin said to the stewardess. "I will persuade her to have them."

"Very well, sir. Shall I get a rug?" she asked.

"I'm sure that would be a great help," Merlin answered.

As soon as she turned to find a rug on the rack above the seats, Merlin slipped the tablets into his pocket and lifted the glass to Romina's lips.

"Just a few sips," he said encouragingly.

Tucked up in the rug, Romina sat with closed eyes until the loudspeaker told them that they were nearly at Athens.

The passengers were told to fasten their seat belts and to put out their cigarettes.

"What do I do now?" she whispered to Merlin.

"Look pale and interesting. And hang on to my arm," he answered.

The airplane came down in a perfect landing at Athens airport and they taxied towards the buildings.

When everyone had left the compartment, Romina moved slowly towards the door and allowed Merlin to help her down the stairs and across the tarmac.

"How do you feel?" Merlin asked in a distinct voice as soon as they reached the lounge.

"Terrible—in fact I feel ghastly," Romina answered, also in a loud voice.

"We shall just have to break our journey," Merlin said firmly.

He disappeared and came back about five minutes later with the information that everything was arranged.

"Now we will go to the best hotel," he announced, "and get you into bed. A good sleep will make all the difference."

"I hope so," Romina answered miserably.

Their luggage, cleared of the Customs, was piled into a taxi and Merlin helped Romina into the back seat.

Then he gave an address to the driver which did not sound in the least like an hotel; but it was impossible for Romina to say anything because it was a very small car and the chauffeur was almost sitting with them.

They drove some way until they skirted the town and started up a luxuriant green valley with the tops of the mountains rising almost sheer above them.

Romina was longing to ask where they were going, but she felt it was wiser to say nothing.

After they had gone for about ten miles, the car turned the road on to a bumpy drive and she saw above them an attractive villa, its windows and shutters painted a vivid blue and its white walls covered with bougainvillaea and clematis.

"Where is this?" she asked almost involuntarily.

"You will see," Merlin answered briefly.

The car stopped at the villa and Merlin got out.

"Wait here a moment," he said to Romina and repeated the same thing to the chauffeur.

She watched him run up the steps to a veranda and what was obviously the front door.

He had a lithe, quick way of moving which had something of the grace of a panther.

'He's not an ordinary person,' she decided.

There was something strange and rather wild about him, as if he had indeed come from the jungle to be tamed in civilization.

The front door was opened and after a few seconds he disappeared.

Then he came out again, and he was smiling.

He was followed by an elderly man who at the very first glance was unmistakably English.

Merlin opened the car door.

"It's all right, Romina," he said. "Our friend is delighted to put us up."

Romina crawled out of the taxi and straightened herself to look into a pair of quizzical blue eyes.

"Jack Harrison," Merlin said, by way of introduction. "And this is Romina."

"I cannot tell you how delighted I am to meet you," the man with the blue eyes said. "Come in and meet my wife while Merlin sees to the luggage."

He led the way up the steps to the veranda and through an open door into a large sun-filled sitting-room.

Romina saw that there were flowers everywhere—mimosa, carnations, azaleas—they seemed to fill the whole room so that the scent was almost overpowering.

And then from the chair in front of the fireplace a woman rose to greet her.

She was over middle-age and yet she had kept her attraction and, what was more, her figure. She wore a thin tweed skirt of oatmeal color and over her shoulders had a cardigan which matched the soft pastel pink of her blouse. She wore a pair of tiny pearl ear-rings and a very small string of pearls, and she looked exactly everyone's idea of a perfect English lady.

"How nice to meet a friend of Merlin's," she said quietly, holding out her hand.

Romina was suddenly conscious of her glaring scarlet coat and her common patent leather bag with stiletto-heeled shoes to match.

Because she felt embarrassed, she looked round for Merlin and was thankful to see him coming through the door looking relaxed and at ease.

"Margaret, this is kind of you," he said to Mrs. Harrison. "Are you quite certain we shall not be a nuisance?"

"Even if I said you were, do you think Jack would let you go?" Mrs. Harrison asked with a little smile.

"If you want to know the truth," Mr. Harrison boomed, "this is the best thing that has happened in a month of Sundays. I have been feeling out of it, old and on the shelf, and the mere sight of you puts new life into me. What are you up to?"

"You will be amazed when you hear," Merlin said.

He suddenly realized that Romina was standing tense and a little embarrassed, and put his arm around her shoulders.

"All right, Romina," he said. "These are friends, real friends. They were both very fond of Chris."

"Chris who?" Jack Harrison asked.

"Chris Huntley—Romina's brother."

"But of course! Good gracious me, it seems only the other

116

day Chris and I were crawling on our stomachs with the machine-gun bullets whizzing over our heads. How is he, by the way?"

Merlin tightened his hold on Romina's shoulder.

"He is dead," he said quietly. "He was murdered, and Romina and I are trying to find out why."

"Murdered?" Margaret Harrison cried. "Oh, you poor dear—how terrible for you! But don't let us talk about it now. Come into my bedroom. I expect you would like to wash and tidy yourself before lunch."

She led Romina away to a small but charming room decorated in white and lilac which overlooked the garden.

A Greek boy brought in Romina's suitcases, and she opened them quickly, hoping that she would find something less flamboyant to wear.

Most of her clothes had been bought specially for their startling effect; but she found a cotton dress which was not too bad after she had substituted another belt and pulled a piece of quite unnecessary embroidery off the collar.

She was relieved to remove her false eyelashes, wash her face and put on only the minimum amount of make-up.

She longed to wash her hair free of the tint which had been put into it in London. At the same time she did not know if she would be required to be Romina Faye again, in which case the brassy tint must stay.

She went back to the sitting-room a little shyly. It was a long time since she had faced Merlin in anything but her 'war paint.'

However, she found he was deeply engaged in conversation.

She was amused to see that he was wearing a pair of Mr. Harrison's gray trousers and a loose tweed jacket, which became him far better than the over-tight suits he had worn as Nickoylos.

Mr. Harrison rose as Romina appeared.

"I have made you a very dry Martini," he said; "I hope that is what you like."

"It will be delicious," Romina said, "after all the beastly champagne Merlin has made me drink."

"If there was one thing I disliked more than anything else when I was in the game," Jack Harrison said, "it was the nauseating stuff one had to drink. I remember once I was on Bourbon for a month—and if there is one whisky that makes me sick, it is Bourbon!"

They all laughed; and then Merlin said quietly:

"But you miss it, don't you, Jack?"

"No, and I can say that quite truthfully. I am perfectly happy here with Margaret. We have our garden and our own vineyard, and have both become mixed up with local affairs. The climate is good, and our friends come to see us."

"Like us?" Merlin said.

"Not always quite such exciting friends, eh, Margaret?—but friends. They come out from London because they need a rest and we send them back looking twenty years younger and very much better in health."

Merlin rose to get himself another Martini at the side table.

"No health cure this time, Margaret," he said lightly; "we leave tomorrow. But before we go, we need a great deal—new passports, new clothes—in fact, new personalities."

Romina gave a little cry of delight.

"This means that Romina Faye is dead," she said. "I could not be more pleased. I always did dislike the girl! If you had called me 'Baby' once more, I think I would have killed you!"

Merlin laughed, and turned to Jack Harrison.

"It was a touch of inspiration when I remembered that you were living here. You see, I was supposed to be Greek—and no one will think it is surprising for a Greek to return to Greece!"

"Is anyone likely to think about it at all?" Jack Harrison asked.

"I hope not," Merlin replied. "I hope to God we have covered our tracks. But there was a woman on the plane who might talk about me when she gets to London."

He told them briefly what the woman had said to him.

"I wonder who she was with?" Jack Harrison said. "He might have been a new Minister to London—or one of the industrial chiefs going over for a Conference."

"So the dope had got a real hold of the woman?" Margaret said. "Poor soul! I am sorry for her."

She saw the look of surprise on Romina's face, and said:

"You don't know what it is like. I have seen a lot of people who have become addicts almost in spite of themselves. It is horrifying. And at the same time, one weeps because a human being can sink so low."

"Have you any idea who is behind it all?" Jack Harrison asked Merlin.

"No," he replied and, rising to his feet, walked over to one of the windows.

"It is so peaceful and lovely here," he continued. "And yet to go on means to risk two lives at least—Romina's and

118

mine. Do you think we would be wiser to go back to London?"

"No!" Romina cried. "Remember Chris . . . remember Paul."

"Just for a moment I'm remembering you," Merlin said.

Margaret Harrison rose to her feet.

"You can't make tremendous decisions of this sort on an empty stomach," she said. "Things always seem worse before one eats. Come into the dining-room. Our house-boy is very punctual. I know the omelette will be waiting for us almost as soon as we get there."

She led the way into a small square room which seemed little more than a conservatory. There were flowers in pots, ferns and strange, beautiful plants with variegated leaves which looked as if they had come from another planet.

"You are looking at my treasures," Margaret Harrison said to Romina with a little smile. "You see, I worked in the Distressed Areas before the war and I thought I would never forget the poverty, dirt and malnutrition—or get the smell out of my nostrils. I promised myself that if Jack ever retired I would become a gardener and grow flowers. So, you see, my dream has come true."

"They are lovely," Romina exclaimed.

"They are my children," Margaret Harrison said gently. "Jack and I have never been fortunate enough to have any."

There was a hint of sadness in her voice, and Romina longed to say something comforting.

But there was no chance.

The men came into the room and the conversation became gay and sparkling as the house-boy brought in their food and handed it round and Jack Harrison poured them out glasses of Greek wine.

When at last coffee had been served and the boy had left the room, their host sat back in his chair.

"Now, then," he said. "What are your orders?"

"Are you quite certain that you are going back?" Margaret Harrison interposed quickly. "Why not go on to England first and tell the General what you have found out?"

"I dare not!" Merlin said, his eyes on Romina. "I would like to—but it isn't possible. You see, if the General knew what was happening he would be bound to take action. He would have to get in touch with the International Anti-Narcotics Bureau. I am not saying they might not be more effective than we are—but there is always the possibility that they would frighten away our prey."

He paused for a moment and played with his glass and then went on:

"If, as Chris seemed to think, they are trying to grow the stuff in Egypt and do not only import it from China, then we have got to act fast. It has got to be stopped before other people besides those already involved find out that it can be done."

"You think this lot—whoever they may be—have kept the secret to themselves?" Jack Harrison asked.

"I am sure of it," Merlin said, "or there would be more of the dope flying around. It is in short supply. Why?—because it is hard to grow. Perhaps even at this time of year they have not yet got into production, but are just relying on what they have smuggled over from China."

"Yet they are building up their clientele?" Jack Harrison suggested.

"That is the way they usually work," Merlin answered. "Once get the demand and you are certain to get your price, however high it may be. But I have a feeling that these people are not likely to take risks if they can possibly help it."

"They have taken one risk, at any rate," Jack Harrison said. "They must have known there would be inquiries about Paul's death."

"Paul put up a terrific struggle," Merlin said. "And who knows?—they might have gone there not intending to kill him. You know how excited Egyptians get—they may have been ordered to frighten him, but when he would not produce the piece of paper which Chris had left, they lost their heads and killed him."

"Yes, that is very possible," Jack Harrison agreed. "Egyptians never expect to go as far as they do when the emergency arises. They always lose control of themselves."

"Well, how can we help you?" Margaret asked Merlin.

"Thinking it over," Merlin answered, "I believe the best thing is for us to go on from here as 'husband and wife.' "

Romina gave a little start, but she said nothing.

"We could take the evening plane to Beirut," he went on, "and there take the first available connection to Cairo."

"It's quite a good idea," Jack Harrison said approvingly. "It should cover your tracks."

"Coming from Beirut," Merlin went on, "people may easily assume we have come in from India."

"Or Persia, Aden—or any of the places east of Suez," Jack Harrison said. "Now what about passports?"

"That's where I am relying on you," Merlin said.

"I have an old one," Jack said, "which Margaret and I had

for a short time when I was doing nothing dangerous. We thought it quite a good idea to have a combined passport."

"Do you know someone who can bring it up to date?"

"Yes—an expert, if it comes to that. He was one of our men during the war; he adores a bit of intrigue. I shall tell him you are going to Beirut to look for someone who has disappeared. You will be 'Mr. and Mrs. Harrison.' What will you do when you get to Egypt?"

"I thought we would go to Luxor and work slowly up the river from there. I've been thinking that there are quite a number of places on the Nile where little notice would be taken of anything which one did—especially if the person concerned had money."

"And if you can't find anything there?" Jack Harrison asked.

"I shall start working the other way," Merlin said briefly. "From Luxor down to Cairo. The trouble is that there is an awful lot of Nile!"

"And an awful lot of swine ready to exploit it!" Jack Harrison ejaculated.

"Now to details," Merlin said. "Margaret, can you lend Romina something decent to wear and then take her to Athens to buy some subdued cotton dresses of the type that one finds in every shop in Oxford Street?"

"I'll do my best," Margaret Harrison answered. "And what we can't find in Athens, Romina can borrow from me. We are about the same height. She unfortunately has a much smaller waist."

"She is young," Jack Harrison said tantalizingly.

"Do you suppose I do not realize that?" Margaret asked. "And I can see, what is more, that Merlin is having to hold up your trousers with a belt!"

"All right, all right, touché," Jack Harrison said. "The trouble is, Margaret is too good a cook. I have put on weight since I left the Service—and I know it."

"You are quite certain that you do not mind doing this for us?" Merlin asked. "You, better than anyone else, realize the penalties if it is found out that we stayed here and that you probably are in the secret."

"My dear boy," Jack Harrison said almost ponderously, "if I had worried about danger I would have been dead years ago—and so would Margaret. I have been through some narrow squeaks one way and another, and I have never regretted a moment of it. I'm not going to miss out on this—I can tell you that, right away."

"Good!" Merlin said. "Now I want a hot bath to get this

121

color out of my skin. And Romina will have to wash her hair, too, before she goes into the town."

"Don't worry about us," Margaret said. "You look after yourself. You look a very oily dago, I can tell you that!"

She rose to her feet and linked her arm through Romina's.

"Come on," she said. "We've got an awful lot of work to do before nightfall."

She took Romina into her bedroom and started to find her something to wear before they went shopping.

"This will do," she said, producing a jumper suit in gray linen. "It has got a belt—I'll find it while you are having your bath."

"Are you sure you do not mind my borrowing it?" Romina asked.

"Of course not," Margaret said with such sincerity that there was no doubt she was speaking the truth.

"It is almost too smart for the part I've got to play," Romina said, picking up the dress.

"We will find you something dull and ladylike when we go into town," Margaret said with a little laugh.

"Who pays for all this?" Romina asked suddenly.

It seemed a terrible waste that everything she had in her suitcase would be discarded now; and she wondered what Margaret Harrison would do with them if they were left at the villa.

"I expect Merlin has lots of money with him," Margaret answered.

"Merlin?"

Romina ejaculated the name almost as if Margaret Harrison had hit her.

"You mean . . . to say . . . that he pays for all this?"

"Well, most of it," Margaret replied. "You see, the agents in the organization are not allotted very much in the way of cash. In fact, they always talk about doing it on a shoe-string. And, unless I am mistaken, Merlin has always financed his own activities."

"He is financing mine, too," Romina said in a grim voice. "Well, I'll pay him back every penny."

"That is quite unnecessary," Margaret Harrison smiled. "I have known Merlin for years. He is rich—very rich, in fact. His father was killed in an airplane at the very beginning of the war and his mother died soon afterwards. Merlin was only a child, of course, and their money accumulated for him. He was brought up by an uncle who, because he had no sons, left Merlin a fortune when he died. So you need not cry about Merlin, I assure you."

"I don't like it . . . I don't like him to pay for me. I want to pay for myself," Romina said.

"I should wait until you come back safe and sound," Margaret Harrison smiled, "then you can pay for anything you want. If you don't come back, I can assure you that Merlin's heirs will not miss the small amount involved."

Margaret was laughing, Romina thought, at her scruples.

Then she remembered that Merlin had bought the clothes she wore as Romina Faye.

It was ridiculous for her to offer to pay for them, as Mrs. Harrison said. And yet a prudish thought was making an angry protest at the back of her mind—nice girls did not accept clothes from men!

It was fun choosing clothes. What woman can resist it? Romina and Margaret went from shop to shop buying not many things but insisting on getting what they wanted. They chose very nice, unexciting, ladylike dresses and the alterations were promised for the next day.

Finally, when they turned for home, Romina stretched out her feet in Margaret's small car and admitted that she was tired.

Margaret took her eyes off the road for a moment and glanced at the girl sitting beside her.

'She's very lovely,' she thought, 'with her pale gold, newly-washed hair and clear skin which owes little of its radiance to make-up.'

And because she was a woman, with match-making never far from her mind, she could not help saying:

"Are you fond of Merlin? I find him a fascinating person."

"Do you?" Romina asked.

She was about to add that she disliked him very much indeed. But then something within her made her suppress the words. It was not true—she didn't dislike him; she admired him—but at the same time she was frightened of him.

There was something ruthless about him. She still remembered his face when he had struck the knife through the man's hand as he lay sprawled in the sand.

"You know, what I like about Merlin," Margaret went on, as if Romina had not spoken, "is that he is so kind. It is not just money—it is taking trouble over people—which means far more. I remember Jack telling me that everyone on his estate adored him; they turned to him with all their troubles, however trivial they might be."

"His estate?" Romina asked curiously.

"Has he not told you about it?" Margaret inquired. "It is

the love of his life. Just as I adore my flowers, Merlin adores his home. He left for some years while he was at school, but now he is living there. It is not very big; but it is a perfect Tudor house. When he is not working, he stays there by himself—and assures me that he enjoys every minute of it."

Margaret paused a moment, her eyes on the road ahead.

"But if you ask me, what that house wants is a mistress. Merlin should get married—I have told him so often enough."

Romina realized where Margaret's thoughts were leading her.

"Perhaps, like me, it is the last thing he wants," she said a little tartly.

"I imagine some people are happier alone—saints and aesthetes perhaps," Margaret said irrepressibly. "And if you ask me, neither Merlin nor you qualify for those particular categories."

She drove her car fast up the rough drive and drew up with a screech of brakes at the bottom of the steps which led to the veranda.

"We're home!" she called as she went up to the front door. "Have you been wondering what had happened to us?"

She entered the sitting-room; and Romina, who was following her, saw her stop suddenly.

The room was empty.

"That is strange," Margaret murmured. "I thought they would be back by now."

There was an undercurrent of anxiety in her voice which Romina did not miss.

Margaret walked across to one of the windows and, picking up a pair of binoculars which lay on the table, put them to her eyes.

"As we live on a hill, one can see for miles," she said. "I often watch for Jack's car leaving the town and then start to lay the table. I can be just ready by the time he gets here."

She gazed out of the window and said nothing more, but Romina could sense the uneasiness in her mind.

"You are worried," she said accusingly. "Why should you be worried?"

Margaret put down the binoculars and gave herself a little shake.

"I'm being ridiculous," she said, "but we've been through so much, Jack and I, that I can't help it. And now, whenever the old things in which he was involved crop up again, I get nervy."

She opened a box on the table, took out a cigarette and lit it with hands that seemed shaky.

"It's absurd," she went on, "and—don't tell me—I am old enough to know better, but I'm still frightened."

"We should not have come here," Romina said uncomfortably.

"No, no," Margaret said. "Please do not say that—I had no right to tell you what I feel. It is my fault—Jack would be furious if he knew. He has been near to death so many times, and this sort of danger makes me creep."

She walked back to the window as if she could not resist watching the road, winding down to the town.

"I should not say this to you—it might only make you unhappy, too, but one longs to be married to a man who has an ordinary job—something nice and uncomplicated; a job where he leaves the house in his bowler hat at 8:30 in the morning and comes back at 5:30 in the evening. I suppose that is what every woman wants—that is, every woman who is in love."

That night when Romina had gone to bed she found herself thinking over Margaret's words and the intonation in her voice as she had said them.

'I suppose I have never been in love,' she thought.

Alex Salvekov had been so good-looking that she had been flattered when he had singled her out and rung her up day after day and contrived to be at the same parties as she went to.

She had believed herself to be half in love with him; but that had been before the night she had let him go home with her, when he had pressed her back on the sofa and found her lips with his.

'I will not think about it . . . I will not!' she told herself.

But she knew, even as the thought flew through her mind, that the memory of Alex had haunted her ever since she had left London.

She found herself wondering what his feelings were when he found she had vanished. Was he upset? Or had he gone out and found another woman—someone more complaisant than she had been?

"I hate him!" she said aloud in the darkness; and remembered her feelings when she opened the telegram which told of Chris's death and saw Alex standing in the fireplace looking at her, like a prince from a fairy tale in his glittering fancy dress.

"I hate all men!" she said firmly.

125

She knew it was going to be impossible to sleep for a long time. Her body was tired, but her brain was racing—remembering things; listening to conversations which seemed to have quite a different meaning when out of their context.

Angry at her lack of self-control, Romina got out of bed and slipped on a glamorous wrap which she had worn in Egypt as Romina Faye.

Tomorrow the wrap was going to be packed away with her other clothes. She had bought a pretty, but plain dressing-gown, which was the kind of thing that every British girl would consider long-wearing and useful.

With rows of lace trailing softly across the floor, Romina opened the French window of her bedroom and stepped on to the balcony.

The moon was high in the sky and the mountains were silhouetted against it, looking purple and mysterious, so that it was easy to imagine the gods of Olympus sitting high aloft and laughing at the foibles and follies of the human beings below.

It was all exceedingly lovely; and yet Romina felt a sudden depression settle on her.

She felt lonely and uncertain, both of the past and of the future. She wanted something to cling to—or was it someone?

Chris had gone. He had left an empty place in her heart. Why had he died so young and so unnecessarily?

"Chris . . . Chris . . ." she whispered beneath her breath. And her whole spirit went out in an agony of yearning for someone who would bring comfort and security to her.

She felt the tears collect in her eyes, but they did not fall.

Then a voice behind her asked:

"Why are you awake?"

She felt herself jump, and she turned round to see Merlin standing there in the shadows of the veranda.

He, too, was wearing a dressing-gown. There was between his fingers a cigarette which he flicked away from him into the garden below.

"I can't sleep," Romina said, almost defiantly.

"Neither can I," he answered. "Funny, isn't it?—you can be tired, and yet your brain becomes a separate entity and ignores the cries of your poor, exhausted body."

"That is exactly what I feel," Romina said. "But I'm depressed as well."

"Why?" Merlin asked.

"I don't know," she replied. "All this killing and unnecessary pain. The world should be a peaceful place—why can't people leave it like that?"

"You know the answer to that, don't you?" Merlin said. "Just two words—money and power. Men want one or the other, and they are prepared to pay any price to get it."

"It's horrible," Romina said.

She looked at him sharply, and added:

"Which do you want—money or power?"

She thought he would refuse to answer her, but after a moment he said:

"I suppose power is the answer—the power to make people behave, to do what they should do, to be kind to each other."

He paused as if he was ashamed at having spoken so seriously, and said:

"It's silly, isn't it, because one can never attain it?"

"It's a good thought, all the same," Romina said.

"Thank you," Merlin said, a smile crinkling his face. "I suppose it is the first compliment you've ever paid me."

"I'm afraid I'm not very good at compliments," Romina replied.

"Neither am I," he said; "but take this as a statement of fact—'moonlight becomes you.'"

"How well I remember that tune," Romina said, ignoring the compliment. "Chris and I danced to it at a Hunt Ball. We had a long, very interesting talk as we did so, as to whether one's reactions to people were chemical or spiritual."

"Unusual for a Hunt Ball," Merlin said dryly.

"That's why I remember it," Romina said.

"And what was the conclusion?" Merlin asked, as though he was really interested.

Romina was leaning across the rail of the balcony.

And now he put his arms on the rail and leaned sideways to look at her.

"Yes—you are lovely," he said, before she could speak. "I did not realize it when I first saw you. Besides, you were so irritable that I only wanted to slap you."

"That is mild to what I wanted to do to you," Romina said.

"Yes, I knew you hated me," he replied. "Well—that seems a long time ago. Can't we be friends, as they say?"

"I don't see why not," Romina answered. "It is easier, isn't it? not to be pulling against each other."

"Much easier," he said. "And so—that is a bargain. We are friends—masquerading as husband and wife. Quite an amusing situation, if you think about it. My old Nannie would approve. She was a great one for not letting the sun go down on one's wrath. 'Come on, Merlin,' she used to say severely, 'kiss and make up, whether you like it or not.' "

Romina laughed, as she was meant to do.

And even as she did so, a strange and unexpected thought came into her mind.

She would like to kiss and make up—she would like to be kissed by Merlin.

CHAPTER NINE

THEY drove into Athens in Jack Harrison's small, rather uncomfortable car.

"We've got a lot to do," Merlin said as they neared the outskirts of the city, "and I think we had better separate. Jack and I will go and see about the photographs and the passport. It should be quite easy to transpose them."

He paused and then continued:

"But on second thoughts, I think it would be better if we had entirely new ones. I know a man who can manage it, Jack, and fortunately I have brought some extra passport photographs of Romina and myself. I have learned of old when one is on the run, it is being photographed that takes time."

"As I have said before—and I am sick of repeating it—you think of everything," Romina told him.

He turned round to smile at her as she sat in the back seat beside Margaret Harrison.

"If you do say it again, I shall slap you," he said. "It is unlucky, or rather it raises my superstitious fears, so shut up!"

"All right," Romina answered. "But you must agree that it is terribly annoying to travel with someone who is always one thought ahead. We will concede you this point—you'll have to get a new passport and photographs, and you know a man who will do them!"

"You must agree, it is annoying," she added, turning to Margaret Harrison.

Margaret laughed.

"They are all the same, these men," she said. "They have got a James Bond complex. Jack lies awake at night planning all the things that might happen. It used to be spies, and now it is whether the roof will blow off in the gales. I sometimes think that we are the most prepared house for any emergency in the whole of Greece."

"Don't say it," Jack Harrison groaned from the wheel.

"I'm just as superstitious as Merlin when it comes to thinking you are safe."

"While you are forging a new identity, what shall Margaret and I do?" Romina asked.

"Shopping, of course," Merlin answered. "That should please you. Do you want any money?"

"No, I don't," Romina said sharply, and then remembered that she had not got very much with her—and there were still several things to pay for which she and Margaret had chosen the day before.

"Well, take this, anyway," Merlin said before she could speak, and passed a wad of pound notes over his shoulder.

"You don't think anyone will be suspicious?" Romina asked.

Merlin shook his head.

"Everyone expects tourists to smuggle currency," he said, "and you'll not be spending them all in the same shop. Surely you'll not want much more? You and Margaret came home laden last night."

"There speaks the eternal man!" Margaret Harrison chipped in. "Romina will want quite a lot more things. You may be a respectable English couple taking a short holiday—but even so, the wife, as they say, will want to take home souvenirs, even in the shape of Greek fashions."

"All right," Merlin said in mock humility, "I'm defeated!"

There was silence for a moment as Jack Harrison negotiated the small car through the traffic.

Then Merlin said:

"As we are not using your passport, Jack—and thanks for the thought—we might as well have a new name. Any suggestions?"

" 'Robinson,' " Jack Harrison said immediately. "That sounds quite ordinary and respectable."

"All right," Merlin agreed. "A rose by any other name . . . I suppose!"

"I shall be terrified that I shall get confused and sign my name as something entirely outrageous," Romina exclaimed.

"It is something that has happened before now," Merlin answered seriously. "Do you remember, Jack, that time in Hong Kong?"

They started to reminisce about an incident which had happened some years previously, and Romina turned to Margaret.

"You are kind to take all this trouble," she said. "I feel terrible having burst in on you without your expecting us."

"Don't worry about that," Margaret Harrison said. "It is a

real joy to have you. To tell the truth, Jack often pines for the exciting life he used to lead. And when he is in one of his 'black' moods, as I call them, I long for something to happen—someone to drop in—especially if they need his help."

Margaret Harrison looked at the back of her husband's head and there was no mistaking the affection in her eyes and the little worried note in her voice.

'She loves him,' Romina thought; and imagined what it would be like to be so happily married that one's only thought was for the happiness of the person one loved.

She had a sudden impulse to tell Margaret Harrison that she envied her and that she personally would give anything to find someone with whom she would be content for the rest of her life.

But there was no time for confidences.

The car was drawing up in the main street outside a large store which seemed to cater for everything.

"This is where I expect you want to get out, isn't it, Margaret?" Jack Harrison asked.

"This will do," Margaret agreed. "Where shall we meet you?"

Merlin looked at his watch.

"We'll be about an hour and a half," he said. "What about three-thirty at the Central Hotel opposite? We'll meet you in the lounge."

"Right," Margaret Harrison agreed. "Take care of yourself—and don't get into mischief."

She got out on the off-side of the car, and Romina stepped out on to the pavement. She gave Merlin a little smile as she turned away and followed Margaret into the emporium.

It was fun, as it had been the previous day, to look at and handle clothes; although neither woman was buying the sort that they really liked or would have chosen in any other circumstances.

"You are too pretty, you know, for this sort of thing," Margaret said a little later when they were waiting in a dressing-room for a fitter. "People will look at you and remember you—and that is the one thing you do not want."

"They'll not pay much attention if I am wearing my glasses," Romina said; "and I'll wear a handkerchief over my head most of the time. It has always been my opinion that it is the most unbecoming thing any woman can do."

"I rather agree with you," Margaret Harrison said. "How I sigh for the days when women of my age always wore glorious hats covered in flowers and feathers!"

131

Romina looked at herself in the glass.

"I suppose I could make my hair a little more mousy," she said. "I had better buy a rinse while we are here."

She spoke reluctantly and she knew, as she did so, that she wanted Merlin to see her hair as it was then—almost like spun glass, fair and soft around her tiny pointed face; the color of corn just as it begins to ripen, or of the first daffodils which appear among the green grass in early spring.

"Don't you think Merlin is good looking?" Margaret Harrison asked her unexpectedly.

To Romina's relief, the fitter arrived before she had time to answer and said that as the workrooms were not busy the dress could be altered within a quarter of an hour.

Romina and Margaret wandered around the store while they were waiting.

There were quite a lot of things which Romina wanted, and she was rather appalled as she finished and collected the things she had chosen the day before to find that she had spent nearly all the money which Merlin had given her.

'I'll put it down on an account,' she thought, 'and he shall have every penny of it returned when we get back to England.'

She did not know why, but she found herself thinking continuously of how Merlin was prepared to finance this sort of adventure.

It was something that she and Chris had often discussed, and Chris had said it was disgraceful that the under-cover men were kept short of funds and that foreign powers often obtained better information just because they were able to pay more.

Romina was not sure whether it annoyed her that Merlin should be rich enough to do as he liked; or whether she admired him for the type of life he had chosen.

Whatever it was, she found herself continually thinking about him and gave herself a mental shake as they went up to the department to fetch the dress which had been altered.

It was ready for them, already packed in a cardboard box; and lingering a little to look at some far more expensive models than they were prepared to buy, they went slowly down to the entrance.

"It is about three minutes to three-thirty," Margaret said with satisfaction. "I bet you the men will expect us to be late, and they will be pleasantly surprised to find us waiting for them."

"On the whole I think I'm very punctual," Romina said.

"I'm not," Margaret sighed. "However hard I try, something always happens at the last moment so that I keep Jack waiting. He is quite used to it now, but when we were first married it annoyed him terribly."

"You're very fond of him, aren't you?" Romina said.

Margaret's face seemed to light up.

"To me, he is the most wonderful man in the whole world," she answered. "And the sweetest. I can never be sufficiently grateful to the fates that let us meet and have made us so happy together."

Romina felt a pang of envy. Why could she not know the love which transformed Margaret's face when she spoke about her husband, and which she had seen all too clearly in Jack Harrison's eyes when they rested on his wife?

The two women walked across the busy street into the Central Hotel.

It had the usual rather gloomy lounge with chairs of non-descript colors and coffee-tables dotted around. There was a reception-desk where a clerk sat picking his teeth and answering inquiries with a disinterestedness which made the most innocuous answer seem rude.

Margaret and Romina sat down where they could see the door.

"We're first!" Margaret said. "Now isn't that a triumph? I bet you Jack is telling Merlin they needn't hurry because we are certain to keep them waiting."

She glanced at the clock over the reception-desk.

"I'll tell you what I'll do," she said. "As we have got a few moments to spare, I'll slip up and see a friend of mine who is sick. I was going to see her tomorrow anyway; and now that you are here, Jack may have other plans. It won't take more than a few minutes because she is not allowed to talk very much. You won't mind if I leave you?"

"No, of course not," Romina answered. "I think I shall be safe enough here."

She looked round the lounge which was empty, except for a very old gentleman who was asleep in the far corner, and laughed.

"There certainly do not seem to be many temptations," Margaret said. "Well, if the men are in a hurry, ring room 302. Jack knows who I am with."

She walked away towards the lift, and Romina got out her vanity case and started to powder her nose.

She was so intent on what she was doing that she did not notice three men come through the swing doors until they had reached the reception-desk.

Then she heard one of them say:

133

"I feel damn' sick—I hate flying!"

He spoke in English with a rather common accent and Romina glanced up casually, expecting to see a cloth-capped tourist.

Three men were standing with their backs to her at the desk and for a moment she did not realize why they seemed vaguely familiar.

Then the tallest of them said sharply:

"You'd better go and lie down. This air-sickness is beginning to be a bit of a curse."

"It's all very well for you, Taha," the first young man replied. "You're always well."

He spoke resentfully and slightly spitefully, and at the same time there was something feminine about him.

The tallest man, who had been addressed as 'Taha' turned a little sideways, and Romina felt her heart almost stand still.

It was the man she had last seen at Sahara City with his three followers—the man she and Merlin had first seen on the stairs of the Pyramid Club, slapping a woman in the face!

For a moment she felt as though she could hardly breathe.

There was something horrible about his tight drain-pipe trousers, pointed shoes and square-shouldered jacket.

Romina thought the whole lounge was swimming around her. With trembling hands she put her vanity case in her bag, keeping her head down, not daring to look up again.

She heard the clerk speaking in English, telling them they could have rooms 220 and 224.

"I'm going up right away," the man who was not feeling well said almost aggressively. "Are you coming?"

"I think I'll have a drink first," the man who was called Taha answered.

It was then that Romina realized that if they sat down in the lounge Merlin and Jack Harrison would walk right in on them.

At any second now they might arrive and Taha would see them and know that he would not have to search any farther.

Quickly Romina got to her feet. She had only to walk straight to the door, keeping her head averted from the man standing a little to the left of the reception-desk.

But as she moved, they moved too; and the man who felt sick went towards the left and the other two took a few steps right, to where she was standing.

There was a coffee-table and another chair in her way. She had to stand aside to let them pass, or brusquely push by them.

She hesitated and was lost.

134

They saw her and stood back politely.

She took a step, keeping her head down. Then, with a click, her bag, which she had fastened insecurely, flew open and the vanity case which she had thrust in hastily on top of her other things fell to the floor.

The other man with Taha bent down and picked it up.

She almost snatched it from him murmuring "Thank you" somewhat indistinctly.

But even as she did so she felt rather than saw Taha stiffen, heard him make a little indescribable sound between his teeth and knew that he had recognized her.

It was then that she lost her head and did what she thought afterwards to be a supremely stupid and unforgivable thing—she ran!

Holding her bag in one hand and her vanity case in the other and leaving her parcels forgotten beside her chair, she ran across the lounge and reached the swing doors.

They were so heavy that for a moment she thought that they would not move, but they swung round and she found herself outside in the sunshine looking at the stream of traffic passing the hotel.

With a leap of her heart she saw a small car edging its way to the pavement. It was Merlin and Jack Harrison.

She ran down the steps and across the pavement, almost colliding with a perambulator and two teenage girls giggling together as they walked slowly in an effort to attract the maximum amount of attention.

She reached the car and dragged open the back door while it was still moving, giving Merlin no time to get out.

"Don't stop—drive on!" she cried wildly. "Quickly, quickly—get away!"

"What's the matter?" Merlin asked, and glancing back at the doorway of the hotel saw the answer to his question.

Standing there looking round were two men, a grim expression on their thin faces and something evil in their darting eyes.

"Hurry!" Romina said, as Jack Harrison pulled into the stream of traffic. "Have they seen me?"

"Yes, they have seen us," Merlin replied quietly.

"They came into the hotel—there was no one else there—I tried to come away and warn you, but . . . but they recognized me."

"Where is Margaret?" Jack Harrison asked sharply.

"She went upstairs to visit a sick friend," Romina answered.

"Then she'll be all right," Jack said. "Where shall we go?"

135

"Keep driving," Merlin said.

He turned round in the front seat and was looking out the back window.

"They are trying to hail a taxi," he said. "They have not got one yet—yes they have—one has just stopped. Keep going, Jack."

"Where to?" Jack asked again.

"Just keep going," Merlin answered. "I'll think of something in a moment."

"Oh, I am sorry—terribly sorry," Romina said.

"It's not your fault," Merlin answered. "I should have anticipated that they might have tumbled to our game of getting off at Athens. They must have had a report from the airport last night that we had not gone on to Rome or London."

"His name is Taha," Romina said.

"The big one?" Merlin said, making it more a statement than a question. "He's obviously the boss. The other little horror is just one of his gang."

"There was another and he was English," Romina explained. "He said he felt air-sick and was going upstairs to lie down."

"That is one less to cope with at the moment," Merlin said. "Keep going, Jack—they are still some way behind."

"We'll soon be out of the town" Jack Harrison said. "Shall I take the main road that goes past the Parthenon?"

"Yes, that would be best," Merlin agreed. "Avoid lonely lanes; remember we have got Romina with us."

"Fool that I am—I didn't bring a gun," Jack Harrison said. "I never for a moment expected anything like this—not so quickly."

"Don't worry," Merlin said quietly; "you're not going to be mixed up in this—"

"Don't be a fool, Jack," Merlin went on, as Jack Harrison opened his mouth to expostulate. "You must think of Margaret—of your own position here."

"And you must think of Romina," Jack Harrison said a little grimly.

"Yes, I've not forgotten," Merlin said. "Now do exactly as I tell you—and please do not argue."

He spoke in a voice of authority and turned to look ahead of them.

They were now out in the open countryside. They were driving on the main road which runs from the town out into the glorious valley which lies behind Athens. From it the

136

mountains rose in the distance, green and beautiful in the sunshine.

On their left was the Parthenon, gleaming white against a vividly blue sky. Crowds of sightseers' cars were dotted at the foot of the plateau on which it was perched, and there was a stream of tourists laboriously climbing the stony hill to view one of the greatest sights in the world.

"Pull up," Merlin said quickly. "Pull up here and let us out."

"What are you going to do?" Jack Harrison asked.

"I haven't time to tell you," Merlin answered, "but I have a plan. Now please do as I say. Drop us and then turn round and go back into the town, pick up Margaret and go home. Don't ask any questions, just behave quite normally. With any luck they'll have no idea who you are."

"You are the boss—but I hate doing it," Jack Harrison replied.

"I know," Merlin said, "but it is the only way. If anything happens to us and we don't turn up in a few hours, get in touch with the General. Tell him exactly what I told you was in Chris's note, and leave the rest to him. Keep out of this, Jack—remember you've retired."

"Damn it! Isn't there anything I can do?" Jack Harrison asked.

"Just stop here, as I told you," Merlin replied. "Come on, Romina, we must hurry."

He jumped out as he spoke as the car was still moving, pulled open the back door and got her out.

He gave Jack Harrison a wave, and taking her by the hand, started to run up the hill as hard as he could go.

Breathless in a few minutes and terribly hot under the afternoon sun, Romina did her best to keep up with him.

She could not help feeling glad that years of riding and hard exercise had made her, as Christopher had often said, as good as any man when it came to an emergency.

Even so the pace was hard, and although she said nothing she stole a glance and was glad to see that perspiration was breaking out on Merlin's forehead.

Finally they reached a large crowd of sightseers who were just reaching the Parthenon slowly and with the least amount of exertion.

"Move in amongst them," Merlin ordered, "and get as near to the guide as possible."

Romina noted that he was able to speak without undue gasping, and did not reply for fear she would sound breathless.

She clung to his hand and he let her pull him in amongst the crowd of fat women fanning themselves with paper fans they had bought from the vendors of such trifles at the bottom of the hill; of old men who had got their coats off and were showing their braces; and young men in open-necked shirts and tight jeans.

The majority were English, Romina noticed, and she apologized to one woman whom she knocked against as she tried to edge her way through the throng.

"I'm sorry, it's a pull up the hill, isn't it?"

"They ought to have a lift," the woman answered. "It's hardly worth it otherwise!"

Romina did not reply, working her way a little nearer the guide as Merlin had told her.

The whole party then stopped, and she could not prevent herself looking back down the hill to see if they were being followed.

The road seemed far away, and then she saw that a taxi had pulled in amongst the other cars and two men were getting out of it.

They had seen them—they were still being followed!

For a moment Merlin, standing behind her, seemed content to do nothing.

The guide started his lecture on the Parthenon, describing its history in slow, ponderous words which had been said so many times before as to become monotonous, even to himself. The tourists listened with hot, unsurprised faces, and gaped as he pointed out each object.

To Romina it was just a meaningless jumble of words as she waited tensely for the two men in black jeans to climb the hill.

The group moved forward, shuffling over the broken marble floor.

It was then, with a little sense of fear, that she realized that Merlin had disappeared. She was alone—alone amongst these strangers!

She moved from the center of the group to the outside. Now she could look back and see that only a little way below the two men were approaching.

They were looking to left and right; searching amongst the pillars, stones and bushes; and Taha had his hand in his pocket.

Where was Merlin—where could he possibly be?

Suddenly Romina saw him, moving swiftly towards the Erectheum, a temple standing on the most sacred ground of the Acropolis. The two men turned swiftly and followed. After a few seconds, Romina could see him half hidden behind a pillar, taking an object from inside his coat and fitting something on to it.

She remembered what Jack Harrison had said in the car, that he did not have a gun with him—and she knew what Merlin was doing.

She had seen Chris several times making the same movements with his arms when he was putting a silencer on his gun!

Merlin was now on the far side of the Erectheum which was on the very edge of the plateau and was therefore out of sight of the approaching men. Then, to Romina's surprise, he jumped down on to the ground and started to walk away in the opposite direction.

In one moment he would be behind some bushes and a great mound of fallen masonry. She felt that he was going to disappear and perhaps she would never see him again. Without thinking, she ran across the hot, bare ground between the Parthenon and the Erectheum.

She reached the smaller temple with its glorious caryatids holding the stone roof on their lovely heads, and as she did so realized that the man with Taha had seen Merlin.

He was beckoning the taller man, and then they both ran towards the piece of masonry behind which Merlin had disappeared.

Romina held on to the caryatid and stood there irresolute, her heart thumping.

Suddenly from the other side of the temple she heard a little 'ping' almost like an arrow whizzing through the air and a sudden cry.

An airplane zoomed overhead and the noise was lost almost as she heard it. She was not even certain that she had really heard the cry—or, indeed, that it had not come from down below where a crowd of children were playing a curious ball game amongst themselves.

Then as she stood—not knowing what to do, frightened and at the same time feeling that it was all something unreal—she saw Taha come round a pile of fallen masonry.

Instinctively she drew back behind the pillar and as she did so there was a little crash and a bang from the statue behind which she had been standing.

For a moment she could hardly believe that she had been shot at.

Tremblingly she made herself slim, not daring to move, her brain as well as her body paralysed with fear, waiting for a second shot. As she waited for death she saw Merlin appear and raise his gun.

It was not until afterwards that she realized that Taha had known where she was and was about to shoot at her again.

She saw Merlin's arm move and heard the ping of the bullet as it left the gun.

Then she swung round and saw Taha. There was a strange, almost ludicrous expression on his face as he toppled backwards into some green bushes which sprouted from the side of the plateau.

For a moment he seemed to lie on top of them, sprawled like a black spider on a prickly web, then very slowly he slipped down through the leaves, falling until there was little to be seen of him save his long pointed shoes.

Romina stared, horrified and unable to do anything but look and go on looking, until Merlin's hand was on her arm.

"Why are you here?" he said roughly. "Another time do as you are damn' well told!"

He gave her a shake that was painful and holding her by the arm dragged her back over the stony floor towards the crowd of tourists who were just leaving the Parthenon.

As if in a trance Romina raised her white face to his.

"Merlin—" she began to say, only to be silenced by his fingers, cruel and hard, pressing into the softness of her flesh.

"Be quiet!" he commanded.

He stood for a moment on the outside of the group, then slowly, without in the least appearing to hurry, he dragged her back the way they had come.

He pointed out something in the roof above their heads.

"Look, you haven't seen this," he said in a conversational tone, drawing her out of the path of a woman who was trying to take a photograph.

"I'm so sorry," he said politely, "I'm afraid we are in your way."

"It's all right," the woman answered. "If you wouldn't mind moving a little to the left."

"Of course we will," Merlin agreed.

Still pulling Romina by the arm, he turned sharply to the left and helped her over the rocky ground.

"Now," he said when they were out of ear-shot, "walk slowly, without hurrying yourself—and don't look back."

He circled around a little to bring them back on to the pathway along which the tourists had come in from their cars.

"Don't hurry," he said again, almost snappily, as Romina instinctively quickened her pace.

If the uphill journey had been difficult, this was far worse.

The effort not to look back, not to hurry, not to ask questions, was almost too much; but somehow after what seemed to her an aeon of time they reached the bottom of the path. They moved through the crowd of souvenir vendors to where the motor-cars, taxis and open carriages were parked.

Men came hurrying up, offering them postcards, pieces of silver, children's windmills and sweets made of honey.

"What about a postcard for your mother?" Merlin said aloud and added before she could speak, "Oh, I forgot—we got some this morning, didn't we?"

"No, thank you," he said smilingly to the man selling them.

He hailed a taxi and tipped a small boy who opened the door.

They got in and Merlin gave the driver the address of an hotel.

The taxi drove off and Merlin linked his arm through Romina's.

"That was delightful," he said. "I only wish I hadn't forgotten my camera. I would like to have some pictures to take home with us to put in our scrapbook."

Romina shut her eyes. She realized that the taxi-driver could hear all that they were saying and that she had to play her part and keep up pretenses until they were alone.

Now she was feeling almost sick with what had happened—the expression on Taha's face as he toppled into the green bushes and sank slowly into them as if they were quicksand.

Merlin had killed him!

She tried to realize that she had seen him murder a man, and she knew it meant nothing to her. Somehow all her senses were numb—as numb as her body had been when she had stood waiting for a bullet to pierce its way through her.

"I expect you are tired," Merlin was saying solicitously. "I have always said there is nothing more exhausting than sight-seeing. Well, the first thing you can do is to go and have a lie down. I expect you'll want to go out tonight and see what gaieties Athens can offer us. I must say I could do with a drink—that Greek wine we had for lunch was not at all bad. We could take a bottle home."

He droned on and on until Romina felt ashamed of her weakness and forced herself to join in. She made desultory conversation until the taxi drew up at the hotel. It was the most difficult thing she had done in her life.

Merlin got out and taking her by the arm helped her up

the steps into the lounge, which might have been a replica of that in which she had seen Taha and his friends.

Romina sat down in one of the soft-seated chairs.

Merlin signaled for a waiter.

"What will you have?" he asked.

"I don't know—a—a cup of tea, I suppose," Romina replied almost wildly.

"Tea for the lady," Merlin said, "and a whisky and soda for me, you understand?"

"Yes, sir," the waiter answered in English.

Romina felt that Merlin had somehow stolen a march on her, and as if he sensed her feelings he waited until the waiter was out of sight and said:

"English ladies drink tea at this time in the afternoon, you know."

"Merlin . . ." Romina said in a low voice, "you killed him!"

"I hope so," Merlin answered. "And another time, don't make yourself a sitting target. Things might have turned out rather differently."

"I'm sorry," Romina said humbly.

"It was an idiotic thing to do," Merlin said in the tone of a good-natured schoolmaster admonishing a small boy. "You knew they were looking for us and yet you went and stood straight in the line of fire."

"I'm sorry," Romina said again. "I didn't realize they were going to try to kill us."

"What did you think they were doing?" Merlin asked. "Bringing us a posy of flowers with their compliments? My dear child, people of that sort enjoy killing. Besides, it is what they had been sent to do."

"Sent?" Romina asked quickly. "By whom?"

"That is what we hope to find out," Merlin answered in the same good-humored voice.

She glanced at him sharply and she realized that he was pleased with himself.

There was a look of triumph on his face. She had seen it there once before when he had thrust a knife through the hand of Taha's boy friend and pinioned him to the ground.

She drew a deep breath.

"What happened to the other man?"

"I got him in the leg," Merlin answered, "in the knee-cap. It will be a long time before he walks again. He did not seem worth killing."

"I thought I heard him scream," Romina said.

142

"He also was a sitting target," Merlin said. "And I've never cared for my game to be too easy."

Romina was silent for a moment and then she said hardly above a whisper:

"Did you intend to kill Taha before he shot at me? Or was it because he was shooting at me that you killed him?"

Merlin seemed to consider it for a moment.

"I'm not certain that I'd care to answer that question on oath," he said, "but if you want your conscience to feel heavy then you can hold yourself responsible for his getting it through the heart—that is, if he had one, which I very much doubt."

He saw her face and added quickly:

"I'm teasing you. Don't think about him. He was about the lowest form of human life—and I should think that we could very likely thank him for Paul's death. Anyhow, he had what was coming to him. And personally on that I intend to celebrate."

The waiter arrived with the tea and Merlin's drink.

He quaffed down his whisky and soda with an attitude of satisfaction.

Romina poured out her tea without thinking.

Then when she had drunk a little she said:

"I have not said 'thank you' yet."

"What for?" Merlin asked.

"For saving my life, I suppose. I'm sorry I disobeyed you—it was a silly thing to do, I see that now. Chris would have been annoyed with me. But thank you for doing what you did."

Merlin looked down at her serious little face. And then he smiled, which made her feel as though the sun had suddenly come out.

"Don't thank me," he said. "I can't afford to lose you. And I don't want to—have you only just realized that?"

CHAPTER TEN

THEIR eyes met across the table and Romina felt that something very strange was happening—something so magical and outside the world altogether that for a moment she could not put a name to it.

She could only stare up into Merlin's face and feel as if she waited for something which would change her whole life.

Then Merlin said softly:

"You are brave—very brave."

She had the feeling that it was not what he had been about to say and that he had changed the words almost as they reached his lips.

He glanced down at his watch, breaking the spell, so that something seemed to snap between them.

"We must go," he said. "We only came here—"

He stopped and smiled at her half apologetically.

"—For me," Romina interrupted, "to get over the shock and my hysterics?"

"You have been wonderful," he answered. "I didn't know a woman could be so courageous."

"I am afraid you have a rather poor opinion of my sex," Romina said, more for the sake of talking than for anything else.

"Perhaps," he said, brushing the question aside as if it brought back memories he did not want to remember. "Anyway, we have no excuse for lingering."

"No, of course not," she answered.

She got to her feet feeling that she left this corner of the shabby lounge with regret. Something important had happened here, something that she had not anticipated—although even now she was not certain what it was.

Outside was the sunshine and reality—the hard fact that Merlin had killed a man and wounded another; if they did not get away quickly there would be a lot of explaining to do.

Impulsively she turned towards Merlin.

"What do you think—?" she began.

"I don't," he answered. "There's no time. Come on—back to action stations."

She was surprised at the happy note—almost one of gaiety and exhilaration—in his voice as he took her arm and led her through the swing doors into the bright sunshine outside.

The pavement was crowded with people, and no one seemed to notice them.

The commissionaire hailed a taxi and Merlin gave the address of the Harrisons' villa.

They got in and Romina resigned herself to silence.

Then to her amazement Merlin reached out and took her hand in his. He held it for a moment as if he did not know what to do with it, then drew a little nearer to her and linked his arm through hers.

It was an affectionate gesture—one which made Romina feel safe and secure.

She stole a glance at him from under her eyelashes.

Now that his lip was not thrust forward sardonically as Nickoylos he looked young again. Gone even were the sarcastic, rather sinister lines which had been in his face when she had first seen him in General Fortescue's office.

Instead he looked—she hesitated and sought in her mind for an adjective—eager and rather excited, like a boy returning home for the school holidays.

As if he felt her scrutiny he turned his face to look down at her.

"Happy?" he asked, with a twinkle in his eye, and she knew from the tone of his voice that it was an impish question.

It was the last thing either of them could possibly be at that moment; and yet, suddenly, inexplicably, she knew that she was. Happy in a strange, fantastic manner that she had never known before. Happy although she was afraid. Happy although she had seen horrors far worse than anything she had ever anticipated.

Yes, she was happy. And why?

Like a flash of lightning she knew the answer. It was the touch of Merlin's fingers holding hers and the warm strength of his palm; the feel of his shoulder, against which with only the slightest movement she could rest her head.

She was happy because she was with him. And she knew then that crazily, incredibly and yet positively, she was in love with him.

For a moment the thought blinded her. She shut her eyes as if to hide her secret from him and from all the world.

Merlin thought she was tired, and tightening his fingers on hers, said consolingly:

"It's all right, we're nearly there."

Romina could not tell him that she was not tired—but pulsatingly, ecstatically alive.

She felt herself tingle, felt a strange thrill within her like a tiny flame flickering somewhere in the depths of her being—a flame which so easily could become a burning fire.

'I'm mad,' she thought. 'Mad after what I have been through. I can't love this man . . . I can't . . . I hate him!'

She wondered why she had felt so antagonistic towards Merlin when they first met, why she had wanted to provoke and quarrel with him all the time.

Was it her reaction after Alex? Was it nothing but a hatred of all men and everything that they stood for?

Or was it something entirely to do with Merlin himself—the strength of his character and personality; the fact that he had opposed her coming with him?

Whatever it was, she realized that now everything was forgotten except this feeling of ecstasy; of knowing herself thrilled because he was so close, because his hand was touching hers.

'He must never know,' she thought, and realized how humiliated she would be if he guessed for a moment that her feelings had changed in such a fantastic manner and that she was no longer his enemy, but a woman who wanted him just as hundreds of women must have done before.

She tried to read into the words that he had said to her as they sat in the lounge of the hotel something more than friendship, more than an appreciation that any man might have for a woman who had shown a courage he had not expected.

She was blinded by her feelings towards him; but she felt that he could never feel the same for her.

"Here we are. I expect they will be pleased to see us," Merlin exclaimed.

The taxi drew to a standstill and Romina opened her eyes.

There was the Harrisons' villa, glowing in the afternoon sunshine; the flowers and creepers vivid splashes of color against the white walls and stony terrace.

It looked so peaceful and so much a part of the countryside that it seemed almost impossible to believe that such a lot had happened since they left it only a few hours before.

Romina stepped out on to the dusty road and Merlin paid for the taxi.

Then as they ran up the steps Margaret and Jack Harrison

came hurrying out of the door, their faces white and lined with anxiety.

"You are safe—thank God!" Margaret exclaimed, and Romina saw there were tears in her eyes.

"Come and have a drink," Jack Harrison said gruffly to cover up his feelings. "I don't mind telling you I'm in need of one myself."

"What happened? For heaven's sake, tell us what happened!" Margaret said. "Jack and I have been sitting here imagining all sorts of horrible things."

"It was not very pleasant," Merlin said in his most matter-of-fact voice, "but I managed to deal with both of them. One rolled down the hill with a broken leg, and the other—the tall chap who Romina told us was called Taha—is dead."

"Dead?" Margaret gave a little cry. "But what about the police—won't they be looking for you?"

"It would be very unlucky indeed if anyone connects us with the incident," Merlin answered, and he explained in detail what had happened.

"Good thing you had your silencer," Jack Harrison said when Merlin told how Taha had shot at Romina and he had finished him off with a bullet straight through the heart.

"I always carry one," Merlin said quietly.

"Damn it all!" Jack Harrison said. "I've lived here for five years now and nothing like this has happened before."

"You should be more careful with your choice of friends," Merlin suggested.

"I was in a terrible state," Margaret interposed, obviously longing to tell her tale. "When I came downstairs, the clerk told me Romina had gone, leaving her parcels behind. I knew something had happened, but I didn't know what to do—so I just sat and waited. Every minute seemed like an hour before Jack appeared."

"That was very sensible of you," Merlin said approvingly.

"Jack always curses if I do things on my own initiative," Margaret answered, "so I waited—and the moment I saw his face I knew something ghastly had happened."

Jack Harrison wiped his forehead.

"I must say, if you had not come back, we were wondering exactly what we should do," he said.

"I told you not to start looking for us," Merlin said.

"It's easier said than done," Jack replied. "Could you have left Margaret and me in the same circumstances?"

Merlin looked slightly disconcerted.

"That would have been different," he said.

147

"How?" Jack asked briefly and then laughed. "You're a humbug, Merlin—you try to appear tough, but you are nothing of the sort! Of course you would have come to look for us—and in another minute Margaret and I were going to do just that."

"I despair of you!" Merlin said lightly, and helped himself to another drink.

"There's no time to talk about it any more," he said as he squirted the soda into his glass. "Did you do the one thing I asked you to do?"

"As a matter of fact, I did," Jack Harrison replied. "The airplane arrives at seven-fifteen, and our man in Rome said he would try to persuade a couple in the party to give up their seats."

"When will we hear definitely?" Merlin said, looking at his wrist-watch.

As he spoke the telephone shrilled and Jack Harrison went to answer it. He picked it up and spoke in such fast Italian that Romina could not understand what he was saying. But Merlin was listening and so was Margaret, and she realized with a little grimace of annoyance that she was the only one to be ignorant of what was going on.

At last Jack Harrison put down the receiver.

"It's all fixed," he said.

"Oh, tell me what's happening!" Romina said impetuously. "I'm being left out of things—I feel like the only child at the party who had never played hide and seek before!"

"Poor Romina!"

It was Merlin who spoke, and she saw that her cry of distress had touched him.

"Tell her Jack, it's your part in the drama."

"It was your idea," Jack Harrison answered. "Well, Romina, it's like this. Merlin and I had a talk this afternoon and even before you fell in with that nice little gang of Teddy Boys we decided it was going to be too dangerous for you two to arrive in Cairo on your own as a couple. Every man and woman arriving together will be scrutinized now that the big-shots are really worried about you."

"I can see that," Romina murmured.

"So Merlin had the bright idea," Jack went on, "that the only way of being inconspicuous was to be one of a party."

"It was because of our talk," Merlin said, "that I thought of slipping in amongst the tourists on the Parthenon."

"Well, it certainly saved your lives," Jack said, "and there is no one for the moment to repeat exactly what happened—unless of course the chap with the broken leg sends for his friends."

"I should think he will be pretty uncomfortable for a day or so," Merlin replied. "A friend of mine was shot in the knee-cap during the war and he was kept under sedatives for nearly a week."

"Let's hope you are right," Jack said.

"Oh, do go on," Romina begged. "What's happening now?"

"I agree with Romina," Margaret seconded. "I've always said you take a very long time to tell a story, Jack!"

"All right, I'll be quick," Jack replied. "Merlin suggested that you both go on a Cook's tour, so I have rung Rome and got a friend there to bribe two of Cook's customers away from a party that is *en route* for Cairo at this very moment. You and Merlin will take their places."

"I think that is very clever," Romina said.

"That's exactly what I say," Margaret agreed. "No one is going to suspect a collection of nice, respectable tourists. They will be looking for something far more flashy where you two are concerned."

"I agree," Jack said. "And don't forget we have no reason to think that they are suspicious that Nikoylos is not what he seems—or that Romina is not an empty-headed film star. All that they know is that Merlin, for some unknown reason, is interested in their precious drug and that Chris had written about it."

"I think we can give them credit for being cleverer than that," Merlin said. "Nickoylos might easily have been a disguise."

"I've always said you should never underrate your enemy," Jack said; "at the same time, it's a mistake to overrate him. If the Egyptians are running this racket, they won't be very subtle."

"But are they Egyptians?" Merlin said. "I've never thought they are for one moment."

"You haven't?"

Jack Harrison was astonished.

"It is happening in Egypt—that's all we know," Merlin replied. "Personally I think—as Chris has already told us—that this is something far bigger and more complex than anything that could be contrived and carried out on the banks of the Nile."

"But he said that—" Romina began, only to be interrupted as Merlin got to his feet.

"We none of us know," he said a little wearily. "Let's leave

149

it at that. It's now nearly five o'clock—we shall shortly have to leave for the airport."

"Yes, of course," Margaret said. "And Romina must pack her things and get rid of the clothes she wore as Romina Faye. What shall I do with them, by the way?"

"Burn them," Merlin said.

"Burn them?"

Both women spoke simultaneously, their tone horrified at the extravagance.

"Burn them," Merlin repeated. "I know it sounds a very nice idea to give them to a theatrical charity or hand them to a jumble sale, but they might be traced. And you don't know that this villa is not going to be under suspicion and might even be searched. Nothing of Romina Faye's or Nickoylos's must be found here. Go and start a nice bonfire in the garden, Jack—no one will think that is surprising, will they?"

"They won't," Jack Harrison answered. "I have one two or three times a week in the spring and in the winter when I am clearing up."

"Well, get going," Merlin said. "Every particle is to be burned. And what won't burn—I need not say this to you, Jack—like buttons and Romina's bracelets—has got to be buried—and buried deep."

"My goodness, I have got out of touch," Jack Harrison said, scratching his head. "It never entered my mind—although I must say I hadn't given it much thought."

"It seems a terrible waste of money," Romina protested.

"It's better to waste money than lives," Merlin said laconically.

She knew he was thinking of Jack and Margaret, and with a little shiver she followed Margaret into the bedroom and they began to unpack out of the cardboard boxes the things they had bought in Athens.

An hour later Romina and Merlin drove up at the airport. Merlin had refused to allow Jack to take them in his car because he said that it was essential that Jack and Margaret should not be mixed up in this drama.

They said good-bye at the villa, and Romina saw there were tears in Margaret's eyes as they kissed each other.

It gave her a very warm feeling that, in such a very short space of time, she had made two friends whom she somehow felt would be part of her life in the future and would always welcome her to their home.

"God bless you!" Margaret said as Romina went down the steps to the taxi.

She heard the gruff note in Jack Harrison's voice as he

said good-bye to Merlin, which told her that despite all his training he could not help showing he was moved and anxious about them.

Merlin gave her explicit instructions before they got into the taxi so that as soon as she arrived at the airport and her passport had been stamped, Romina went straight to the Ladies' Cloakroom. She was to stay there until she heard over the Tannoy the arrival of the airplane from Rome.

"Give the passengers time to disembark, because they refuel here," Merlin said, "and then mix with them and proceed back to the airplane without paying too much attention to me. I shall be there—but just for now we don't want to look like a couple."

In the cloakroom, which was empty save for a Greek woman sitting in the corner knitting, Romina stared at herself in the looking-glass over the wash-basins.

It was pleasant to see herself without false eyelashes and exaggerated make-up. Nevertheless, she could not help wondering whether she had not looked more attractive from a man's point of view than she did now. She looked a lady—but a rather dull surburban one.

There was one thought in her mind—would Merlin find her attractive?

Then she smiled at herself and found that, after all, make-up made very little difference. It was only the superficial difference between Romina Faye and Romina Robinson—and the latter was very much more like the real Romina, the Romina whom Chris had known and whom other men had found exceedingly attractive.

Her thoughts veered away to Alex Salvekov. Despite all that had happened, the wound was still there, the humiliation still worried her.

How she wished it had never happened! How she wished she could have fallen in love with Merlin and felt there was nothing sordid and unpleasant in her background!

It was not that he would ever know. Perhaps he would never realize she loved him. But she knew this feeling within her was something new and very different from anything she had experienced before.

She had always scoffed at the idea that love should be a wonderfully ecstatic and sacred thing. And yet she knew at last what all the poets had meant when they wrote about it.

"I love you," she whispered, and felt the tears gather in her eyes.

So much had happened to her in such a short space of time. First the loss of Christopher; and now her love for a man

151

who, despite the fact that he seemed to like her a little better than at first, she was quite certain would never love her as she loved him. Why should he? To him she was just an encumbrance—someone who had forced herself upon him.

A nasal voice announcing the arrival of a B.E.A. airplane from Rome came noisily over the Tannoy.

Romina washed her hands to waste time, fiddled about in front of the looking-glass, then, when she thought the right amount of time had elapsed, peeped into the lounge.

As she had anticipated, it was crowded with people—some of them hurrying towards stalls where Greek souvenirs and newspapers were displayed, others going into the cafeteria, and some just sitting on the large leather sofas, prepared to wait patiently.

Romina walked boldly out, as Merlin had told her to do, knowing that it was wrong to behave surreptitiously. She saw an empty seat on one of the sofas and sat down on it.

Beside her was rather a nice-looking middle-aged woman with a tired face and a B.E.A. bag already filled to capacity with souvenirs.

"What sort of flight have you had?" Romina asked conversationally.

The woman turned towards her eagerly, and Romina thought that with any luck this passenger was alone.

"It's been lovely," she said. "But I bought so many things at Rome that I haven't much room for anything more. Is there anything here worth having? Native things, I mean, that one can take home?"

"I should wait until you get to Cairo," Romina advised. "You will find lots of things there—some of them quite cheap, too."

"Will I really?"

The tired voice seemed to brighten.

"Or so I have always been told," Romina corrected herself. "I had a cousin who was there last year and he brought home some splendid things—but he said you've got to bargain to get them at the right price."

"That's what I have been told, too," the woman said.

They went on talking, and out of the corner of her eye Romina saw Merlin standing at the bar in conversation with two or three men.

It was not long before the flight was called and the passengers were asked to return to their seats.

As everyone rose, Merlin moved towards Romina, put the boarding-card in her hand, and went back again to finish his conversation with the man with whom he was sharing a bottle of beer.

He said nothing to Romina, but she knew what she must do.

Still clinging to her new-found friend, who was telling her about her life in Horsham and how she had saved up for this trip because she had always wanted to see Egypt, Romina moved with the crowd towards the exit and across the tarmac towards the airplane.

The sun was getting low in the sky and there seemed to be a golden glow over everything.

Romina noted the other passengers and decided that she looked very much like them.

They were mostly quiet, middle-aged people who had very little money and who had saved up for a long time to make this one exciting trip to see the wonders of Egypt.

The Cook's courier was checking over the passengers one by one. He hesitated when he saw Romina and asked her name.

"Mrs. Robinson," she told him, after only a second's pause.

"Yes, yes—of course," he smiled. "I hope you and your husband will enjoy being with us."

"Thank you very much," Romina answered and climbed the gangway into the airplane.

As she seated herself and took off her gloves and saw the narrow gold wedding ring that Margaret Harrison had remembered to lend her at the last moment, she felt a little tremor of fear at the thought of going back to Cairo.

What lay ahead? She remembered Paul lying dead on the floor of the room where Chris had worked. She thought of Taha falling into the bushes, and the ludicrous expression on his face. Two deaths—three if you counted Chris—and all over some ridiculous drug which people took because they were unable to face the world as it is and wanted to find a dream world of their own.

'Fools!' Romina thought scornfully, and wondered if they were worth fighting for and if, indeed, it was worth risking her own life and Merlin's merely to save people who in most cases did not want saving.

There was the usual scuffle for seats inside the airplane and Romina noticed that her friend had found a seat next the window.

"Shall I sit next to you?" she asked moving over. "I don't know what has happened to my husband."

"Yes, do, dear," was the reply. "It would be nice to have someone to talk to. Not that there aren't some very nice peo-

153

ple on the trip, but some of them are already paired, if you know what I mean. They have either come with their husbands, their children, or a friend."

"Why didn't you bring a friend?" Romina inquired.

"Well, I meant to, as a matter of fact," the woman replied. "I had it all planned to go with an old school friend of mine who is nursing, but at the last moment the patient she was with had a relapse and she could not leave him. I suppose some people might have insisted as we had made our plans. But Rose is ever so conscientious—we used to laugh at her when she was at school and say she was the perfect perfect—she always does the right thing."

"How sad for you," Romina said in a sympathetic voice.

They were in the tourist part of the airplane and now she realized that Merlin had joined her on the seat nearest the gangway.

"Oh, here you are!" she said in a matter-of-fact tone which she felt any wife would use to her husband in the circumstances.

"I'm not feeling much better," he said rather disagreeably in a loud voice which told Romina that he wished the people around them to hear.

"Oh, aren't you?" she replied. "I am sorry."

"I thought a beer would help my headache," he said, "but it has only made it worse."

"Has your husband got a headache?" Romina's friend in the inside seat asked brightly. "Perhaps he would like an Aspro? I have some here in my bag."

"That is kind of you," Romina said.

"As soon as we start," the friend went on, "we will ask the stewardess—she is such a nice girl if it's the same one we had from Rome—to bring him a glass of water, although I expect there will be something to eat and drink."

"I expect there will," Romina agreed.

Merlin palmed the Aspro deftly so that only Romina saw him do it.

Then dinner was served on the airplane and after that everyone seemed rather sleepy and disinclined to talk.

Certainly there was no sign of tension and nothing to make Romina or Merlin feel there was anything unusual in this crowd of rather weary sightseers nearing the end of the first part of their journey.

The bus was waiting for them at the Cairo airport and the guide, who had hurried them through all the Customs formalities at the maximum speed, shepherded everyone on board and they set off at quite a good speed towards Cairo.

It was then for the first time that Romina began to wonder what would happen when they arrived at the hotel. She supposed that Merlin would cope with the situation. Had he thought, too, of the possible embarrassment of sharing a room together—a double room for a married couple?

When they arrived in Cairo, the Cook's party were packed into a large bus and taken to a small, second-class hotel in an unfashionable quarter of the town. It was clean and comfortable. Romina had no complaints, save for the fact that they were registered as 'Mr. and Mrs. Robinson.'

Looking very like a 'Mr. Robinson' in his worn tweed jacket and unfashionably full gray flannel trousers, Merlin locked the bedroom door behind them and smiled.

"Well?" he asked.

Romina felt the color rising in her cheeks.

"What . . . what do you mean?" she inquired.

"What do you think of our little honeymoon suite?" he asked.

She looked towards the twin beds separated only by a small bedside table.

"It . . . it's all right," she said, angry with herself for fluffing her words. "I've had to share a room with Chris before now."

"You're not embarrassed?"

She had the feeling that he was deliberately making things worse by asking questions.

She managed to turn away her head in what she hoped was a disinterested manner and answered:

"Of course not! One expects this sort of thing."

"You speak as if you were very experienced."

This time she could not help turning round to look at him with questioning eyes.

"Why do you say that?"

"Perhaps I am trying to find out about you. You've not told me much about your past."

"I've not had much opportunity."

"No, that's true," he agreed. "You sound a woman of the world! Some girls would be calling coyly for mother if this happened."

"I'm sorry to disappoint you," Romina said, "but after all we've been through today sharing a bedroom really seems the least of many other evils."

"How do you propose we should arrange things?" he asked.

155

She felt his little moment of being difficult was over and she tried to force herself to think of something sensible.

"Suppose you go downstairs and get a drink," she said. "And I'll get into bed and after that I'll keep my eyes shut."

Merlin threw back his head and laughed.

"I like that," he said. "It's the modern girl's perfect solution to what would have given the Victorian spinster screaming hysterics."

"I'm glad you think it is so funny," Romina said huffily.

His laughter died away.

"I'm sorry—I'm being a beast. You've been through a hell of a lot today. I've no right to tease you. But you were so obviously trying to put on a matter-of-fact 'this doesn't worry me' air when we came in that I just had to be annoying. Forgive me?"

There was no mistaking the genuineness of his apology and Romina flashed him a glance of appreciation.

"Of course I forgive you."

"Very good," he said, "except that I am not going to bed just yet."

"Oh, Merlin."

Romina got up from the stool on which she had been sitting in front of the dressing-table and came towards him.

"You're going out," she said accusingly. "You're not to do it—you hear? There is nothing left to discover in Cairo—you must wait until we get to Luxor."

"How can you be sure of that?" Merlin asked.

"Because it is obvious. And if they see you now, all that we have done—all this subterfuge and play-acting—will be wasted. We've got back without their realizing it and it would be mad, absolutely mad, to throw it away at this moment, to let them see you and suspect something, or . . . or even to get killed."

Her voice vibrated with the intensity of her feelings, and Merlin seemed to consider what she had said with an amused look on his face which she could not understand.

"You don't want to be left alone," he said. "That's it, isn't it?"

"Of course it is," she said, snatching at a straw. "Of course I want you to stay with me."

"That seems reasonable enough," he said, and crossing the room, he sat down on one of the beds.

Romina turned back towards the dressing-table. She was shaking with emotion and she could not keep her hands still. She knew the truth, although she did not reveal it, was not

...at she was afraid of being left alone, but that something
...ight happen to Merlin.

She could not bear it—she could not bear him to be killed
... Christopher had been killed, or left as Paul had been with
...pen, staring eyes.

She loved him—oh, God!—how she loved him! And yet he
...emed determined to run into danger, to risk his life.

She tried to tell herself that thirty-six hours ago she would
...ot have worried so much, there would not have been this
...earing agony within her breast—or the dryness in her mouth
...ecause she was afraid she would say too much and let him
...now how deeply she really minded.

She knew he was coming to a decision, and she waited for
...is reply with almost bated breath.

"All right," he said at last. "I won't go—but it seemed to
...e to be rather a good opportunity to scout around."

"We know what there is to see here," Romina said fiercely.
A lot of men waiting to peddle the dope which has not
...ome. Wait until we get to Luxor. And by the way—how
...oon do we get there?"

"We're in luck," Merlin answered. "This tour is scheduled
...o as not to interfere with another one which started two
...ays ago. I gather it is rather more expensive so they get all
...he priorities. We are to spend a day—only a day—in Cairo
...nd we leave for Luxor tomorrow evening. Then, after three
...ays there, we come back to Cairo for a further two days'
...ightseeing. After that—home."

"Oh, that fits in perfectly!" Romina said in a tone of relief.
Let us sleep tonight and get out of this place alive—that's all
...ask."

"Very well," Merlin agreed. "And by the way, I have been
...stablishing with the party that I'm not feeling at all fit—a
...ouch of fever which I got when I was serving in Malaya.
...hey are all very sorry for me. It means, I'm afraid, that I
...hall not be able to go sightseeing tomorrow."

"That's clever," Romina said quickly. "There will be no
...hance of anyone seeing us."

"You can go, if you like," he said.

"No, no! I have a wifely duty," Romina replied. "I shall be
...utting ice on your forehead—or whatever the right remedy
...s."

"It doesn't really matter, of course," he said, "because we
...hall have the opportunity to see all the sights on the return
...ourney. The guide has already assured me that I shall miss
...very little."

157

"Then we'll stay here," Romina said with a little sigh of relief. "That means tonight, too, you understand?"

"I heard, Madame," Merlin said, making a mocking salaam towards her.

She felt for one moment that she had got the upper hand of him.

"You go downstairs," she said, "and make an excuse that want a Coca Cola, or something. Asking for newspapers rather too obvious. And give me exactly five minutes."

"Your servant, Memsahib," Merlin answered mockingly.

He went from the room and Romina hurriedly undressed. She slipped into bed, turning off all the lights save for one on the table between them.

She heard his tap on the door and felt herself give a little start. Then he was once again in the room, locking the door behind him.

"I've brought you your Coca Cola."

His voice was almost over-casual.

He set it down on the table between the beds.

"It's the Arab variety—and I should imagine quite undrinkable."

Romina was lying with her back to him, her face turned towards the window.

"I'm ready to shut my eyes," she said.

"I'm not modest," Merlin told her. "I once had to pretend to be a nudist—it cured me of any illusions about the human body."

She felt herself giggle.

"Don't say that in front of my new friend," she said. "She would be terribly shocked."

"I like your friend," Merlin said. "By the way, it was clever of you to pick her up."

"Believe it or not, her name is Leonora Huggins," Romina told him.

"I'll believe it," Merlin said. "And I think it would be wise if you went down in the morning and confided in her how ill your husband is feeling."

"All right," Romina said.

She heard him get into bed, the springs creaking a little as he did so. Then he reached out his hand and turned out the light.

"Good night, Mrs. Robinson," he said.

"Good night," she answered.

She half hoped that he would say something more, that they would talk together in the darkness. But almost immeditely she heard him breathing quietly. He must have fallen very quickly into an exhausted sleep.

She lay for a long time listening to him, thinking about him, wishing she could look at him.

There was no sound except for his quiet breathing.

"I love him," she whispered soundlessly into the darkness and thought with a sudden glow of happiness that for to-night, at any rate, they were safe.

CHAPTER ELEVEN

"I'M afraid this is very boring for you."

Merlin spoke from the bed where he was lying propped up on several pillows, a three-days'-old Daily Telegraph in his hand.

He spoke kindly and without the sarcastic note in his voice which would have been there a few days ago.

Before she answered Romina rose from the chair on which she had been sitting and walked towards the window to stand looking out with her back towards him.

She did not want him to see her face because she was afraid that he would see all too clearly the truth. Just before he spoke she was thinking how happy she was.

It seemed to her, sitting in the quiet, rather shabby bedroom, with the sun-blind half down to exclude the hot afternoon sunshine, that she had found a sudden haven of peace.

It was like being married, she thought—Merlin reading in bed; she sitting in a comfortable chair; and the conversation between them calm and unexceptional. It was the kind of talk any married couple might have.

"No, I'm not bored," she said at last cautiously. "I think we had enough excitement yesterday to last us for a very long time."

There was silence for a moment, until Merlin said unexpectedly:

"I wonder what you are thinking about? You have a habit of shutting yourself away, of letting down a shutter between yourself and the person you are with. It makes me curious."

Romina wanted to say that she was glad he was interested in her, but somehow she could not find the words. Instead, because he had brought back all too vividly the danger surrounding them, she said impulsively:

"Are we mad, do you think, to do this alone? Supposing we went back home and told Guardie all we knew, wouldn't he send out more experienced people to cope with the situation?"

"I expect they would send me," Merlin replied without conceit, making it just a mere statement of fact.

Romina shut her eyes against the sunshine outside.

She knew then that nothing would make her leave him now. Whatever lay ahead—danger and perhaps death—she would rather be with him than sitting at home in safety and tearing her heart out with anxiety.

"Romina," he said urgently, "go home—I don't want you to be mixed up in all this. You are too nice and far too pretty."

"Thank you for the compliment," she replied a little dully, "but I intend to stay."

"I thought when I first saw you," Merlin went on, "you were one of those hard-boiled Society girls—the type I most dislike."

"I'm sorry I gave you that impression," Romina answered.

"It wasn't only what you said," Merlin continued, "and of course I realized at once that you had taken a dislike to me—it was those orchids all over the floor—the fact that you had been out with that 'Debs' Delight,' whatever that Russian bounder calls himself. I've always been wary of Society—I got caught up in it once or twice and loathed every moment of it and all the people in it."

"It sounds as if you have got a chip on your shoulder," Romina said lightly.

She was determined not to discuss Alex with him; the mere memory of that evening when Chris's letter had come to the flat made her feel slightly sick.

"I suppose I have in a way," Merlin replied, surprisingly good-humoredly. "My mother was always keen on my meeting the right people—what she meant by that was the right type of girl who would make me a good, respectable and extremely unexciting wife."

"What sort of wife do you think you would like?" Romina asked. She managed with tremendous effort to make her voice sound disinterested and slightly amused. It was a question anyone might ask in the circumstances, she thought.

Merlin did not answer for a moment, and then he said:

"I suppose the true answer is I want someone pure and unspoiled."

It was not the reply she had expected. She felt as if he had struck her. So that was what he wanted—someone who had not been mauled by other men, someone in fact who did not have purple orchids sent to them by a man who was known to be an international womanizer!

She wanted to cry out that only once had she been so stu-

161

pid. She wanted to tell him that something strange had come over her that night—perhaps it was because she was lonely and some clairvoyant sense had told her that she would lose the one person she had loved more than anyone else in the whole of her life. But she knew that these were excuses—excuses for behavior that was despicable, weak and sordid.

"You are very quiet," Merlin said.

"I was thinking," Romina replied.

"Of the past, or of the future?" Merlin asked.

"The future," she lied because she was afraid of her thoughts.

"We had better start planning something about it," Merlin said in a matter-of-fact tone. "What time did the courier say we had to be ready?"

"The airplane leaves about six o'clock for Luxor," Romina replied. "We leave here at half-past four."

"It's half-past three now," Merlin said. "I'll go and have a bath and dress in the bathroom. Have you got any powder or anything that I can rub on my face so that I can look pale and interesting? After all, I'm supposed to be ill."

"I'll find you something." Romina promised.

He got out of bed and put on his dressing-gown, collected his clothes and went from the room, closing the door behind him.

Romina sat down in the chair and covered her face with hands.

"I love him," she told herself. "I love him and it's hell to be here in these circumstances."

Even as she whispered the words, she knew that on the other hand it was heaven to be with the man she loved, to see his lined brown face, his dark eyes looking down at her.

She wondered why she had never noticed when she first met him the twinkle which always lay in the corner of his eyes, the little twist of his lips which told her when he was amused.

She had thought then that his face was cynical and sardonic, but she knew now that it was stern and yet sensitive.

She picked up the tweed jacket he had been wearing and held it close to her. There was something comforting in the feel of it; something, too, which made her think of England and home.

"We'll get back," she promised herself, "we'll get back and go down to the country. Perhaps if he saw me in my home with the fields and garden as a background, he would like me better."

It was a forlorn hope; and yet she knew that like all

162

women in love she would go on hoping, hoping that he would begin to like her, to need her, to want her as she wanted him.

Merlin came back looking clean and sprightly.

"I feel better now," he said. "I really think that I shall just be able to endure the trip to Luxor."

Romina laughed.

"You look far too healthy to be convincing," she said. "You will find the powder on the dressing-table—you had better rub it well in."

He did as he was told and then deftly penciled dark lines under his eyes. She had to admit it made him look as if he had not slept well for several nights.

"That's better," Merlin said with a sigh, standing back to admire his handiwork. "Now what about my lady wife?"

"Nobody will notice me," Romina said, combing her hair back from her forehead and putting on her sun-glasses.

She had on a plain, rather dull cotton dress and a pair of low sandals which she and Margaret had bought in Athens.

Merlin looked her over.

"You know, the trouble is," he said, "whatever you do with yourself you still look a very pretty girl."

"Oh, shut up!" Romina said laughingly. "You are making me nervous. I think the men in our little group are far too old to be interested in me anyway."

"They'd better not try," Merlin said grimly. "I should be a very outraged husband indeed."

Laughing and teasing each other, they packed their few belongings in their suitcases and then went downstairs a few minutes before half-past four to find nearly everyone assembled in the lounge.

"You've missed a real treat, Mrs. Robinson," Leonora Huggins told Romina. "We saw the Citadel and the chief mosque. I kept thinking to myself what a pity for you and your husband to miss it."

"We will try and see it on the way back," Romina said reassuringly. "My husband is better for the rest, I'm glad to say."

"Poor man! We've all been sorry for him," Mrs. Huggins told her, and one or two other people came up to say how sorry they were.

The courier, fussing about like a broody hen, hurried them into the bus which was to take them to the airport.

Romina could not help remembering the huge limousine in which she had last traveled this way along the same road, and hoped that the fact that they were with a British party would make them of no interest to anyone who might be snooping about the airport.

It seemed that her wish was granted, because with the exception of the airport officials, no one appeared to take the slightest notice of them.

After a very short wait they were shepherded across the tarmac and into a Dakota of Arab Airlines which was to carry them to Luxor.

As Merlin was supposed to have been ill, Romina fussed over him a little to impress Mrs. Huggins and various other women in the party, and insisted on his sitting in the inside seat.

As the airplane rose, she saw him looking back at the airport and knew that he was hoping that they had escaped undetected.

It was not a long journey to Luxor, but by the time they had arrived the sun had set and it was dark as they taxied towards the airport buildings.

"Keep with the mob," Merlin whispered in her ear, and she nodded as she undid her safety-belt and bent over to help him with his.

Once again Mrs. Huggins was useful.

Romina walked beside her as they left the airplane and soon inveigled her into talking confidentially and earnestly so that a casual onlooker would not realize that she and Merlin were together.

The bus carried them along the narrow, dusty road which led from the airport to Luxor. Now the darkness seemed to have a translucent quality and there was a dry fragrance in the air that was quite unlike anything Romina had known before.

She felt herself thrill with a sudden excitement. This was Luxor, which she had always longed to see; and the thought of Pharaohs and their secret tombs seemed to put everything else out of her mind.

It was only when they were alone in the big, high-ceilinged bedroom that Romina could voice her thoughts.

"We're here," she said. "It's exciting, isn't it?"

Without waiting for Merlin's answer, she walked across the room and stepped out on to the balcony which overlooked the front of the hotel.

Below was a blaze of lights which brought the insects fluttering in thick clouds. A number of other people from their party were still seated on the veranda from which the red stone steps led down to the road. On the other side of the road was the slow-moving river, and beyond, only just disernible in the light of the moon, were the mysterious hills in which lay the Valley of the Kings.

"It's absolutely breathtaking," Romina said excitedly.

Then she realized that Merlin was not listening to her. He was sitting at a small table, spreading something out in front of him. She came in from the balcony and walked across to see what he was looking at. It was a map.

"What are you looking for?" she asked.

"This is a map of Luxor," he said in a low voice. "While we were coming here in the bus I managed to ask the attendant a few questions. He was obviously quite unsuspicious—he thought I was the usual tourist who always wants to know something different."

"What did you ask him?" Romina inquired.

"I wanted to find out if there had been any new houses or villas built lately," Merlin replied, "and he told me with great gusto and not a little pride about a huge villa which had just been completed to the north."

He pointed as he spoke to the map in front of him.

"As far as I can ascertain," he said, "it is just behind the ruins of this temple. Of course this is an old map and would not show it. But he described it very vividly and from what he said—yes, that's the place—I'm very curious to see it."

"You mean—?" Romina began.

"I mean," Merlin said, looking up at her, "that if anything is going on here, that's where we are most likely to find it. He described a wall to me—a very big wall—and he said no one is allowed inside."

Merlin sat back for a moment in the chair.

"Of course, I may be reading more into his words than he meant. If it is a Sheikh—as he seemed to think—who built this, they all like privacy. For one thing, they have to keep their wives from being seen—and all Orientals have a horror of being overlooked by their neighbors."

"All the same, you think there is something in it?" Romina suggested.

"I am certainly going to have a look," Merlin replied.

"When?" Romina asked.

"Tonight," he replied.

"Tonight?"

She did not know why, but she was surprised.

She glanced at the two brass bedsteads standing side by side with their white mosquito nets covering them.

And then quickly, almost too quickly, as if she were afraid of her thoughts, she said:

"Of course—the sooner the better."

But Merlin was not listening to her; he seemed to be considering something.

After what seemed a long pause he said:

"I don't think this is the moment for any type of disguise. We'll go as ourselves—two tourists stumbling about in the moonlight. It's as plausible an explanation as anything else."

"Yes, I think you are right," Romina agreed.

He glanced at his watch.

"We don't want to go yet," he said. "Unpack your box and leave the room looking quite ordinary. We don't want the servants to think that anything looks at all strange. And then I suggest we walk down the steps openly. If anybody asks why we have come down again, we'll say we feel we must have a breath of air—that again is quite a feasible explanation."

"All right," Romina agreed. "Quite frankly, I could do with a little air."

She went into the bathroom which adjoined their bedroom and washed her hands. She stared at herself in the glass over the basin and thought she looked rather frightened.

She went back into the bedroom to find that Merlin was ready, having changed his shoes for a pair with rubber soles.

"You'd better put on those lace shoes Margaret lent you," he said, "you will find the sand very uncomfortable in sandals and we may be walking over quite a lot of it."

Romina did as he suggested, then they walked downstairs out of the front door and on to the veranda.

"Hello, Robinson!" one of the men said as they passed his chair. "Thought you were going to bed."

"It's pretty hot upstairs," Merlin replied. "I thought I'd get a breath of air before I turn in."

"They are building a new hotel with air-conditioning," someone remarked.

"Yes, but that'll be for the millionaires," Merlin quipped, and they laughed as he and Romina walked down the steps and into the roadway.

They stood for a moment staring at the Nile, then walked slowly along the path which bordered the water.

Other people were doing the same thing. There was nothing to make them conspicuous in any way from the other couples perambulating in the warm evening.

Merlin walked slowly, linking his arm through Romina's and drawing her farther and farther away from the hotels, houses and little line of shops along the road.

Soon the path on which they were walking became more

andy and the tarmac on the road seemed to be covered with
ust and sand as if it was seldom used.

"How far is this villa?" Romina asked, trying to peer
hrough the darkness and seeing little except the palm trees
ilhouetted against the stars, and the small green bushes
which bordered the banks of the river and appeared surpris-
ngly verdant against the sand which pervaded everything
lse.

Merlin looked around him. There appeared to be no one in
sight.

"I think we can move a little faster now," he said in a
quiet voice, and set off at what was a normal English walking
peed.

They met a man astride a very small donkey and a woman
n a black millaya-luff carrying a stone jug on her head. Then
hey came across some small children who stared at them cu-
iously but did not beg for alms.

Soon the path and the road were left behind and they were
walking on thick gritty sand and having difficulty in avoiding
he small clumps of cacti which were extemely painful if one
tood on them.

Nothing is more tiring than walking on sand, and after a
while Romina complained:

"You're going too fast!"

"Hush!"

Merlin turned on her almost sharply, and then she saw just
head of them there was a high dark wall.

She longed to ask questions, but Merlin's "Hush!" had
een imperative.

He stopped and she saw that he was taking his bearings.

The light of the moon was getting stronger every moment
nd her eyes were growing more accustomed to the dark.
Now she could see quite clearly that the wall ran right down
o the water's edge and back for a very long way over the
and until it was lost in the darkness.

It was a very formidable wall—high and with broken glass
on the top of it which would make it very difficult for anyone
who wished to scale it.

Romina could not be sure, but there seemed to be a jetty
built out in the river, and she thought she could just discern
what appeared to be a number of small boats bobbing beside
t.

"Come on," Merlin said, taking her hand, and he drew her
along beside him. They moved inwards away from the river
following the direction of the wall.

It looked impregnable and Romina wondered what Merlin had in mind.

On they walked, the sand sinking into her shoes and hurting her feet, but she was too nervous of Merlin to ask if she could stop and shake it out.

At last after walking a long way they came to the end of the wall and turned sharply, and Romina could see that it went some considerable distance before, she imagined, it turned again.

Merlin drew her nearer until they stood at the very corner, then he looked down and she could see that he was smiling.

"Native work," he whispered in her ear, "is always shoddy."

She wondered what he meant until she saw him put his foot on the corner of the wall and find a foothold.

In a second he had managed to spring up and by placing his hands carefully amongst the broken glass was able to look over to the other side.

He stayed there for a long time, just looking, then he jumped down to her side again.

"It's quite easy," he said. "I'll help you over."

"Do you mean that we are going to climb that?" Romina asked in a tone of dismay.

"Of course," he said. "Don't worry—it's not difficult. There is somewhere for you to put your feet, and then you can lever yourself up."

"What—on to the glass?" Romina asked.

"My coat will protect you from that," he told her. "And, as I have just said, native work is nearly always shoddy, and the glass at the corner is not half so sharp as it is nearer to the river."

He took off his coat as he spoke and threw it on top of the wall; then he showed Romina where she should put her feet in the broken concrete.

"Now," he said, "I'll go over first and help you down on the other side—is that all right?"

"Yes, of course," she answered, hoping her words sounded convincing.

He sprang up on the wall with an ability which she had always suspected in him. For a moment she saw him astride the top, then he slipped down the other side.

Nervously, because she was afraid of falling, she did as he told her and to her surprise found it quite easy.

She could feel the glass through his coat, but it did not pierce the tweed, and although it was uncomfortable it did not hurt her.

168

She hesitated at the top.

"Come on," Merlin whispered urgently. "You'll be seen if you stay up there."

She slithered as far as she could go and then dropped and felt his arms catch her securely.

Just for a moment she felt breathless at the impact but as he pulled her tightly to him she felt something else—a fluttering flame of excitement and desire which ran through her irresistibly and uncontrollably.

"Oh, Merlin . . ."

She heard her voice clearly breathe his name, and then she was looking up at him and his mouth was very close to hers.

She felt her whole being cry out to him. As if, in that moment, he knew what she felt, he bent his head and kissed her on the lips.

She felt a sudden leap of ecstatic joy within herself; and then, as quickly as his lips had taken possession of hers, he raised his head and she was free.

"Good girl!" he said, and she thought that his voice was a little unsteady as he turned to pull down his coat from the top of the wall.

Just for a moment she could hardly remember where she was; nothing seemed to matter save for the fact that he had kissed her. The night . . . the darkness . . . the place where they were . . . all seemed to whirl around her, and she could remember nothing except the happiness within her and the burning flame of her love.

"Come on."

Merlin spoke roughly, and she came back to earth with a bump.

They were in the midst of some bushes which had obviously been planted at that end of the garden as a kind of screen. They were not very big or overgrown and it was easy to walk between them and the wall.

Merlin was doing just this and she followed him, longing for the touch of his hand—too shy to seek it on her own initiative.

They moved almost silently for a few moments until Merlin stopped and she was able to look through the bushes into the garden itself.

What she saw was surprising, because the ground was laid out entirely as a water garden with small round ponds, each about ten feet across, almost touching each other and extending across a huge area. They were fed by little streams and what appeared to be pipes, and Romina guessed that they all were connected to the Nile, and perhaps the water was pumped from the river.

It was very quiet, and there appeared to be no one about.

The villa, which was large and sprawling, gleamed white in the moonlight, but there were no lights in the windows and it had a deserted look as if no one was living in it.

The moonlight glinted on the ponds and now Romina could see that something was growing in them, a plant of some sort—rather like watercress, she thought.

She was about to speak to Merlin when he turned toward her.

"I must get hold of that plant," he said, and she knew they were both thinking the same things.

He moved swiftly forward, and she saw him kneel down and put his hands into the water.

And then suddenly, without any warning, the garden was flooded with light.

For a moment it was dazzling. Great floodlights and searchlights turned everything from being silver and soft in the moonlight into something harsh and garish.

Merlin started to his feet, and instinctively Romina ran forward to stand beside him. They saw in the brightness of the lights that men were appearing from all round the garden.

'They must have been on guard,' Romina thought, as more men came running from the villa.

There were at least twenty-five of them, some carrying rifles, and with one quick glance Merlin realized that to try and get away was hopeless. He reached out and took Romina's hand.

"It's all right," he said reassuringly, but she knew by the pressure of his fingers that he was not as confident as he sounded.

The men hurried up to them, but without noise, without speaking, which in itself was frightening, for the Arabs are invariably noisy.

Then a man appeared from the house. He was Egyptian but he wore tight black trousers and short leather boots. His shirt was white, but a wide belt round his waist was red.

He looked them over and his dark eyes seemed to glitter.

"What are you doing here?" he asked in English.

Romina saw that he had a revolver in his hand.

"I'm sorry if we are trespassing, but we thought that the house was empty," Merlin said courteously. "I'm afraid we were just curious. We are tourists and only arrived in Luxor tonight with a Cook's tour."

"You have no right here," the Egyptian said sharply.

"As I have already told you, we're very sorry if we have offended you in any way," Merlin said. "We asked at the hotel and they told us there was nobody living here."

"I think that is a lie," the Egyptian replied. "But come—"

He gesticulated with his revolver, and Merlin and Romina had no choice but to walk along the path.

The other guards were still absolutely silent, and Romina felt that this was more sinister than if they talked and abused them for coming into the garden.

She felt frightened and she noticed that Merlin, who had been carrying his coat after he had pulled it down from the wall, now slipped it on and she guessed it was because he had his gun in the pocket and wanted to have it handy.

In silence, broken only by the sound of feet on the paved path which ran beside the water pools, they walked up to the villa. The door was open on to the garden and Romina could see there was a bright light inside, and the reason why the place seemed deserted was because every window was covered with shutters.

The Egyptian with the revolver motioned them inside and they entered a large room which was comfortably furnished. Standing in the center of it was another Egyptian also dressed in European clothes.

He was an older man and there was something extremely unpleasant about him as he contemplated them with an insolent look on his face.

"We have been expecting you, Mr. Nickoylos."

"I don't know what you are talking about," Merlin said in a bewildered tone. "My name is Robinson and this is my wife. Here's my passport, if you don't believe me."

He held it out, and the Egyptian took it from him, glanced at it and chucked it contemptuously on the floor.

"You are Nickoylos," he said. "We were told you might be coming here." He turned to the young Egyptian. "How did they get in?"

"Over the wall," the Egyptian answered.

"Now what is all this nonsense?" Merlin expostulated. "My name is Robinson. My wife and I are staying at the Imperial Hotel. If you don't believe me, send for the courier from Cook's and he will certainly vouch for us. I admit we were wrong in trespassing on your property, but we thought the place was empty and that it would be rather fun to see what an Egyptian villa was like inside."

He spoke very convincingly and just for a moment Romina

thought there was a flicker of indecision in the Egyptian's face.

"What do you suggest we do?" he said, turning to the young Egyptian.

"He had his hand in the water," the younger man said.

"Then you are Nickoylos," the older man repeated to Merlin. "I was told in Cairo that you might try and come back."

"I honestly don't know what you are talking about," Merlin replied. "As I've already told you, if you don't believe who we are, send to the hotel. It won't take long for one of you to go and fetch the courier—his name is Wren, by the way."

The younger Egyptian said:

"He was pulling one of the plants out of the water."

"I was doing nothing of the sort!" Merlin said. "If you want to know, I got my hand dirty getting over the wall—put it in some birds' muck or something—and so I was cleaning it."

Again, Romina thought, the older man seemed almost convinced.

But the younger man moved his gun in a menacing way.

"Dead men tell no tales," he said. "I suggest we hold their heads under water until they drown and then chuck them into the river. Their bodies will drift downstream and it will look as if they had a boating accident. You can even upset one of the boats if you like."

"Oh, no!" Romina exclaimed. "Why should you want to do such a thing? We have done no harm."

The elder Egyptian again seemed undecided. He bent, picked up Merlin's passport off the floor and turned and looked at it.

"They are easily faked," the young man said scornfully.

Romina looked at him.

There was something in his face which reminded her of someone, and then she knew who it was. It was Taha, and she wondered whether, in fact, they were brothers. There was the same sinister set of the eyes, narrow, tight lips and sharp, evil features.

She wondered if Merlin had noticed it, too; and then suddenly realized with a sense of horror that their very lives hung in the balance.

The two Egyptians had drawn apart a little and were talking. They were speaking in Arabic, and Romina could see that Merlin was listening and knew that he understood what they were saying.

Their voices were low, and then they began to argue and get excited.

There was something almost violent about the younger man, and because he was so frightening Romina slipped her hand into Merlin's.

He had released her when he had searched in his pocket for his passport, but now he took her hand again and held it closely, and despite the terror of their position, she felt the thrill of his fingers.

"What are they saying?" she whispered.

He shook his head, and she knew he was too intent on listening to have time to answer her.

Finally, the younger man turned round and roared at the guards who were standing about:

"Search him!"

Merlin made a quick movement but he was too late. Several men held him tightly and one of them dragged his gun from his pocket.

"A gun! Do you think that tourists carry guns?" the younger Egyptian screamed.

"So you are Nickoylos," the older man said. He walked across and slapped Merlin hard across the face with the back of his hand.

Romina gave a little scream.

"I'm not—and you can't prove it," Merlin answered. "I've carried a gun ever since the war, especially when I'm in a country like yours. One never knows what sort of things one may meet about the place."

The man hit him again. This time the ring on his finger cut open Merlin's cheek, and Romina saw that he was wearing the snake ring with the three pearls on it just like the one which Merlin carried in his notecase.

Merlin must have noticed the ring at the same time; and then suddenly in quite a different voice he said:

"All right—the play-acting is over. Let me free and I'll show you something."

"Another gun?" the young Egyptian sneered.

"No—something more important," Merlin answered. "A ring, such as you are wearing."

The two men looked at him uncertainly.

"I've got a story to tell you," Merlin said; "and something which will interest you both very much. Now then—are you going to let me tell it?"

The older man looked curious and gave the order for the guards to stand back.

They released him, and moving his shoulders as if their

173

hands had hurt him, Merlin pulled out his notecase and shook the snake ring on to the palm of his hand.

"You see?" he said.

"You must have stolen it!" the young man who looked like Taha's brother said accusingly.

"On the contrary," Merlin said, "I was given it for a reason."

"What reason?" they inquired.

"I was told to come here to find your Chief," Merlin said. "I've a proposition to make to him—from an American syndicate."

"I do not believe it!" the man who looked like Taha cried. "He is a liar—he has lied about everything! He said he was Robinson—he is Nickoylos!"

"I'm not Nickoylos—whoever else I might be," Merlin answered. "As a matter of fact I've been trying to get in touch with your Chief in London, and failed; so I hit on the idea of coming here to see if I could get a chance of seeing him."

"A likely story!" the younger man said; but the older appeared to be listening.

"Who gave you the ring?" he asked at length.

"That I'm not allowed to reveal—but it was one of your own people, I promise you. And my request is genuine enough. There's a lot of money to make in America—a lot of money indeed. What would you say to a million dollars?"

Romina saw the younger man's eyes glint greedily.

"Who sent you?" he said. "Tell us the names, otherwise we will not believe you."

"I'm afraid they are so important that I'm not allowed to reveal their names to anyone except the Chief of this business," Merlin replied. "Of course, if you aren't interested I can go back and tell them so."

The younger man laughed loudly.

"That is one thing you are never going to be able to do," he said.

"Then I'll tell you what I will do," Merlin said. "Take me to your Chief and let me tell him what I want—and if he isn't interested in the money—well, then, you'll doubtless have his permission to hold my head downwards in the water, or whatever nice little solution you have to this problem."

He spoke contemptuously; and the young Egyptian raised his hand as though to strike him.

"No—no!" the older man said. "I think that it is only right that we let the Chief decide about this. After all, he is coming here."

"Tonight, I understand?" Merlin said.

"How did you know that?"

The older man turned on him almost ferociously.

"My people are well informed," Merlin said suavely, "otherwise they wouldn't have a million dollars to offer you."

"I say kill him!" the young Egyptian snarled. "Get rid of ,im—and the woman, too!"

The older man looked Romina over in a way which made ,er shrink a little closer to Merlin.

"It would be a pity if she should die too quickly," he said, ,nd the leer made her more afraid than she had ever been ,efore.

"It is understood that I see the Chief?" Merlin asked ,uickly.

"If he will see you," the older man said.

He turned to the guards and gave an order in Arabic.

The men came across the room, and taking Merlin and Romina by the arms, thrust them forward out of the room down a passage.

At the end of it there was a door, and as it opened Romina ,aw there was a flight of stone steps going down into the ,ellars under the villa.

They all clattered down, the guards holding her so tightly ,hat she felt their fingers digging into her flesh, and at the ,ame time she was afraid that they would push her so that ,he would slip and fall.

They reached the bottom, and here the ceiling was so low ,hat Merlin had to bend his head as they moved along.

One of the guards had a key and he opened a door which ,was stoutly made.

"Get in there!" one of the men said in broken, rather guttural English as he kicked Merlin and sent him flying ahead ,of them.

Then they thrust Romina in after him and she heard the ,door slam and the key turn in the lock.

It was pitch dark inside the room.

Romina fell forward and she could feel that the floor was ,stone. Now she struggled on to her knees and put out her ,hand.

"Merlin . . ." she cried a little piteously.

"I'm here," he answered. "It's all right."

She felt his hand come out to her in the darkness. Then ,suddenly from the corner of the room another voice spoke in English.

"Merlin who?" a man's voice asked sharply.

CHAPTER TWELVE

FOR a moment there was a stupefied silence.

And then in a voice which seemed strangled in her throat, Romina cried almost hysterically:

"Who is it? Who are you?"

Her words seemed to echo in the darkness before a man's voice replied, also a little tremulous:

"It can't be—it . . ."

Before he could say more, Romina gave a cry which seemed to come from the very depth of her being.

"Chris! It . . . it is Chris, isn't it?"

"Romina! What are you doing here?"

The darkness seemed full of vibrations and emotions.

Then the voice from the corner said shakily:

"Wait a minute—don't move—I've got some matches here—"

Before he could finish speaking, Merlin had flicked open his lighter and the tiny flame illuminated his face and Romina's as they stared wide-eyed in the direction from which the voice had come.

There was the sound of a match and they could see a rather unsteady figure lighting the stump of a candle.

"Chris, darling Chris, you are alive!"

Romina ran forward and threw herself down beside a man sitting in the corner of the cellar on what appear to be a rough mattress.

The candle, set on a small ledge on the wall, flared up and Merlin stepped across the stone floor to put his lighter beside it.

It was Chris—but a very changed, very emaciated brother, whom Romina would have hardly recognized.

He was terribly thin; his clothes which had once been white were dirty and torn. He had a rough beard on his chin and there was a great gash on his forehead where the oozing blood had matted his hair.

But nothing mattered for the moment except for the fact that he was alive.

"Oh, Chris! What have they done to you?"

"It's all right," he answered, and stretched out his hand which seemed too big for his bony, emaciated wrist, and laid it on her shoulder.

"You're alive . . . you've alive . . . !" Romina murmured, tears running unchecked down her cheeks.

"Only just," he said with a twisted smile. "What the hell are you doing here?"

Merlin, who had said nothing until then, answered him:

"It's good to see you, Chris," he said. "We've been trying to find out why you 'died.' "

"Damn your curiosity!" Chris flashed. "Why couldn't you have kept away?"

"Did you really think I would?" Merlin asked.

"No, I might have guessed you would come, pushing your long nose into it. But why did you bring Romina?"

"I made him bring me," Romina interrupted. "He didn't want to—he's tried to get rid of me all the time—but I had to find out what had happened."

"So now we are all in a mess," Chris said.

"How bad a mess?" Merlin asked quietly.

"As bad as it could be," Chris replied, "and we haven't much time."

"Tell us what has happened," Merlin said. "We'll give you all the explanations afterwards."

"If there is an afterwards," Chris retorted.

"What do you mean?" Merlin inquired.

The eyes of the two men met in the light of the flickering candle.

"It's the end of the road," Chris said, "the Boss arrives to-night."

Romina knew why they were communicating with each other in tense voices.

"Don't worry about me," she said. "I'm only so happy to see you again—nothing else matters."

Christopher gave her a little hug as she knelt beside him on the mattress.

"Look—we've got very little time," he said. "What do you know about this set-up?"

"Only what you left in Madame Goha's charge," Merlin answered.

"So you got the paper, did you?" Chris said. "I hoped she'd have the intelligence to give it to someone like yourself."

"They killed Paul," Merlin said quietly.

177

Romina knew by the sudden hard pressure of Chris's fingers what this information meant to him.

After a moment he said:

"I've told you the Boss arrives tonight. I've been kept alive only because I wouldn't give them the information they required."

"Which was?" Merlin asked.

"Who told me about the drug."

"Tell us about it!" Romina begged. "We've gone on speculating, trying to think what it can be—and all we know is that you thought it very important."

"It is important," Chris answered; "so important that I see now I was a fool to have kept the information to myself for even a moment."

"Tell us," Merlin said, almost in a voice of command.

"Well, I knew I was on to something big when I wrote to Romina," Chris began; "but I had no idea then just how vast and terrifyingly damnable it really is."

"You should have told Guardie," Romina said.

"I know," Chris answered humbly, "but I was so pleased with myself for finding out what I had that I was conceited enough to think I could find out the rest all on my own."

"Go on," Merlin said briefly.

"I managed to get one of the small fry to take me to a place where a lot of the distributors met," Chris continued. "It was a kind of night-club—a pretty exclusive one—and I kidded him into believing that I was going to help them."

"Was it in Cairo?" Merlin asked.

"Yes, of course," Chris answered. "There were the usual ghastly types. Then a fight started with a man who was one of their chief agents—a revolting specimen known as Taha."

"He's dead," Merlin said quickly. "I killed him."

Chris's thin face broke into a smile.

"That's the best bit of news I've had for a long time. I couldn't bear to die, knowing that he was still walking the earth. Anyway, he was very much alive the night I first saw him. He stared a fight with another man there. I don't know what it was all about—they both lost their tempers—but finally Taha brought out his gun and shot the other man."

Chris paused, his mouth set in a grim line.

"He had a silencer on the gun, but there was such a noice going on that at first I did not realize what had happened until Taha's gang picked up the man and started bundling him out of the door. The person who had taken me to the club pulled me quickly out of another. I've never seen a man as frightened as he was—sweat was running down his face and he kept murmuring something about Taha not liking witnesses."

"Taha was a beastly man," Romina said, remembering his evil-looking face.

"My friend sprinted off," Chris went on, "and I hung about for a bit. I guessed they had dumped the shot man—and sure enough, about a quarter of an hour later I found him in an alleyway bleeding profusely. I realized that he was past any medical aid, but I asked him if there was anything I could do for him."

"That was so like you," Romina said, "getting into trouble because you wanted to help someone."

"There was no one about and it seemed safe enough," Chris answered in a matter-of-fact voice. "Well, to cut a long story short, the man, who was actually little more than a boy, had been a Catholic. He wanted a priest so that he could make his last Confession—but I realized there was no time to fetch one."

Chris paused for a moment and then he said in an embarrassed tone:

"He wanted to make a last Confession—so I heard it."

"What did you hear?" Merlin asked.

"I heard everything I had been trying to find out—he told me exactly what this organization meant. Of course it only came out in breathless gasps, but I could fill in the gaps with what I already knew."

"What did he tell you?" Merlin persisted. He had drawn nearer to Chris and was sitting on the dirty floor, his hands clasped round his knees.

"He told me," Chris answered and dropped his voice still lower, "that the drug is being grown here in Egypt because it requires a certain type of mud. It is, in fact, the most revolutionary type of narcotic that has ever been discovered. For one thing, it has a dual purpose. The flowers and seeds, when brought down to powder, produce in those who take it a feeling of supremacy—a feeling of superiority as if they are supermen—or gods in human form."

He paused for breath, coughing in the hollow, heart-rending way of a man who has been knocked about. With an effort he went on:

"The root on the other hand, when dried and powdered produces in those who take it an inertia—a complete sapping of the will and a kind of vague, moronic happiness."

"Good Lord!" Merlin ejaculated.

"It seems incredible," Chris said, "but it works—that's what I've got to impress on you—it works."

He took his arm from Romina's shoulder and took one of her hands in both of his.

"You see what they are trying to do?" he said. "And by 'they' I mean the devils who have learned of this drug—they are trying to rule the earth."

"Are you serious?" Merlin inquired.

Chris nodded.

"They have a ring which is issued to the chief distributors—in fact the supermen themselves."

Romina gave a little exclamation, and Merlin said:

"I've got one—but never mind—go on."

"Then you've seen the three pearls on the snake's tongue?" Chris said. "Well, I'll tell you what they stand for—Suppression; Segregation; and Supremacy. Those are the aims—the goal—of those who wear the ring; and of the man who issues them."

"And who is he?" Merlin inquired.

"That's what I have been trying to find out," Chris answered. "He is coming here tonight."

"Is it a Communist plot?" Merlin asked.

"Might be," Chris replied. "Or it might be just the wild ambitions of one man. But whatever it is, the whole thing is dangerous beyond words, beyond expression."

"The only hope is that they are short of the drug," Merlin said.

"They aren't short," Chris replied; "it's just that the plant is not yet in flower."

"No, of course, it isn't," Merlin agreed. "We came through the garden—we saw the plants—they are green."

"They will flower in about a fortnight from now," Chris said. "Two weeks—and by that time it's very unlikely that I or you will be here."

"But surely—" Merlin began, only to be silenced by a gesture of Chris's hand.

"It's no use kidding ourselves," he said. "These men are utterly ruthless. They've wanted to kill me ever since they took me away from my lodgings. I under-estimated them, you see. I did not realize they had seen me in the club. Everyone who had been there that night must have been silenced very effectively."

"You mean . . . they killed them all?" Romina asked.

"All," Chris said. "Taha took no chances."

"Why didn't they kill you?" Merlin asked.

"Because of the first two sheets of the letter I had written. As I expect you guessed, I was just going to put it into code when they walked in. They knew as soon as they read it that

I must have had an informant. They tried very hard to make me tell them who it was."

Chris moved as he spoke, as if remembering what had happened to him. His tattered shirt opened a little more and Romina saw the marks on his chest.

"Chris! What have they done to you?" she cried.

He looked across her bent head at Merlin.

"It wasn't very pleasant," he said grimly, "but I knew as long as I could keep silent I wouuld remain alive. They didn't realize that it was the man who had been killed who told me; and they were determined to find out who it was and give him all he deserved."

"They beat you," Romina whispered.

"It could have been worse," Chris answered. "They were well up in all the good old Nazi methods—cigarette-ends; cold water baths; being kept awake for hours on end—they tried them all! I have never been so grateful for my Commando training which made me pretty resilient to that sort of thing."

"What chance have we got of avoiding it?" Merlin asked, and his eyes were on Romina.

"A slim one," Chris answered. "They have told me in no uncertain terms that tonight I speak—or die. They have also indicated some of the tortures they intend to employ on me."

"I hated those men the moment I saw them," Romina murmured. "They are evil."

"Zarifa, the older man, isn't so brutal as Hosaris, the younger one," Chris told her. "He's a real little swine—drunk with power, and the drug makes him sadistic to the point of madness."

"And the rest of the people here?" Merlin inquired.

"Don't you understand? They are doped!" Chris said. "They obey orders. They have lost the power to think—to do anything on their own. Whatever they are ordered to do, they will do it."

"I thought there was something queer about them," Merlin said.

Chris gave what was almost a chuckle.

"Your understatement is typically British," he said. "They are morons, almost zombies; and in their way, perfectly happy. Can't you understand what the world would be like if the men who control this drug succeed in their scheme? We should all be suppressed; they would be absolutely supreme; and we should have no desire to do anything but to obey."

"It's fantastic—it's impossible," Merlin exclaimed.

"Is it?" Chris asked. "I'm not so sure."

"The whole nation—the world, can you imagine it?"

"In a way I can," Chris replied. "They are working on the important people first—the diplomats, politicians, heads of industry—gradually and insidiously coming down to the people. Women, of course, are easy game."

"My God! We've got to stop it!" Merlin said.

"But how?" Romina whispered. "How?"

"What's the time?" Chris asked.

Merlin looked at his watch in the candlelight.

"About twenty minutes to eleven," he said.

"And the Boss is due about eleven o'clock."

"What can we do?" Romina cried. "We can't just sit here and wait to be killed!"

Again the men's eyes met across her head.

"Have you got any money?" Chris asked unexpectedly.

"Of course," Merlin answered. "I thought it was strange when they searched me that the men did not take it."

"They were not ordered to do so," Chris answered. "Give it to me."

Merlin drew out his notecase.

"There's about fifty Egyptian pounds," he said.

"Give it to me quickly."

Chris almost snatched it from Merlin; then getting to his feet with difficulty, he walked across the stone floor of his cell.

He was limping, Romina noticed; and then her eyes rested on his back which was naked except for a few pieces of his shirt.

She forced back the cry that rose to her lips. Her brother's back was a criss-cross of weals from which the blood had congealed.

Chris went to the door of the cell, rattled it, and he shouted at the top of his voice:

"Nahas!"

For a moment nothing happened. Then they heard footsteps coming down the passage. Chris spoke through the door in Arabic.

Romina looked at Merlin for an interpretation.

"He's saying that he wants to go to the lavatory," Merlin said, "and he is telling him, also, that he has something to give him."

They heard the key turn in the lock, the door opened a little way, and Chris stepped out.

Romina drew a deep breath, and almost pitifully she asked:

"What's going to happen?"

Merlin moved to sit down beside her on the straw mattress which Chris had just vacated.

"Whatever it is," he said quietly, "I know you will be brave."

"I'm not brave," she answered in little more than a whisper. "I'm a coward—and I'm afraid."

"We're all afraid," he answered gently.

She looked up at him, and then in the light of the candle saw an expression on his face that she had never seen before.

"Romina," he said, and his voice was very low and deep. "If we've got to die, I don't want to do so without telling you that I love you."

"Merlin . . ." She hardly breathed his name because she was so surprised.

"I love you," he said again. "In fact, I think I've been hopelessly in love with you from the very first. I love everything about you—even that defiant little gesture with your chin; even the hostility in your eyes when you have been hating me. Yes, I love you, Romina—and now it's almost too late to tell you so."

"Oh, Merlin . . . Merlin . . ." His name seemed somehow to have been set to music. "I thought you hated me."

"Only at the very beginning," he said, "when I didn't want any woman tagging along. I suspected that because you were so pretty—no, not pretty—utterly, exquisitely lovely, that you would be a nuisance and get in my way. Instead of which you only got into my hair."

He looked down at her face raised to his, and somehow there was no need for her to answer him. He saw in the expression in her eyes, in her parted lips, what she was feeling and what she was trying to tell him.

For a moment his eyes widened, and she knew that he, too, was astonished, until with an inarticulate sound which was half a groan and half a cry of triumph, he pulled her close to him.

He rested his cheek against hers and it seemed to Romina that that in itself was an ecstasy beyond anything she had ever known. His lips sought hers, tender and gently at first as if he was a little in awe of her; then suddenly passionate, hungry and possessive.

She felt the world whirl round her, forgetting where she was and the dangers that surrounded them. She only knew a joy beyond expression, a wonder and a glory that had never before existed for her.

Merlin raised his head and looked down at her.

"I love you, my darling," he said, and his voice was hoarse

183

and broken. "I love you as I have never loved anyone before."

"And I love you . . . too . . ." she whispered. "I've loved you for days—or is it years? I love you so much that I can't find words . . . to express it."

He pulled her so close to him that she felt as if he squeezed the very breath from her body. And then he was kissing her again—wildly, almost feverishly, like a man who knows he is going to lose that which he most prizes, but for the moment it is within his grasp.

Suddenly he set her free.

"God in Heaven!" he said. "We've got to get out of here! I'm damned if we'll die like rats in a trap!"

He jumped to his feet and walked towards the door, but as he did so there was the sound of a key turning in the lock and Chris came back.

Without words both Romina and Merlin realized there was something different about him. There was an assurance in the way he moved; a new expression on his face; and Merlin said what was in both their minds:

"There's a chance, isn't there?"

Chris nodded.

"So slender," he said, "that it's going to need a lot of imagination to believe it might work. Still, one never knows."

He moved towards the mattress where Romina was still sitting.

"What's the time now?" he asked.

"Eight minutes to eleven," Merlin answered.

"Well, then, listen because we haven't much time," Chris said. "I've been working on Nahas ever since I've been here. He's better educated than the rest, he was a student at the University in Cairo, and his one aim in life has been to get to England. He has brought me the few luxuries that I've had, like a candle and enough food to keep alive, only because I paid him for it. He couldn't care a damn whether I live or die—but money will buy him his freedom and he has stopped taking the drug."

"You persuaded him to do that?" Merlin asked.

"What is more important, I've persuaded him now to give us our only chance of escape," Chris replied. "There's a motorboat which Zarifa and Hosaris use which is kept at the end of the jetty. It's a very fast boat—faster than anything else around here. Nahas has promised that he'll have it running at the end of the jetty from the time we go in to see the Boss until such time as we either join him—or die. The only

184

stipulation he made is that if we escape we take him with us."

"If we escape—" Merlin repeated. "Any other plans?"

"None," Chris said. "We've just got to wait and see what turns up. Have you got a weapon of any sort?"

"They took my gun," Merlin answered, "but I've got a knife—the good old Commando trick—strapped to the bottom of my foot."

He bent down as he spoke and shook off his shoe.

"I've only got one thing," Chris said. "You remember that I used to be able to charm snakes? Romina will—"

"Yes, of course, I remember," Romina interrupted. "You seemed to do nothing else all the time you were in India. It used to give me the creeps."

"Well, I've been trying my powers since I've been here. Unfortunately I've not been very successful. There were no snakes, but I did manage to charm a scorpion."

"A scorpion!" Merlin ejaculated as he removed a small flick-knife from under his instep.

Chris went to the shelf on which the candle was burning.

"She's here," he said. "In a matchbox. I call her Fatima, and I suggest that we give her to Romina."

"I don't want it," Romina said quickly.

"I think you do," Chris said gently. "The men upstairs are not very pleasant to women when they are under the influence of the superman drug."

Romina shivered. She was remembering what Hosaris had said about her not dying too soon.

"Very well, I'll take it," she said and put out her hand.

"Be very careful not to open the box by mistake," Chris said. "Remember that if a scorpion stings you, you die very quickly and unpleasantly, and Fatima works fast."

"I'll remember," Romina promised.

She took the box from him gingerly and opened her white handbag and put it inside.

As she did so, she saw her vanity case, and instinctively she took it out, opened it and began to powder her nose.

Then when she saw her tear-stained face she flushed that Merlin should have seen her looking so disheveled. She wanted to look lovely for him.

She glanced up at him and saw he was watching her. Their eyes met, and for a moment they both forgot everything, even Chris.

"Are you two in love with each other?" Chris asked suddenly.

They both smiled, and there was no need for an answer.

"Then damn it! We've got to get out of here!" he said. "I don't want to miss being best man at the wedding of my greatest friend and my kid-sister."

Merlin glanced at his watch and said quickly:

"What do you know of the lay-out of the house?"

"I've never been in the front rooms," Chris answered. "But Nahas tells me there is a kind of veranda in the front, as in most Egyptian villas, and there are steps leading straight down to the jetty. There's no access to the place except by water."

"Jolly useful for their purpose and for secrecy," Merlin said. "Did they build it?"

"I don't think so," Chris answered. "I gather it belonged to a Sheikh or someone who was very jealous of his wives. He died before it could be completed. The Boss came along and made it his headquarters."

"Surely someone local might have suspected something was going on?" Merlin suggested.

"Why should they?" Chris said. "The men in the household, the guards, the gardeners, etc., don't go home. In fact, most of them have been brought from other parts of Egypt. They are happy; they have nothing to complain of."

Merlin wiped his forehead.

"You're right," he said. "The whole thing is terrifying."

"It could be happening all over Europe and America," Chris said, "while the Chinese take care of the East."

There was a sudden sound of footsteps and voices.

Romina gave a convulsive little gasp, shut her handbag and held out her hand to Merlin.

He took it and pulled her to her feet. As he did so, she saw him slip the knife into the pocket of his coat. Chris was standing tense and alert in the center of the cell.

The door was unlocked and thrust open.

Hosaris stood there in his tight black trousers and open-necked white shirt, and the red belt holding his pistol was around his waist. In his hand he had a short black whip, and behind him were two of the guards, looking, Romina thought, rather stupid and imperturbable.

"Bring them upstairs!" Hosaris commanded.

Romina noticed that Chris and Merlin managed to get on either side of her and Chris led the way through the open door to follow two of the guards down the passage.

As he passed Hosaris, the young Egyptian flicked out the whip like an evil snake and struck him on the shoulders.

Chris's thin body shuddered, but he said nothing, and then the whip cracked again, on Merlin's back.

186

Neither of the men spoke, and they progressed slowly up the stairs on to the ground floor.

Hosaris barked a word in Arabic, and the guard ahead of Chris turned sharply to the left and through an open door into a magnificently furnished room with windows overlooking the Nile.

There were big soft couches, satin cushions and low coffee tables. And at the far end of the room, seated on a bigger couch than all the others—a table in front of him laden with food—was the man they had come to see.

He was eating and did not raise his head as they entered. Romina barely glanced at him as she tried to take in the room, seeing the open French windows on to the veranda which undoubtedly led, as Chris had described, to the river.

Then the man at the far end of the room spoke, still without raising his head.

"Send the guards away!" he said sharply. "It is necessary only for you and Zarifa to hear who had betrayed us to this man."

As he spoke, Romina gave a little gasp and stared across the room as if she had been turned to stone.

It could not be! It was impossible!

Then she saw that she had not been mistaken at the sound of the voice.

It was Alex who sat there! Alex Salvekov—eating unconcernedly the food in front of him, as if he were seated in a Mayfair dining-room or in one of the smart restaurants that he patronized in London.

She felt as if she could hardly breathe; as if the mere sight of him was enough to make her feel that she was suffocating.

When he had finished what he was eating, he put down his knife and fork and raised a napkin to his mouth. As he did so, he looked up for the first time and saw her.

There was no doubt that he, too, was surprised. The astonishment on his face might have been ludicrous, but it was swiftly transformed into another expression—one which Romina was afraid to put a name to, even to herself.

"Romina! This is indeed a surprise!" he said silkily. "I had no idea that you were the lady guest I was told was waiting to see me."

Romina did not answer and he turned to look attentively first at Merlin and then at Christopher.

"Ah, I see," he said suavely. "This is your brother, and, of course, Nickoylos. How very stupid of me, I might have guessed. But my colleagues are not very good at pronouncing

187

names. I think perhaps he was traveling under a pseudonym, is that not so?"

He glanced at Hosaris, who said in a loud, aggressive voice:

"He had a passport in the name of Robinson."

Alex Salvekov lay back and laughed.

"A little unimaginative," he said. "I have always suspected names like Robinson and—let me see, what was the other?—Harrison."

He put out his fingers and washed them delicately in a finger bowl in which were floating the heads of several small blue flowers.

"No, Romina," he said. "You were very stupid to involve yourself in this sort of thing. It is a pity, because through it we missed some very pleasant hours together in London. I was looking forward to the meeting you had promised me that night you sent me so arbitrarily away from your flat."

"I promised you nothing," Romina said hotly.

"Not in words perhaps," Alex Salvekov said, "but your lips! Your lips, my dear, promised me many things."

"Don't speak of it!" Romina stormed. "How could I have been such a fool . . . such an idiot?"

"Why be so heated?" Alex Salvekov asked gently. "Come here, Romina."

"I would rather stay where I am," she answered. She put out her hand quickly and felt for Merlin's.

"I think if you want to be helpful to the two gentlemen who accompany you," Alex said, "you will do as I ask."

This was something she could not refuse; and reluctantly, feeling as if she was walking on a morass on which every step was dangerous, she drew slowly near the table.

"Sit down," he said. "Sit down and join me in eating these delicious strawberries. If I remember rightly, you enjoy strawberries."

He picked up a plate and held it out to her. As he did so, something snapped in Romina's memory—and she remembered. That same gesture . . . the plate of strawberries . . . it had happened to her before.

She could see Alex doing it . . . see flashing rings on his fingers as he held the plate, the rings he had worn as an accompaniment to his fancy dress of a Russian nobleman. . . .

And she could hear her own voice saying:

"Oh no, thank you. I don't want any more to eat."

"Just try them," Alex had said, "they are delicious."

"But you've put sugar on them," she protested. "I don't like sugar with fruit."

"It's only a little," he replied, "you won't notice it."

To please him, and because it seemed such a fruitless argument, she had eaten one or two of the strawberries and, as he had said, she did not notice the sugar.

Now she knew why he had been so anxious for her to eat them.

"The drug . . . your drug . . ." she stammered. "It was on the strawberries you gave me at the ball. That was why I let you . . . why, when you came back to my flat . . . I . . ."

"My dear," Alex's voice interrupted her, "must you really behave like this in front of an audience?"

"You tried to dope me," Romina said accusingly. "And if Chris's letter had not dropped through the letter-box at the very moment it did . . ."

She gave a little shudder and put her hands up to her face.

"Quite unnecessarily dramatic," Alex said. "But since you mention it, let us take up the charming little episode where we left off."

Romina took her hands down from her face.

"Never!" she said. "I would rather die."

"Do you really mean that?" Alex asked. "Have you ever thought what dying means? It's not just extinction, as many people presume. Not out here at any rate, not with my friends Zarifa and Hosaris about. They have very peculiar ideas about the way people should die."

He smiled, and his voice deepened and warmed as if he enjoyed what he was saying.

"Hosaris, for instance," he went on, "enjoys beating people to death—something I have never really taken to, myself—but to him it is the height of enjoyment. The Romans went in for it a lot, I believe, and Hosaris is determined that he is the reincarnation of a Roman; perhaps he is!"

He glanced towards the young Egyptian who was tapping his thigh impatiently with his black whip as if all this talk bored him and he was longing to get on with the job.

"And then there is Zarifa," Alex continued. "He has much more subtle methods. He learned them in China, I believe, and he calls them 'the thousand agonizing steps to heaven.'"

"Be quiet!" Romina cried. "How can you talk like this? You are civilized. I've met you in decent people's houses, and all the time . . ."

"All the time I was planning what will prove to be the most dramatic and magnificent era the world has ever known," Alex said. "Can't you see, my dear Romina, when directed by me, how much more peaceful and pleasant life will be for everyone?"

189

"You're mad!" Romina said accusingly. "You'll never get away with this."

"I wonder who there is to stop me?" Alex asked. "Not you, my dear, and certainly not these rather fierce, glum-looking gentlemen with you. But why fight against the inevitable? Sit down and enjoy my strawberries—you'll feel quite differently about everything then. And while you eat them, your brother can tell us the little tale I have been waiting to hear of who gave him the information about my plan and what he did with the piece of the letter my men were unable to find."

He looked up at Hosaris. The Egyptian raised his whip and Romina heard it swish through the air as he brought it down with all his force on Chris's back.

Chris, taken by surprise, stumbled and a little groan came from between his lips.

"Stop! Stop!" Romina cried. "You can't do this! You can't be so cruel, so bestial! Please, Alex!"

She was pleading with him with tears in her eyes and now he looked up at her with a triumphant smile on the corner of his lips.

"That's better," he said. "Now you are beginning to talk like a woman. What about these strawberries?"

He pushed them towards her, and Romina stood irresolute, not knowing what to do or what to say.

And because she was ashamed of the tears in her eyes, she tried to open her bag to find her handkerchief.

As she groped for the clasp, she suddenly felt it snatched from her hand and Alex opened it and turned it upside down on the table.

Her things fell out, tinkling amongst the dishes, glasses and cutlery—her vanity case, lip-stick and comb, the little medallion she always carried of St. Christopher, her handkerchief, the small gold pill-box which contained vitamins and the matchbox which Chris had given her down in the cell.

They all lay among the plates of food Alex looked them over and gave a short laugh.

"Just what I might have expected," he said. "For a second I thought perhaps you were carrying something more dangerous."

He laughed again as Romina put out her hand and picked up her handkerchief to wipe the blinding tears from her eyes.

As she did so, almost in a dream she saw him take a cigarette from the carved ivory box which stood on the table, and instinctively pick up the matchbox as it lay in front of him and open it.

It was all done so quickly; if it had not been, she thought afterwards, she would have cried out a warning without knowing that she did so.

But even as her lips parted, it was too late.

The box opened and something angry and swift slipped from the matchbox and down the sleeve of Alex's coat.

He gave a cry which was almost like the shriek of a bird. He sprang to his feet, shook his arm, and then the cry turned to the sound of an animal in mortal fear.

Zarifa and Hosaris at the other end of the room moved forward towards him, and as they did so Merlin's knife plunged between Hosaris's shoulder-blades.

Zarifa tripped over Chris's outstretched foot; and the side of Chris's hand, hard and straight with all the force of a desperate man, came down on the back of his neck. He fell forward on the carpet, killed as neatly as a gamekeeper might kill a rabbit.

Then Romina, trembling and unable to take her startled eyes from the writhing Alex, who by now was throwing himself about on the couch in agony, felt Merlin take her arm.

"Come on," he said and started to drag her towards the window.

She ran because she had no alternative, even though her knees seemed to have turned to jelly. She ran faster than she had ever run before, hearing Chris panting and wheezing behind them, and then, just ahead, at the end of the jetty they saw the motor-boat.

The engine was purring gently like a cat asleep in the sunshine and as they sprang into the boat—Romina tripping so that only Merlin's arms prevented her falling headlong—it burst into life.

Hardly a second passed before they started moving at an almost incredible speed down the river.

"You have done it!" Romina heard the young Egyptian at the wheel say triumphantly. "You have done it, sir!"

It was impossible for Chris to answer. He was doubled up in the effort to get his breath, like a man who has been rowing a race.

Then Romina felt Merlin's arms around her and his face was very close to hers.

"We've done it," he said gently. "We're safe, darling—do you realize that? We're safe."

She was too exhausted and breathless to answer him, and could only lay her head back against his shoulders and feel a relief that was too wonderful to be believed.

Then she felt his mouth seeking hers and she knew that nothing else mattered—there was nothing to say.

They were going home, they were going to be together . . . and she loved him.